GUANTANAMO JIHAD!

By
Niall de Souza

Published by
Editorial Schaumberg Fontaine Salva S.L.
(Donostia Marseille Wien Dublin)
Publishing@Europe.com

First published December 2005 by
Editorial Schaumberg Fontaine Salva S.L.

Copyright 2005 Niall de Souza

The moral right of the author has been asserted.

All characters in this publication other than those clearly in the public domain are fictitious and any resemblance to real persons, living or dead or to actual events, locales or marine vessels is purely coincidental and beyond the intent of the author or publisher. The events described though plausible are mostly imaginary. Most geographical locations however are real.

All rights reserved.

No part of this publication may be reproduced, stored in a retrieval system, or transmitted, in any form or by means withouts prior permission in writing of the author and is sold subject to the condition that it shall not, by way of trade or otherwise, be lent, re-sold, hired out or otherwise circulated in any form of binding or cover other than that in which it is published and without a similar condition including this condition being imposed on the subsequent purchaser.

A CIP catalogue record of this book is available from the British Library.

ISBN-10: 0-9552082-0-3
ISBN-13: 978-0-9552082-0-1

Cover design by Brian McCarthy at www.artinprint.com
Typeset by Stephen Jeffery at Bounty

English language edition printed and bound in the Republic of Ireland by Colour Books Ltd at www.colourbooks.com

Reorders from from Editorial Schaumberg Fontaine Salva S.L.
(Donostia Marseille Wien Dublin)
by email: Publishing@Europe.com

Acknowledgements

To literary scholar Senator David Norris for his support and enthusiasm.

Dedication

To those found guilty by suspicion who are deprived of freedom, hope or life.

Niall de Souza discovered early his enjoyment of writing and had his first story published in his teens. Leaving the craft of short story writing behind, this is his first novel, motivated by 21st century events becoming a disturbing repeat of history, both recent and ancient. He lives in Ireland. He is married to Deirdre and has three children, Carl, Daragh and Keith.

"In the name of Allah, most benevolent, ever merciful.

O Prophet, urge the faithful to fight; if there are twenty among you with determination, they will vanquish two hundred and if there are 100 then they will vanquish 1000 unbelievers, for they are people devoid of understanding."

THE HOLY QU'RAN   (Al-Anfal 8:64)

CHAPTER 1

Samia leapt up the external starboard stairs, two steps at a time and continued running along the Boat Deck towards the front of the liner. As she came up to the last forward Lifeboat station, she paused at the deck rail to catch her breath. Then hearing Gino coming up the stairwell after her, she grabbed the low neckline of her dress and ripped it completely open to reveal firm dark breasts of the same mahogany hue as the rest of her Eritrean skin. As the obese Gino began running towards her, she then swung her leg over the rail and stood facing him in the exposed area of the Lifeboat bay, her hot face full of passionate contempt.

The heavily panting Gino spoke as loudly as he could. "What in the name of …what are you doin' in there?" as he sucked in lungfulls of warm Caribbean night air.

Samia viciously roared back "DON'T COME NEAR ME PIG, STAY WHERE YOU ARE!"

She took hold of the Lifeboat's side rope and in one athletic movement levered herself onto the boats tented cover. Pulling her black fashion shoes off, she tossed them over the side and walked barefoot on the canvas cover until she got to it's ridge. There, in the middle of the cover she knelt down, legs astride the ridge, balancing herself, pulling her long dress up her thighs.

Samia was glad to be out of reach of Gino who had spent the previous half hour fondling her intimately with both hands in the men's bathroom of the ship's Monte Carlo piano bar. As Samia now looked below at the fresh milky foam streaming past the huge ship she wished she could jump in and clean herself of Gino's infidel saliva he had slobbered over her. She was now relieved that the most personally awkward and unholy part assigned to her in this mission was over. She also now realised however that if she lost her balance on the lifeboat cover gritted with salt crystals, the 30 metre fall could well kill her as her trainer Hakeem Belbachir had reminded her months earlier in Bou Saada camp, Algeria.

She steadied herself and shouted down to Gino "KEEP AWAY, YOU HAVE DEFILED ME. UNLESS YOU CALL THE SHIP'S SECURITY I WILL JUMP

IMMEDIATELY......CALL THEM NOW!"

Gino was dumbstruck "What the hell are you sayin'? If this is a joke you bitch, no-one is laughin". I didn't touch you ……….. well, whatever I did….. it was with your consent! No chick but no chick baits Mr.Gino Calvoni's sirloin piledriver just for a tease.... D'YA HEAR! REMEMBER it was YOU who brought ME to the men's bathroom WASN'T IT?"

He paused for a moment and then murmured looking at Samia "Jeez, what kind of goddam crew is on this ship? A full metal deep-ender this one is anyway and she's about to prove it!" Gino decided to rush for help realising he'd better be the first to explain what had happened before the ranting Samia had an audience listening to her allegations about him. At stake was not only his successful bid to supply all ham and sausage to the new ship's kitchens, but his reputation as a pillar of Miami's Italian American community. He was an invited guest on this maiden voyage of the Fantasea of the World, grossing at 114,000 tons and the latest marine leviathan to cruise the Caribbean seas. On honeymoon with his third wife, she had gone to bed feeling unwell as the ship rolled in a gentle undulating swell in the Florida Straits. Gino Calvoni was a small rotund man in his late forties who over-ate his own food ingredients and who cultivated a fearsome reputation. He liked to explode into temper with slow payers, which he preceded by abdominal straining to redden his face for added effect. Born Calvi he changed his last name to Calvoni after a conference on 'Effective Product Branding' and was proud of his name promoted almost

State-wide on Florida's minor highway hoardings.

He now hurried down the outer stairwells, his heart pounding, torn on the one hand between an inclination to disappear and go back to his cabin and if Samia jumped, no one would be the wiser.

On the other hand his instinct was also to stay and use his persuasion skills to talk her down but he still had her allegations to answer if he succeeded. What, he thought, if she didn't jump and he pretended he'd never met her in the Piano Bar. She'd pick him out as the weak 'buffone' who had ignored a woman in distress; he'd be the Italian American who had turned his back and walked away. That might expose his family to a lawsuit for millions of dollars by the girl's family, whether she jumped and survived or even survived long enough to implicate him.

He burst through both double doors of the Klondike Casino, chest heaving for air and grabbed a croupier's arm, spilling neat stacks of gambling chips everywhere. "There is a woman about to jump overboard! Right now! Call security immediately... she is on the lifeboat deck ……..on the right hand side. She's nuts and ………..is half stripped off and ready to dive in. I recognise her as ...I think she is one of your crew! She says her name is Samia or somethin'. She's also ravin' on about passengers including me touchin' her up, Jeez, I just wanted to pull her back from the edge……a total screwball!"

Before the male croupier had time to take in what this panicking passenger was saying between gasps, Gino was grabbed from behind.

"Lost a little too much Sir"? asked a man firmly while pulling Gino's arms behind his back.

"LISTEN TO ME"! he roared and then paused to calm himself, "one of your crew is goin' to jump overboard, don't you understand what I'm sayin"?

The plain clothes security officer restraining him didn't reply but then twisted and pushed Gino's left arm upwards, forcing him painfully down onto one knee. Onlookers worried he might go into cardiac arrest. At that point the officer took out a small radio out of his jacket. "Chief this is Hank 228762 here, in the Casino. I've a passenger here, seems upset.....says we've a jumper, Starboard lifeboat decks, he says she's goin to dive off a lifeboat, can you send someone else to check it out? I'm gonna cuff the passenger, bring him to the Casino staff room then I'll be up there right away"!

Little did Gino Salvatore Calvoni know that he was just someone in the wrong place at the wrong time and the first accessory to what President Castro would later declare in an address to the Cuban people, to be an "insanely provocative act of religious war: an act of so called holy war unseen in the western Hemisphere since the moors conquered Spain in the 8th century."

CHAPTER 2

The previous day at 0400 hours on a calm tropical night, Samia's commander Hakeem Belbachir had led the thirty strong Guantanamo Martyrs Brigade, all heavily armed, onto the shores of the tiny island of 'Ile à Vache' off the Haitian coast. As the brigade surrounded the village of Pacq the rhythmic trills of cicadas were hushed briefly by the barking of dogs, frenzied in alarm at these figures quietly wading towards them. Around the cove, fumes of stale wood smoke from cooking fires hung in the still air. Passing the fishing skiffs hauled up on the beach, pungent whiffs of putrid fish filled their nostrils until they took up positions inside the village amid the wafting stink of latrine shacks.

Never intending to offer resistance the villagers had little problem in being held captive by these strange speaking men. Most villagers had been quietly awoken with a welcoming gift of a $100 dollar bill which was thrust into whatever ragged pocket the dark skin travellers could find, much with the same purpose as Columbus had when handing over gifts to the natives on reaching this land of old Hispaniola. Suspicious and fearful of the armed visitors at first, the villagers were nonetheless grateful for the dollars which when changed into local gourds and centimes was more than a year's pay. They might have received more if not for the brigade's concerns that someone might flee in a skiff to the mainland to invite others in on the pay off.

Never before had such an odd group of disciplined, young men arrived during the night, moving silently about the village talking quietly between them in French, Arabic, Russian and English. All were dark and heavily bearded except one with fair hair who had a sparse growth of stubble. Soon after sunrise each put on identical small dark sunglasses.

Usually the inhabitants of Pacq would be held to ransom by smaller crews blown ashore on coasters adrift with engine trouble. Plying the long drug run from Santa Marta or Baranquilla on the Colombian coast, drifters would burst into the shanties of these fisher folk helping themselves voraciously to dried fish and house rum. Nothing was usually offered in return by these narcotraffickers except menace and insults backed up by a holstered pistol. This night however, these visiting boatmen had purposely moored their faded blue shrimp trawler in the shallows at Pacq. Each man shouldered an AK47 assault rifle, with a bullet belt wrapped loosely around the waist or draped, sash like, across the chest.

Strangely for the local girls and younger women living further away from the village the men did not confront them but turned to ignore them once the dollar bills were dropped at their bare feet wherever they stood whether inside the shacks or outside the latrines.

At first the younger women thought it was a down payment for favours; one pretty girl lifted her skirt immediately but was knocked backwards to the ground by a powerful punch in the face from a martyr's fist. He then kicked her raised skirt back to cover her genitals and slender legs while loudly swearing in Arabic at her. The villagers assumed that this was just a staging post of a spectacularly valuable consignment of cocaine that must have filled the trawlers weathered hull, heavy at anchor in the turquoise Haitian waters.

The apparent leader of the group was a big framed marine engineer softly introducing himself as Hakeem. Cleanly dressed in new grey khaki, still bearing creases, he was the only one of the group to wear a matching jungle hat. His full upper and lower lips, partly obscured by overgrown black moustache had chapped into bright pink after the long sea voyage from their base near the port of Tuapi on Nicaragua's Mosquito Coast. Red pock marks showed through thin cheekbone hairs at the top of a cascading beard bush. Later resting in the shade of the beach tree line he took off his sunglasses revealing dull olive black eyes set in bloodshot whites, showing the need for sleep missed the previous nights. He then took off his soldier's boots and walked into the hot shallows up to his ankles. Craning his neck he looked up to the sun and with eyes closed, he saw the hot crimson of his own blood, the very same bright red that he remembered gushing from his nephews little heart exposed by shell shrapnel that winters day two years earlier in Rafah refugee camp,

Gaza; his nephew had been on the look out all day from the rooftops for his return home after six months at sea. Hakeem remembered his own tears dropping deep into the boys smashed chest cavity; he remembered shielding the slippery beating heart with his cupped hand, as it pumped less and less against his palm. When the heartbeats ceased he would never forget it's last spasm hitting his lips and blood sodden moustache. He would not forget the boys clenched hand opening out as if to gently offer a farewell 'high five' between parting souls.   He had in those hours shed his life's tears for the boy and that watery sap of compassion had run dry that day forever.

Suddenly he was startled from inner thought by the scratching of a rat crawling through netting on a skiff. He watched it entrap itself hopelessly, rest, then burrow further into the net pile, only to enmesh itself more. He then walked away from the skiff and took out of his jacket pocket a cell phone, switched it on and paused for a signal reception. He put the phone away assured that cell phone communication was as he expected, a discovery a long way off for the inhabitants of Ile à Vache.

Heavy but agile, Hakeem had earlier rushed from hut to shed to tree-shack not just introducing himself to each family but checking if there was any radio receivers about. Hakeem knew that if there was anything the locals had in their homes from the boats foundering all year round on the island's sandbars, it was a radio receiver. When the powers of the local potions failed to heal a wound, a local priestess would be called up on mainland Haiti; she was then asked to intervene and with the promise of a couple of gourds she would work up to a trance like chant, broken into crackles over the radio, seeking the restorative attentions of whatever Spirit was invoked.

Hakeem, now aware of being observed in silence by the villagers ashore, turned around and carefully pulled a magnum pistol from a hidden chest belt. He was weary already of salutes and smiles and gestures of thanks from the villagers. It was leading to a familiarity which left him uneasy. He had long learned to trust no one and if he ever thought twice that there was treachery in the making, he always acted decisively first; mistaken or otherwise he would be the survivor. Choosing the moment of his own death would be nothing less that heroic in a battle between the great Mudjaheddeen and the Infidel. He lined up the pistol sight with his right eye, paused, and with one shot exploded the rat into fragments of flesh among wood splinters. Its spine lay metres away, a limp piece of coral pink necklace twitching with life momentarily before a last writhe and arch on the hot sand. The men women and children stepped quickly off the cool piles of seaweed and slipped back into the tree cover. Hakeem then highstepped through the water out to the trawler and climbed the rope ladder.

Emerging from the wheelhouse a minute later he

sloshed slowly ashore while holding a laptop computer flat on his head. He went to sit on a lobster basket embedded above the shoreline. Opening up the laptop it whirred into life to the gasp of a distant child believing he had seen a television.

Unknown to Hakeem an old woman had shuffled across the soft sand and boldly stood behind him. She then burst into laughter in a mocking cackle at him as he tried to wave rat hairs away. Not seeing the humour he looked around and was startled by the sight of a hairless old woman, her dark brown head covered in scaly nodules. Her ears were deep purple and swollen so much they sagged down into her neck covered in beefy red ulcers. One eye bulged out upwards like a shiny egg and oozed out of both corners.

"Moi, Madame Leprosa", she mumbled hoarsely as she held out a gangrenous claw hand to him, her toothless cavernous mouth forcing a smile. "Roh T Kaoud" he replied spontaneously in Arabic, telling her to "fuck off". She wasn't getting any money or a handshake. His angry tone was enough to send her hurriedly shuffling off the beach. That frail Madame was the villagers only defence against the narcotraffickers seeking a hideaway. No one ever lingered for long in Pacq after meeting her and tried to avoid a return visit. Hakeem however unlike the traffickers didn't panic and flee upwind of the old woman. He regained his composure watching the laptop screen flicker with new images. A graphic appeared on its screen, being a three dimensional image of the superstructure of the new cruise ship Fantasea of the World, whose keel had been laid three years earlier at the Vrytinen Shipyard of Finland.

Competition to build this latest and most luxurious cruise ship for Festival Cruise Lines had been intense. The burglary 18 months earlier at the offices of the Naval Architects, Levio Marintech in Helsinki had been assumed to be an attempt at commercial espionage by a competing French shipyard. The break-in had been executed as the Finns celebrated the arrival of New Year with street fireworks setting off hundreds of alarm sensors across Helsinki. The alarm bells muffled by heavy snow, no one much cared or was too drunk to drive. After New Year's a sharp eyed technician had spotted the disturbance of the disk sequence in the marine CD cabinets. After some discussion about the firm's reputation, and the fact that the only disks available, and probably copied, were merely 3-D presentations of the completed ship for their client, it was agreed that reporting the matter would be seen as a waste of police time.

In the heat of the Haitian midday, Hakeem, sitting on the embedded lobster pot above the shoreline shouted over his right shoulder "ZADOR, COME OVER!".
A thin fair haired figure with a gangly step came out of the cool shade of some drooping palm fonds and flicked his Russian 'smoke' away. "Get the others" ordered Hakeem.

"I'll wake everyone" replied Zador in a thick Chechen monotone.

Zador was Mustafa Zadorozhna. He had trained with Hakeem in Algeria after fleeing the Russian advance into Grozny. He was left newly born at the backdoor of Grozny city's orphanage Number Four. At the age of 11, he was ejected for good after burning the chicken house where he had locked in a hated mother warden. Leaving the orphanage, his possessions consisted of the Holy Qu'ran, a spoon and the note that was pinned to the blanket over him when left as a newborn at the door of the orphanage. The Holy Qu'ran and spoon mattered little to him unlike the note which was his relic guarded with his life. He got used to hiding it in a bullet case. The case was either held in his armpit by a bandage or if he was picked up by the police or ended up asleep in dormitories or shared prison cells, he shoved it well up his rectum.

Before joining the Chechen rebels he lived off the meagre proceeds of protection payments from market stalls and cigarette kiosks. More often he just accepted fruit or smokes for later sale or barter. He came to the attention of the Chechen Kommando after recklessly lobbing a petrol bomb through the front hatch of a stalled Russian tank. Unlike Hakeem who was a qualified seaman, Zador earned his place on this mission at Bou Saada training camp in Algeria by his cold indifference for his own skin in combat. With dwindling opportunities for arson in bombarded Grozny he took to living for days deep in the city's sewers from where he would come up to garrotte Russian soldiers asleep at night in their barracks.

His brilliant memory of the sewer network had earmarked him for this special mission where knowledge of a labyrinth of decks and a detailed memory of the new ship's layout was required. With a squint in his left eye, now small and sunken after years of trying to centre his eyeball with his thumb, he did not have the shooting accuracy nor patience of Hakeem who was a self trained crack shot sniper. Zador's poor shooting accuracy did not bother him in the least. He had long earned the wary respect of his fellow martyrs in his expert use of his favourite but cumbersome weapon which he carried everywhere: an old Russian liquid Plamya Obretz 50 Flame Thrower; it's three fuel tanks when full weighed 23 kilos which Zador left harnessed on his back for hours on end. As part of his own training routine he would also sleep in the tank harness, fully refuelled. Not only did this ensure a permanent stench of diesel off him but also meant he was ordered away from his comrades campfires at gunpoint if in harness. He never ever got a light for a smoke from anyone except Hakeem.

Hakeem had first come across Zador on the outskirts of Grozny mistaking the fair haired armed civilian coming out of a sewer manhole for a Russian deserter. Moments before Hakeem was about to execute him, Zador seemingly unconcerned for his plight of summary execution, calmly asked for a last wish that he could finish biting a finger nail. He then recited a verse of the Holy Qu'ran as he lay prostrate with Hakeem standing over him, pistol pointing at the back of his head. Learning verses from the Holy Qu'ran was the extent of his short education at the Orphanage until Hakeem taught him English in Algeria from a translated Qu'ran text and old American movie reels projected onto a tent cover in the desert.

Hakeem Belbachir had from an early age sought a career at sea to escape the choking ghetto of Rafah were manic fervour for liberation squatted easily in a nest full of the desperate and the forgotten. Weary of being involved in small scale skirmishes in a forgotten Chechen war, Hakeem left Chechnya for Algeria to develop his idea to 'bring war crashing through the gates of Satan's infidel fortress, the United States of America'. He had convinced his fellow martyrs how unique opportunities could be exploited across the Atlantic where he would "slit open the weak Caribbean underbelly" of America. Hakeem had carefully studied American influence politically, geographically and militarily in the Carribean with Cuba at its centre. He knew Cuba well as a marine engineer having worked on Russian oil tankers docking in the port of Matanzas.

Like Zador the rest of the Brigade were already awake from Hakeem's pistol blast at the rat and began appearing from the undergrowth at various distances up along the cove as the locals retreated between them. The other martyrs were a mixture of young Chechens,

Syrians, Hamas Palestinians, Sudanese, Yemenis, two Iraqi Fedayeen, and a veteran mudjaheddeen from Bosnia. Unpaid, all were mercenaries of Allah, preparing for payment in life after death in paradise where martyrs were honoured heroes for all eternity.

Hakeem got up off the lobster basket heading for the shade with his open lap top with Zador joining up with him.

"Hey Zador, I just met a Haitian beauty who could be your mother. See over there, just leaving the beach, she didn't get money. She's the last one, go after her."

Zador looked over at a stooped figure now wearing a tattered straw hat, leaning on her stick with her back to them. Zador turned to Hakeem "At least I know my father wasn't a big confused camel, you furry bastard!" replied Zador angrily.

"Enough" said Hakeem putting his hand on Zador's shoulder. "She just looks Chechen, a Babushka, she has a bit of frost bite. Give her a few dollars and then we will all go through our mission objectives together. Here's the money, go."

Zador went off taking it as a command but was bored anyway and was getting increasingly edgy as the day passed.

Hakeem called the others to gather round.

"Okay, the rest of you, Suleyman, Amir, Khalil, Alif and Badshah, each of your units will be four martyrs instead of five. Me and Zador, we will be two units with five men in each. In less than eighteen hours the beaches of Florida will run red long after sunset with the filthy blood of Americans and Jews".

Hakeem opened the computer disk's programme for the layout of the ships crew compartments which came up a vivid blue 3D graphic. Areas highlighted included the Bridge deck, a crew gymnasium next to the Engine Hall and blocks of crew sleeping quarters set amidships in the lower decks.

"I want each of you not just to tell me where you will attack but where you expect the other units to be at the same time if you need help." continued Hakeem.

Suddenly a roar coming from the end of cove interrupted Hakeem. It was Zador, his unmistakable Chechen accent shouting "HAKEEM, HAKEEM YOU BROWN LUMP OF DESERT SNAKE SHIT! SO YOU THINK THIS IS FUNNY? YOU CALL THIS DISEASED VOODOO WITCH A CHECHEN MOTHER?" he raged, getting louder. The whole gang came out onto the beach led by Hakeem.

Alif replied mockingly to Zador "Give her a gun Zador, she'd still shoot straighter than you!"

Zador went apoplectic with fury, drew out his pistol sending everyone running for cover. He fired several shots in different directions, some bullets flicking up sand with much the effect of a thrown pebble. Hakeem dived for cover behind a tree "Forget it Zador and don't waste ammunition, that's my command. She is either a real leper or a voodoo zombie. Keep away comrade."

Zador turned around, stormed up to the woman kicking the sand angrily. He took a second Luger pistol from his chest belt. The woman had slumped over with her face in the sand once the firing had started. He put the gun to the back of her head and hesitated with his finger pressing back the trigger. He paused for a moment realising he might be splattered in pus and bits of lesions instead of just bloody bone shards and clumplets of brain lobe. He looked over in the direction of his Flame Thrower for a moment. Then he straightened up, turned around and looked over at Hakeem.

"You know something Arab martyrs?... this witch has no self pity unlike your wailing Palestinian women. Yet like a Chechen, she is ready for death every day."

Zador walked away from the woman toward the rest of the group. Most of the other martyrs hadn't known Zador too long but long enough to be wary of this unpredictable and trigger-happy misfit on this mission.

Without warning, Zador then turned about and quickly fired off all pistol chambers into the woman, all over her back. Faking a cheeky smile he stared at the group then reloaded and holstered his pistol "That was my act of mercy for today comrades, no?" asked Zador, now with a mad wide eyed grin, which further unsettled the others unsure if the gun would stay holstered.

Khalil caught up with Hakeem, saying within earshot of Zador. "That's all we need, a useless psycho following no-one's orders except his own."

"Don't worry Khalil" said Hakeem quietly "Tomorrow he will be loose among 1,200 passengers; we need to watch carefully the crew of that ship. That's your only task Khalil. Just keep the crew separate from the passengers. I haven't checked the crew for Jewish names. Do that for me once all the crew is under your control. I hope to have at least one hundred Jew prisoners from the passengers alone. We need all Zionists, American, Israeli or from wherever. We will talk about it later."

Hakeem returned to the shade with the full brigade "Okay everyone, let us concentrate from this moment on. Zador, ESPECIALLY YOU! Put your temper in your holster with your pistol. With discipline we will be more effective, our enemies are not old lepers but arrogant rich American infidels, but as blind as lepers to the suffering of the Islamic nations. The Americans have yet to learn that the power and will of Allah is greater than their military might; for all their new weapons they are still afraid, afraid of death and warriors afraid of death are not God's warriors. To die in battle for Islam is glorious! Hour by hour God brings us this opportunity ever closer. We will bring Satan to his knees, and all his earthly money and power will never defeat our courage and determination to succeed in our sacred mission. Let the world remember us for our bravery and honourable death in Jihad. Then the King of the Day of Judgement will grant us a special place by his side. We need to rest now comrades and focus on our heroic mission. We will need our bodies to be strong if we are to achieve our first objective to capture the ship quickly."

Hakeem looked around as each man listened

attentively, the younger commandos nodding to confirm their readiness. "Let's begin with Amir, what is your target?"

"The security center and weapons lockers." he replied.

"Okay Amir now take the computer and report on the positions of your comrades on the ship." Amir clicked open a multicoloured graphic of the entire ship and rotated the 3-D diagram 360 degrees.

CHAPTER 3

That same day, the Fantasea of the World, 18 decks high with her Bridgedeck a full 17 storeys above sea level had been nudged astern and hauled at her bow by tugs out of Miami harbour. All four of the eighteen ton propellers idled as she was brought out to the tide, escorted ahead by two honour tugs. The tugs hoisted fire hose fountain sprays which dusted the ship in misty rainbow plumes to Port and Starboard. Her hull and superstructure was liveried in Cruise ship white save for a band of gold paint encircling the ship at Promenade Deck level. The band of gold swept up to the large intertwined FCL letters of the Festival Cruise Lines logo at the bow.

Bedecked from bow to stern with the flags of the world the passenger compliment on this, her maiden voyage, was limited to twelve hundred souls, on board by special invitation and occupying the best of the ships nine hundred state rooms. The Guest of Honour was the Governor of Florida and his guests from the Florida State Legislature and State administration in Talahassee together with the President of the Florida Bar Association. The Governor was a champion of positive gay discrimination who would later officially open the ship's controversial 'Gay & Straits' Night Club. Completely unpublicised was the presence of a dozen girls from Miami Executive Escorts who were available as personal hostesses to the several Investment Brokers and a party of men from the ship's Insurance Underwriting syndicate all embarked without partners. The girls were not to approach the men until the ship was outside US Territorial waters and Floridian jurisdiction. The Fantasea of the World promoted itself as an 'All in One' resort for families, couples and singles. It offered a private members Topless Poolbar & Playclub licensed to the President of PlayBabe Publications, who was on board with a dozen of his favourite models for an inauguration party and photo shoot.

The sounds of the harbour side marching bands began to fade in the warm breeze and as the tow lines were let off, the ships fog horns awoke from their slumber with two thundering groans. Then, with her single smoke stack spewing bog brown puffs, her turbines whined into life. Surrounded on all sides by bobbing yachts and launches, her sirens whooped, alerting the small boats to the eruptions of churning white water. As her chief engineer powered up her 64,000 horsepower turbines at the click of a mouse button, giant frothy balloons of cream foam welled up from the midnight blue depths.

The crisp English voice of Captain Rodney Hamilton, formally of Her Majesty's Royal Navy came over the tannoy:-

"Distinguished Governor and fellow Captains of Commerce, Tourism and Travel, Ladies, Gentleman and lucky children, this is Captain Hamilton speaking. May I ask for a few moments of your attention…firstly to very warmly welcome you all on board the newest and largest cruise ship of Festival Cruise Lines and to celebrate with me her maiden voyage. The Fantasea of the World, for your information, has a gross tonnage of 114,000 tonnes, a length of 1,126 ft and beam amidships of 110 ft. Most importantly she has a cruising speed of 28 knots, the fastest Liner in the world. On this trip, not fully laden we may achieve with her four turbines 30 knots in the calm seas forecast. Please familiarise yourself with the safety procedures and your Muster station on board in the event we need to implement an evacuation, however unlikely. Our 632 crew on board for this trip will be delighted to assist you in safety matters and of course in any requests or special needs that you may have to make this cruise unforgettably enjoyable for every one of you. I look forward to meeting many of you in the coming three days that we have the pleasure of your distinguished company. I shall be in the King's Galleon Saloon for dinner at seven o'clock. Now, if you would please stand for the anthem of the United States of America ... as we hoist the stars and stripes."

As the rousing music died away the Captain concluded: "Thank you everyone and before I say a few words to the children for whom this ship is also catered, I should inform you that we will have a fire drill in the course of the cruise as a practice for our crew and I ask you for your full co-operation during the short exercise. Now boys and girls, listen carefully as I will answer some of your many questions now."

Captain Hamilton, a man in his mid-fifties, fit and tanned, took a deep breath "I have crossed the Atlantic 205 times, the Pacific 87 times, I have never been shipwrecked, never hit rocks, icebergs, another ship, never been lost overboard, never had a mutiny or been sunk or eaten by sharks or shanghaied by pirates and don't want to be. The ship will shortly be doing 22 knots and could do more if she was going faster you will be able to go ashore when we are at anchor and not before and I never watch movies about disasters at sea, sorry you can't steer the ship or come to the Bridge and I hope to retire from the sea this year."

In a crescendo roar he finished "IS THERE ANYTHING ELSE YOU WOULD LIKE TO KNOW?"

The Public Address tannoy went silent as crew and passengers laughed heartily "Enjoy the cruise everyone and thank you for your attention." the Captain uttered as he recovered his breath.

Captain Hamilton was glad to be retiring early after this cruise as he had been planning to leave his wife after 18 years and was looking forward to setting up a new home in Barbados with Olga the ship's fitness instructor. He could then put behind him the double life he had been leading for the past ten years. This latest commission was a farewell honour by Festival Cruise Lines which he had reluctantly accepted. He had to undergo further training to familiarise himself with more new marine technology and power control by computer joystick with software programmed overrides. With more and more ships becoming floating theme parks, he saw little point in cruise ships leaving port as every on-board entertainment was internal and the farthest any ship need sail in his view would be the territorial limit allowing the casinos open. Games on the high Hurricane Deck needing skill to deal with the ship's roll in a strong Trade wind were now receding memories for Captain Hamilton which he would never revisit. He insisted on still calling the Sports deck with running track the Hurricane deck.

While the passengers were left joking and laughing at the Captain's speech, Samia Badoud was nervously faking laughter. Samia was newly employed as a "Child Counsellor" and was assigned to the Family Entertainment Centre. Unknown to Samia, another 'sleeper' martyr was working as a kitchen hand in the ship's lower galley. In spite of just starting his duties, Abdul Babar was already sweating profusely even before the baker had yet to start the ovens for Afternoon Tea. On the spur of the moment after clumsily toppling a saucepan stack he took another tranquilliser pill from his inner trouser pocket. Abdul was edgy; he had been given a key but minor role in his holy mission. His critical acts of Jihad would trigger a co-ordinated and unstoppable sequence of terrifying actions onboard the liner and both in Cuba and the small town of Chichester, England.

The Fantasea's destination anchorage was eighteen hours sailing away, with mooring due not long after sunrise in deep water off a private Festival Cruise Lines island renamed Key Fiesta. The island was a previously unmapped piece of sandy scrubland but now trumpeted as 'Your key to a private fiesta in paradise'. The Cruise Line had spent over a hundred million dollars creating a medieval themed island of 'Tamed Savages, Conquistadors and Pirates'. Awaiting the ships passengers on this maiden voyage was a 'Meet and Greet' party of 'savages' bearing gifts of fruit and flowers. As with the other Festival Cruise ships calling at the island there would be the usual groups of young Mexicans dressed by the cruise line to look like wild Amerindian natives who awaited the ship's arrival on outrigger canoes.

As the passengers disembarked from the liner onto the launch tenders these 'natives' in vivid plastic head-dress would dive in for coins thrown overboard by some passengers.

The dimes and quarters would glint in the bright turquoise waters as they frisbeed downwards while the 'natives' already clutching coins pretended to snatch the coins as they sank into the gloom. When they surfaced holding up a coin the waiting passengers would respond with whoops of delight though eventually throwing coins further out to be rid of the incessant pleas for quarters and dimes. Later the 'natives' would dive deep collecting their bounty of small change.

The crew rostered for this maiden trip on the Fantasea of the World numbered 632, mostly new hires. The unskilled tasks were assigned to a mixture of Philippinos, Indians, and Mexicans. They met the company's requirements of understanding English and offering not just service with humility but also the unique added quality of servility long disappeared in Europe and America. Being servile came easy to them as the buying power of their lowly wages at home bestowed a local dignity, aside from the status of working for an American company and more, working on a luxury cruise ship. Passenger relations, entertainment, front line employees in retail and administration were a mixture of American trainees and experienced crew from Festival Cruise Lines WHQ in Miami. The officers and mechanics on board were mostly of European origin predominantly Greek and Polish. The first and second officers were American and seconded for this maiden voyage of VIP's from the

Festival Cruise Lines older sister ship, The Fantasea of the Americas.

In keeping with the stated company policy to promote international diversity, among the other trainees hired from the two dozen or so different nations were Samia and Abdul hiding behind false French identities of Samia Compte and Abdul Durand. Their applications for the jobs had been emailed in several different names from internet cafes in Europe. Samia's successful application was sent from Café Connex in Marseille and Abdul's from the Cyber Kaffe in Leipzig. At the Festival Cruise Lines "New Hires Welcome and Induction Party", neither knew nor met the other. In the hurry to recruit and train new staff in time for the maiden voyage, the use of Computer Assisted Staff Profiling (Casps) Version 2 had only been used randomly by Fantasea Lines in new hire selection. Both Samia and Abdul's repeated training in Algeria in interview and interrogation techniques had not been needed before being selected; French language was a 'must have' for the Cruise Line and there was nothing unusual about Arab looking French speakers of whom there were dozens employed on every ship. After training for their roles in Hakeem's base in Algeria, Samia and Abdul had both received military training in separate camps in Yemen where they were given new family and life histories. Upon leaving Yemen for their holy mission they were sworn never to visit a mosque, utter a word in Arabic or pray except during actual martyrdom.

There was nothing remarkable in either's luggage coming on board the liner though Samia jokingly passed off her collection of Miami City and Dade County community newspapers as a souvenir hoard. Her combat clothing on which she had stitched a large fashion label was passed over without remark. Once on board in her cabin she began to cut out articles and gossip columns detailing the famous and wealthy Jews who had booked on the liner's maiden voyage. Just before sailing, she had managed to send some information by email to Yemen along with some attachments downloaded from the Miami Herald about politicians and celebrity passengers.

Now she thought she was the sole martyr on board and would have to rely on her own judgment as to which other passengers would be valuable to Hakeem, in addition to those passengers targeted in replying emails from Yemen. As well as fulfilling her role of assisting children around the ship she had to locate the state rooms where these targeted passengers were now accommodated. Also concealed in the luggage of Samia and Abdul were satellite phones and each had strict instructions to turn on the phones at precise times for incoming calls and to receive further instructions. The calls would be quick to conserve battery power and coded to protect from an accidental or deliberate eavesdrop by ships in the region or on the Fantasea of the World itself.

CHAPTER 4

On Ile à Vache it was nearing high water at 21.30 hours, local time and shipboard time on the liner. Hakeem and the brigade weighed anchor and motored away in the shrimp trawler at a walking speed of three to four knots. At the bow was Hakeem using an infrared night scope looking for signs of wavelets spilling over any sandbars ahead. These might be just hidden under the full tide in the otherwise flat calm sea and he was very aware of the unreliability of the outdated Haitian coastal navigation charts. As the put-put sound of its marine engine echoed away along the coast, the only light showing in the darkness was the yellow glow of dim wheelhouse light as Hakeem had covered the trawler's red and green side lights. Occasionally Hakeem flashed his torchlight indicating a turn to port or starboard for Khalil to steer clear of a reef or a possible sandbar. Once in deeper water, Khalil would be relying on the echo sounder and the newly fitted radar while Hakeem studied the old charts; they were better than nothing to guide them as they brought her up to a full speed of fifteen knots.

Hakeem had earlier calculated the approximate arrival time of the cruise ship coming through the deepwater shipping lane between Eastern Cuba and

Western Haiti which was named the 'Windward Passage' on the charts. He based his calculations on the liner's departure time, the nautical distance from Miami using the shipping channel through the Windward Passage to Fiesta Island and an estimated cruising speed, sailing with the tide, to reach the island's sheltered waters at 0800 in calm conditions. Not to miss the liner, Hakeem had deliberately overestimated her speed calculating that her propellers may be kicking out twenty five or twenty six knots.

Once in position the brigade knew they would not have a long wait before the liner would appear on radar. The liner would also pick them up on her radar and they needed to uncover the trawler's red and green lights to avoid attention. Holding the trawler's position drifting in the straits of the Windward Passage against a running tide meant throttling up the engine every couple of minutes and then idling as the tide carried her back. Soon he would have to continuously motor against it. Hakeem expected that the actual speed of the liner coming through the Passage on a fast current could be an overall five to eight knots faster than the liner's gauge reading.

Trailing in the wake of Hakeem's trawler was an inflatable rib boat. At the back of it there was a 60 horsepower outboard motor capable of carrying five adults at a speed of 40 knots. The inflated rib, undetectable by radar would carry the brigade's small advance party once the liner began to slow down. It was critical to the attack that the liner's engines stop and stop long enough in the Passage strait to allow the trawler come alongside later when the rest of the brigade would board the ship. Once tied alongside they would then also transfer the trawler's cargo of 500 Glock pistols with ammunition, 9 shoulder fired rocket propelled grenade launchers, one M60DX extendable bipod heavy machine gun with 16,800 rounds, 10 kilos of Hexogen explosive and 4 small red cylinders marked 'Mercaptan'.

On board the liner, Samia and Abdul each had their different instructions with both awaiting a call on their satellite phones to act. Abdul was relieved when the main galley finally closed, ending an evening of shouting, being shouted at, panicking staff and bodies in collision. He knew that the plush dining saloons and tranquil guest lounges would soon be engulfed in a similar chaos. Left alone in the pastry kitchen he had pocketed a meat cleaver and three new carving knives. That would do for battle in the event of his discovery but he looked forward to arming himself with the pistol he expected later from Hakeem. Fully armed he would immediately dare the American pastry Chef to again call him a "deadbeat sand nigger" when the Chef would be staring into the barrel of that pistol. Abdul's eight hour shift was now over and he made his way to the Trash Center carrying a bag of left overs. He diverted to make for Pilotage Door number four, on the same deck level and just two metres above the liner's water line. After ending up in dead end passageways twice he finally saw the door with its single small porthole, the purpose of which allowed crew to see the arrival alongside of a Harbour Pilot. As he came up to the Pilotage Door he had seen in an instant the ceiling corner CCTV camera, the large door lock and adjacent small red box with fire key and the 'Door Open' sensor wiring which led off up to the Bridge. As he hesitated at the door to memorise the details whilst pretending to be lost, a voice came over the intercom speaker from the liner's Security Center.

"Crewman, if it's the Trash Center your looking for, go back to the red passageway and take a left. That's the red passageway and on the left."

Abdul waved meekly in humble thanks at the CCTV camera looking long enough to notice that it was fixed facing the pilotage door and was not swivel mounted. Abdul duly found the Trash Center and was relieved to see only sprinklers and no cameras. It was there he intended to hide under the trash bags waiting for instructions once he had retrieved his satellite phone from his cabin.

Meanwhile, fourteen decks above, Samia though tired, continued her work in Juvenile Passengers Ship Orientation, already working beyond her shift without taking a break. She had reconnoitred the crew and passenger area layout as best she could and tried to recall from memory what she had seen from drawings in the training camp in Algeria. Leading groups of precocious teenagers dressed in contrived shabbiness around the ship, some teenagers dropped out along the way at the Network Games Center and at the Arcade

Electronic Games. Others stayed at the Rock Climbing Wall or hung back to book seats at the Planetarium while the last of the teenage girls invaded the Viennese Pastry Terrace. Samia's beautiful dark features betrayed her Horn of Africa parenthood, her thin ebony hair in daylight reflecting a glossy bluish sheen. Most striking was the flash of her glacial white teeth in a broad full lipped countenance. Samia was born an Eritrean Falasha Mura, a tribe of Ethiopian Christians converted from Judaism throughout the 20th Century. Her parents had tried hard to convince the Israelis of their Jewish ancestry before Israel's rescue by airlift of Ethiopian Falasha Jews during the famine of 1984. After her parents and younger brother later died of cholera, she applied again as a twelve year old orphan during another airlift of Falasha Jews in the 1991 'Operation Solomon'. Further rejection by Israel's Ministry of Immigrant Absorption led to her decision to renounce Judaism and Christianity and become a zealous teenage convert to Islam.

On board the liner, Samia's engaging dimpled smile drove the older boys to flirt with her, play pranks and ask the most stupid questions hoping to trigger a rare smile. In her strong French accent she had explained about the pool hours, the opening hours of the Toy Games and Software shop, the 3 to 8 years dining room, the 9 to 12 years dining room and how not to hog all the seating in the 24 hour 'all you can eat' Planet Pizzeria without ordering something.

As she passed the MTV video wall, the Ping Pong and Volleyball Courts she had explained the rules about drinking on the decks, the restricted adult only bars and the over 21 age limit for access to the casino. All the while she was noting in her mind the position of CCTV cameras for the mission to come. Some teenage boys insisted that the beautiful Samia "chill out" with them under the Glass Atrium and Aquarium otherwise they jokingly threatened her that they would follow her back to her crew cabin. Thankfully for her she was eventually relieved of her duties by two male Child Counsellors whereupon she then hurried back to her shared cabin to pick up her list of passenger targets.

She found her cabin door unlocked on arrival and saw her cabin companion lying in the top bunk. "Hi Bonnie" Samia called out wondering if she was yet asleep. Bonnie murmured drowsily, "Samia I'm bushed, wake me up next week."

Samia sat quietly on her lower bunk and collected her list of passenger names. "I will see you in a while Bonnie, I am going to the ice machine". Samia walked briskly down the corridor heading for Passenger Administration. On her way she stopped by the bank ostensibly to ask about any special exchange rates for crew. Her actual intent was to memorise the bank tellers face and shiny name badge which was inscribed *'Janice'*.

Arriving in Passenger Administration, she found the office door ajar and a weary elderly clerk rubbing her eyes, her spectacles pushed up to her forehead. Samia paused at the door to show her full child counsellor uniform of yellow shorts, blue blouse and embossed baseball cap.

"Hi" said Samia feigning cheerfulness. "just wondering if there is a special list of all children on board with their ages?" she asked.

"Err....nope honey. Just one big manifest print out for all passengers over there! The one with all the scrawls in red all over it, you can see how many changes we had to make. Too many big heads that needed bigger state rooms! Little heads with little brains are a whole lot easier. You should be thankful!"

Samia tried to smile. "I can imagine" she answered.

"And so many important people on this first cruise," Samia added as she leafed through the manifest ending with the passengers in the Grand Suites at the back of the ledger.

The lady sighed quietly "It's not just the ship's maiden cruise, it's a maiden cruise for a lot of VIP freeloaders as well sweetie … you'll know all about it during the fire drill. They won't know one end of the ship from the other!"

Samia left Passenger Administration wishing the clerk luck and returned to her cabin to prepare to bring about a situation where the Captain would order the ship to a dead stop. In the cold glare of her bunk's wall light she had put on a modest black knee length but figure hugging dress. On her face she used a little matt blusher, electric blue eye shadow, black eyeliner and a wet shine ruby lipstick. She then checked her watch coming up to 22.30 hours.

It was time to switch on her Global Star satellite phone, a neat hand held model which she put into her black patent handbag. She slipped quietly out of the cabin, walking quickly to reach the nearest crew elevator. She was hoping to arrive in the passenger area unnoticed by any crew en route. She was aware of the ship's policy explained to all crew over 3 days of shoreside training that the crew could freely mingle with passengers when off duty. But she knew that as an off duty child counsellor, her stunning wealthy looking appearance would raise eyebrows on this, the first night of the voyage. However the ship had now become quiet. The only noises came from slight vibrations of wall panels in the crew passageways. She finally reached the 'Monte Carlo' piano bar alone and as intended, unnoticed.

At the entrance she stopped. She adjusted her eyes to the soft lighting between the randomly placed sofas. It was busy though mostly with couples and she had to find a man, any man, on his own and seemingly available. With her back resting against the bar counter she ordered an orange juice and turned again to face the room becoming a featureless and anonymous silhouette surveying the passengers. She observed a heavy man leaning towards a table lamp leafing quickly through the pages of a magazine, while the pianist was on a break. She waited for several minutes for the pianist to begin playing and half way through the first melody she walked over to him hesitantly.

"Is this seat free sir? This is one of my favourite tunes." she said. The large man in a white open neck shirt, looked up at her and briefly at her figure. "Absolutely, sit down, the music is wonderful here." he replied. The man was in his forties, she guessed.

He put his magazine down. "So you like 'Lara's Theme' he continued "Have you seen 'Dr Zhivago', its one of those sorta timeless classic movies?"

She turned towards him and crossed her legs "I just like the music" never having heard the tune or of the movie before. She forced her eyes to linger on his eyes longer than she had wished. This was part of the mission she had despised. Both listened intently until the tune was finished.

"Are you one of our special guests?" she asked.

"Special, maybe." he replied. "Actually I am in the food business, we supply a lot for this magnificent vessel.

Samia replied "Wonderful." nodding her head looking impressed. "I am just one of the new crew. This is my first day at sea. It is quite lonely for me." she paused. "I have no parents and my only friends are back in France. Are you alone too?"

"Eh no, I have my wife with me, actually she is my third wife. I suppose deep down too, ... I am alone also, always lookin' for the right woman for me. I gotta compliment the company for selectin' such a beautiful charmin' woman as you". Samia faked a smile at him whereupon he opened out the centrefold of the magazine on the table. Samia looked away from the huge photograph of a naked woman stretched across the pages.

"My name is Gino, actually Gino Calvoni the Third but friends call me G, and that's only for friends....... close friends." You might have heard of 'Calvoni the only Pepperoni' it's our slogan everywhere, we've even an advertisement on Cable TV."

"Samia Compte is my name. I am Samia Compte…….. the first!…from France."

"ENchantay Mamoyzelle. I'm gettin a drink, can I get you anythin" he asked her as the waiter passed. Samia declined politely and kept her head bowed while pointing to her still full glass of orange juice, preferring to remain unrecognised by fellow crew.

After his drink arrived they listened in silence as the pianist played out a medley of songs. Gino slowly turned over the pages of his magazine, revealing more poses of tanned naked flesh. Just as the pianist finished, a loud beeping sound came from her handbag drawing glances from everyone in the room. She dropped her full glass in nervousness as she hurriedly pulled her phone out and pressed the answer button. She stood up and went straight to the Ladies Restroom holding the phone by her side.

Once inside she brought the handset up to her cheek, took a deep breath: "Hello, everything is FANTASTIC here now, I am fine. Where are you?" she spoke in the coded wording as agreed, her voice echoing in the green marbled splendour of the piano bar bathroom. It was Hakeem on the other end of the phone and whose soft gutteral speech she had last heard in Yemen six months earlier. He spoke slowly and loudly in halting clear tones: "We - are - ready- to - fish. We - can - see - your - boat - now - on - our - radar. Go - and - check - your - position - from - the - stars - at - 23.30." he added.

Samia looked at her watch, showing 23.00 and replied "I will check my position from the stars at 23.30." Hakeem abruptly ended the call. Samia stuffed the phone hurriedly back in her handbag and put her hands on the cold marble; they were moist but cold. She ran the hot tap and dried them off. She then composed herself for a moment and looked into the mirror emotionless save for a slight movement of her full lips. She had whispered under her breath in Arabic "Death to Satan".

Gino stood up as she returned to his table. "Everythin' okay?" he asked adding "Was that one of those world phones workin' off satellites?"

"Yes, we share a few between us on the ship." she replied "and now you must listen to me very carefully Monsieur G………come closer to my face. I like your magazine very much. Now I want you to follow me into the men's room. Gino's eyes widened and he put his half empty glass on the table. "You want me to what?"

"I said I want you now to follow me into the men's bathroom, not the ladies bathroom but the men's bathroom .....I have something special to show you." Only in there will you see it. You will like it. It is very special. Come".

Gino took his glass and gulped back the remains of his whiskey "Okay Samia ...if that's what you want I will follow you in to the men's room but....maybe we could go to....."

Samia had got up from the sofa without listening to Gino's mutterings and went swiftly towards the men's room turning round once to check that he was following her. She waited for him to catch up. When she entered the room she instantly grabbed his shirt and pulled him roughly into a cubicle. A fellow passenger realising what he had just seen quickly zippered himself up and left the room murmuring "wow" to himself.

Inside the cubicle Samia lifted up Gino's shirt and pressed her lips against his, thrusting her tongue into his mouth. Without hesitating he lifted up Samia's dress and slipped his hands inside her panties to grope her smooth buttocks. He was becoming very aroused and strongly manhandled her, getting rougher by the minute. Realising that she might lose control of the situation she grabbed his hand and violently pinned him back by his wrists against the side wall of the cubicle. "Will you come outside with me for some fresh air?" she asked catching her breath. Gino was panting also and replied "Absolutely, if you want. I can't bring you back to my cabin but ...." Samia immediately opened the cubicle door with Gino following behind rapidly fixing his clothes.

They headed straight for the flights of stairs, Samia leading the way moving quickly. One flight and then two flights and soon they were outside on the Promenade Deck cooling off in the night air.

Gino came up beside her breathless but trying to conceal it. "Lets go higher!" she said. Before he had replied she had taken his hand and led the way rushing up another outside stairs to the Weather Deck. By this time Gino was flushed and hyperventilating.

"Is that it or …do you want to climb …the goddamn mast too?" he puffed. It was then that Samia raced on ahead of him heading for the next starboard stairs up to the Boat deck.

CHAPTER 5

Within minutes of Gino convincing Casino security that Samia was on a lifeboat threatening to jump, three casino staff had arrived watching Samia. She was sitting on the ridge of the lifeboat cover, and screaming repeatedly at the staff in well acted hysterics, "WHO are YOU? WHO are YOU?" Samia wanted more than red jacketed croupiers looking at her but knew that it wouldn't be long before the ship's security would be taking over. Everything was unfolding as Hakeem had predicted. Seconds later the Chief of Passenger Security arrived calling up the Bridge on his lapel microphone as he did so. "We have a problem with a passenger here, could be personnel. Lifeboat deck, starboard side, close to Muster Station A. The girl apparently goes by the name of Sammy or something."

As soon as the First Officer on Watch heard the message he looked back from the starboard side Bridge wing and replied to the Chief "get Human Resources if you think she's crew and get the Sea Marshals in on this whether she is crew or not. Also throw a life jacket to her and ask her to at least hold the jacket." The First Officer then hung up and dialled the Chief Engineers phone. "Full Astern until Dead Stop." he ordered abruptly. "Affirm Full Astern until Dead Stop sir."

replied the Duty Engineer. The First Officer then dialled the Captain's quarters.

The Captain was wide awake and busy with Olga's legs around his neck. "Captain I have to disturb you about a safety problem.... we have apparently a member of the crew or a passenger threatening to jump overboard. A young girl. She is balancing atop starboard lifeboat number one. If she survives the fall we don't want to lose her so I have reversed all props for a Dead Stop sir."

"Damn" uttered the Captain, concealing his heavy breathing.

"Just bow thrusters only on Full Astern please. The stern props on Full or even Half could pull the youngster under. Cordon the deck from all passengers and non-marine crew except Security. I will be there in a minute."

By the time the Captain had reached the Bridge Samia was holding the life jacket thrown up to her. From the Weather Deck below, the sounds of walkie talkie beeps interspersed with male voice radio chatter grew louder until four men appeared at the top of the Boat deck stairs. They walked briskly up to the rail beside lifeboat number one.

"Okay guys, stand off. Get a ways back, give the girl some space," Hank the senior sea Marshal said loudly, in between breaths, making sure Samia would hear him.

After a few minutes surveying the problem he turned

to the Chief of Passenger Security and in a quieter voice told him to post a guard at the bank and the jewellery shops as she could be a decoy. Just as Hank took a final breath before speaking to Samia, he hesitated. Frowning in puzzlement he turned again to the Chief and whispered sideways to him. "Did you ever hear of a suicidal jumper wearing a parachute? What's she doin' holding a life jacket…do you think she really wants to be shark feed?"

"Most suicides are a cry for help Marshal, no more, lets get her down." replied the Chief.

"Young lady we are United States Law Enforcement Sea Marshals, my name is Hank Kruger and here is my ID………….. I am here to help you."

Samia had guessed who they might be and she concealed well her relief that everything was still going to plan. The Captain had now arrived on the Bridge and was observing the situation. He spoke to the First Officer. "Once we're drifting we will be running fast, keep us in the channel. One stern prop please, DSA."

"Dead Slow Astern Sir" replied the First Officer. As soon as the liner began to respond the Captain continued "All Bridge Officers to stations. Stand by to launch portside rescue launch. Four man crew please. Prepare for a Man Overboard …get some life rings and smoke floats ready to throw in after her if she jumps before we're at a halt…………and oh, all deck lights off on the starboard side please, we don't want any passenger concerns gentlemen or as you might say in the U.S., "no rubberneckers.""

Less than 2 kilometres across the dark Caribbean ocean Hakeem Belbachir, Commander of the Guantanamo Martyrs Brigade was observing the ship through his binoculars balancing himself on top of the trawler's wheelhouse. He noticed that the bright cluster of lights moving slowly in the night had come to a stop. The Fantasea of the World would now drift slowly towards them into his trap while the trawlers engine ran constantly to hold position in the strong tide, as if fishing. Unknown to Samia acting hysterically on the lifeboat she was accompanied by companion martyr Abdul Babar who was quietly sweating profusely under the full plastic sacks of the Trash Center. One of the sacks which he pulled on top of him tore in the process spilling what he guessed were probably pizza crusts, fries, prawn shells, or rib bones. Whipped cream or congealing meat stock seeped into his open shirt as he lay horizontal. He pressed the satellite phone face down into the fat of his stomach to muffle the loud beep of an imminent call. He knew the mission was underway as soon as the gentle throb of the ship's engines and the rattling of a loose ventilator grill in the Trash Center had stopped.

On his mind continually was the strength of both phone signal and radio traffic interference during the call. He was below more than a dozen metal deck floors and Hakeem had explained to him in Yemen about the thicker metal plating and double skin of the ship's hull at sea level. Hakeem also had mapped out for him several times the position of the Trash Center and the pilotage doors which were just two metres above the water line.

As the ship became motionless the silence began to unnerve Abdul. In the dark of the trash centre his eyes were fixed on a chink of light coming through the door he had left open. Whatever food remains had fallen over him were now sliding off him in streams of sweat. Without the soothing sound of the sea rushing past outside he was now alone in the quiet, his heart thumping like a drum. He was unavoidably thinking about death. His burial in the dark under the rubbish concentrated his mind on how he was going to spend what probably were his last worldly hours. While he might die unceremoniously in this world, in the afterlife he would however be a Great amongst Greats in the war against the unclean and ungodly. He would find his place alongside the giants in the history of Islam and if God spared his life on this world for another mission he intended to change his name to Salaheddeen whose life was spared in victory after victory against the crusading infidels a thousand years earlier. Death will be glorious.

As the minutes passed his thoughts turned to evening prayers in France and memories of joking with his brothers over coffee in the decrepit boarding house in Choisy le Roi. He would not now pray however as he lay prostate on his back in the Trash Center. He was getting sleepy from the effects of tranquillisers and the build up of heat from the plastic trash sacks on top of him. He had to stay awake and began to remember happier memories of his childhood. He would at all costs avoid an insult to Islam by praying surrounded by the waste from the tables of Satan though he wondered in what direction lay the holy city of Mecca.

Suddenly Abdul's entire body jumped with the shock of the loud beeps of the incoming call on the satellite phone. In seconds he was outside the Trash Center with pieces of gristle and limp French fries falling out of him. "Hello, everything is FANTASTIC here, I am fine, how are you?" asked Abdul excitedly. The voice on the other end of the line was Hakeem.

"We - are - ready - to – fish. Open - the - net. Open - the - net. Do - you - hear - clearly?"

Abdul responded. "The net will be open in a few minutes, the fish have not seen me, everything is FANTASTIC."

Hakeem hung up first , always conscious of satellite phone chatter being monitored by U.S. listening stations. Abdul immediately headed to the pilotage door number four, carrying a large trash bag on his shoulder which would conceal his face from the CCTV camera.

As soon as he came into the view of the camera he pushed the bag against the camera lens and pulled from his jacket a wire cutter cutting the CCTV cable instantly blacking out one of the forty monitors in the Security Center. The Center monitored every safety sensitive Passenger Activity Zone, both internally and externally, including the pilotage doors. Atop the ship's mast one rotating camera gave a bird's eye view of the entire ship. As Hakeem had guessed, the drama on the starboard lifeboat deck had drawn the attention of all the security staff. Through his binoculars he was even more pleased with the decision of the Captain to turn off all starboard lighting which would provide further welcome cover from the cameras. As Samia continued with her threats to jump from the lifeboat a large detachment of security staff were dispatched to protect the cashiers in the casino. A second detachment was deployed at the ship's bank, though closed.

The next critical part of Abdul's mission was to cut the 'Door Open' sensor cable linking the pilotage door to the Bridge. That done, then with one stab of the cutters, he smashed the glass box holding the Pilotage door lock emergency key. The lock turned easily with two motorised deadbolts withdrawing into the doorframe. With both hands he grabbed the handles of the heavy reinforced door and clipped it back to the hull. Below him, less than two metres down, he could see the creamy streaks of foam gliding silently past. Looking out into the black night he could see little other than wavy melting reflections of cabin lights gliding across a polished ebony membrane. He began to panic not seeing any sign of Hakeem's boat. He went back inside and began to inhale deeply when the life jacket locker caught his eye. He immediately prised open the door and pulled on a life jacket. He looked anxiously at his watch showing 00:17.

CHAPTER 6

With the five hour time difference the time was now 05:17 in the English village of Chichester, a couple of miles from the Port of Southampton on the English Channel coast. The village boasted its own post office but the bank had long gone and not long afterwards its tiny police station had also closed. Most of the village's 160 residents commuted to work or shop in Southampton.

The Guantanamo Martyrs Brigade knew that a stake out in such a small location would be very conspicuous and quickly draw suspicion from the local folk. To avoid being attracted by anything other than the normal routine, several different brigade members had hired different cars in Southampton and driven past number 13 Blackheath Road, several times every day.

No. 13 Blackheath Road was a pretty bungalow with flower baskets hanging from the eaves. In the driveway was Mrs Hamilton's red Volkswagen Polo bearing the same registration numbers and letters that Hakeem had shown them in photographs back in Chechnya. The martyrs were further reassured by the large brass ship's bell hanging in the porch. The brigade had to enter No. 13 Blackheath Road and restrain their first hostage of the entire mission before she could use her mobile phone. She was observed nightly to go to bed around about midnight and normally left the porch light on. The martyrs weren't sure if they had to deal with any dog in the house but the fillet steak that had been thrown in the garden three days earlier had remained uneaten and none of them had seen a dog as they drove by or walked past the house on rainy days under cover of an umbrella. As the men's watches came up to 05:30 they opened the door of the hired truck that was parked outside the house. The first one out carried a sledge hammer and ran straight up to the hall door. In the bright light of the porch two well aimed blows landed on the door lock and within seconds three men were inside the hall. They were unsure which room to enter first until a light went on at the end of a corridor and Ms Hamilton nervously called out "who's there? who's that?"

In an instant the men, wearing balaclavas, were in her warm fragrant bedroom. She was immediately knocked back onto her soft cerise duvet and a sticking bandage was bound around her mouth. After a few seconds of muffled screams she stopped to catch her breath through her nose. She was pulled up on her feet and her brushed cotton dressing gown thrown over her head. Her arms were tied behind her with rolls of plastic packaging tape. Again she squirmed hopelessly, pausing again to breath deeply through her nose. One of them then crudely stuck a fully charged syringe of Propofol anaesthetic into her neck and in a couple of seconds she dropped limply to the floor. The men then carried her out bodily through the porch, smashing the porch light as they did so and bundled her into the back of the truck.

Some time later she woke up. Drowsy and disorientated, she gradually realised she was seated and bound with barbed wire to a toilet bowl. A fresh newspaper had been taped to the front of her dressing gown. As her vision began to focus in the semi darkness she could see a figure looking through a camera on a tripod who began taking photos of her, the flash causing her to wince and turn her head aside. She knew the unmistakeable smell of heavy marine oil. With the barbed wire wrapped around her tearing into the newspaper each time she moved, she was sure that if she remained quite still she could faintly hear the sound of the sea. Through the open toilet door she could see she was in a derelict warehouse, maybe in Southampton docks she thought.

She looked down at the newspaper taped to her and made out the title name of 'The Southampton Globe Newspaper'. Sitting on the toilet bowl she slowly realised she could be left unattended for hours or days and could be hand fed like an infant or have to grab and bolt food off a plate like a dog if she was to get any food.

While Mrs Hamilton was coming round in the grey English dawn the Caribbean darkness was vividly broken by the ship's sparkling white lights laced in tent like curves from stern to masts to bow. Captain Hamilton ordered the portside rescue launch lowered into the water, out of sight of Samia, its crew of four hoping to pick up Samia as soon as possible if she jumped; if she did they would expect to fish out a lifeless body shattered by the high fall from the lifeboat deck.

Hakeem now at the helm of the trawler, slowly manoeuvred the trawler around to approach the ship dead ahead from the front. He could see the starboard side in near darkness and watched as the portside rescue launch was lowered into the water. As he expected, the rescue launch then motored around the stern to stay out of sight of Samia. He looked at his watch and shouted to Zador and Khalil to pull in the powerful rib alongside the trawler to board it. In a couple of minutes the inflatable rib with a total of five men on board was speeding towards the liner's portside, the speed climbing rapidly up to 40 knots. The attack had begun.

Hakeem had to move very quickly to ambush the rescue launch before it's crew alerted the Bridge. At high speed he circled around the liner staying in darkness. Then he lined up the rib for a direct run in under the ship's huge stern, the martyrs gunsights fixed on the rescue launch. In the launch the luminous orange life jackets of the crew were easy visible targets for Hakeem. The rescue crew stood up and turned around to see what was coming out of the darkness.

Hakeem holding an Uzi machine gun in one hand and the wheel in the other, sprayed the crew in a single prolonged burst of fire, the impact of the multiple hits flipping all crewmen backwards over the launch into the water. The crackle of rapid gunfire went unheard on the ship, as the loud piped music played on throughout the decks.

Hakeem then throttled back the inflatable rib to reduce it's waspy engine noise and stealthily brought the boat along the port side of the stationary liner making for the open pilotage door number four. There in the doorway stood the lonely figure of Abdul silhouetted against the bright light of the passageway. Abdul was craning his neck anxious that the approaching engine sound was that of the martyr's boat whose appearance he had been waiting for, it seemed, an age. Abdul, whispering prayers to himself, got down on his knees and grabbed Hakeem's hand pulling him up out of the inflatable into the ship. Next was Zador, unwieldy in his LPO-50 fuel tank harness, his AK47 strapped to the flame thrower barrel. He was followed by Amir, Badshah and then Khalil, also with AK47's and each had a grenade launcher belted around their back. All five on board, Hakeem tied the empty inflatable to the opened door hinge, engine off.

Hakeem, shouldered his Uzi to quickly embrace Abdul before drawing his pistol and heading for the upper decks.

On the Bridge, Captain Hamilton decided to make a

quiet information announcement over the speakers in the Passenger Activity Zones still open.

"Good Morning to all passengers still enjoying the ship's facilities and yet to go to bed. For your information we have decided to reduce our speed and hold our position as due to the fact that we are running in a strong current, we will be arriving in Key Fiesta too early. We have a special welcome for you at Key Fiesta, which is to coincide with our planned arrival at 0800 hours. Do enjoy the calm and quiet while we wait here off the Haitian coast. We will be underway again shortly. Thank you and goodnight."

Zador stayed with Abdul by the pilotage door, called up the trawler on his satellite phone and issued a command to the rest of the brigade on the shrimp trawler. "Full speed to the ship. We are ready. The mission begins."

Hakeem ran up all the external portside stairs, pistol in one hand, Uzi in the other. Reaching the Bridge deck portside, he paused for a moment looking through the forebridge door. He saw Captain Hamilton looking into the compass binnacle. Hakeem pulled back the door and jumped in holding the pistol in his raised hand aimed straight at the face of Captain Hamilton roaring "GET BACK! HANDS BEHIND YOUR HEAD.........., NOW!... OR YOU DIE, NOW! BASTARD INFIDEL!"

The suave Captain Hamilton stumbled backwards, eyes wide, his mouth open. "Good God, what do you want?" Hamilton retorted defiantly.

"This ship is now under my command Hamilton and YOU will be my First Officer." Hakeem answered loudly. "And if you do not obey I will let your old brain get some fresh air instead of rotting quietly in retirement with Mrs Gwendolen Hamilton.

"Are YOU mad man, ME, hand over MY ship to ………." Hamilton's voiced trailed off.

"Gwendolen Hamilton?" he enquired. He then continued firmly "I have no concern about anyone NOT on board. My only concern is my passengers and my vessel carrying them. Harming or even killing me will serve you no purpose. You need ME more than I need YOU, whoever you are, you miserable piece of stinking criminal flotsam."

Hakeem came up to Hamilton, pressed his pistol barrel up under Hamilton's chin, his face inches away. "You need me Mr Hamilton because Gwendolen needs YOU, she is gone from the pretty cottage in Chichester and like your pretty flowers hanging in those copper baskets from your green tiled cottage roof she will need some water soon. Yes, Hamilton, I know all about you and your command of the British Navy frigate 'Valiant' and your medals for invading the Malvinas, an island of penguins, recaptured from Argentina for the honour of the British Empire. Yes, the great empire that makes and breaks nations, that helped make the state of Israel and destroy Palestine. Yes, when death comes to you, it must not be honourable, Hamilton.

For now, you and Gwendolen still alive in England and all the passengers and crew of this ship are prisoners, prisoners of our Holy War". As my prisoners I will respect them or most of them, more than I ever will respect you Hamilton!

Hamilton's mouth began to quiver in a mix of rage and panic. "What's happened to my wife, what's going on?" Hamilton asked angrily.

"Nothing yet. You will do EXACTLY as I say Hamilton" ordered Hakeem. "We know all about you Hamilton. We have been following your wife and watching your house for a long time. Mrs Hamilton could soon be a widow if you're not careful. For now we need you more than we need Mrs Hamilton. So if you want her to live you will obey ALL my commands. Is that clear Hamilton?"

Suddenly Khalil pushed open the door, excited, AK47 at his hip. "Hakeem, we have control over the Security Center, Amir is there … and all the ships weapons, now, … how............ about this smart sea dog...... helping me identify the ships police?"

"No, he stays on the Bridge. Samia will do that, get her!" commanded Hakeem.

As Khalil left the Bridge one of the deck officers spoke up, "Who are you? What are you looking for? Weapons? Diamonds?"

Hakeem looked over and raised his pistol aiming for the deck officer. "Who said you could speak? I am now in command of this ship.... did you not hear me? Next time you will say to me "permission to speak SIR" or I will lower you into the water above the stern propellers and when I order "Full Ahead" you will lose first your legs then your belly and finally your head ...... just like a big American milkshake with real chunks of American filth."

Captain Hamilton suddenly lunged at Hakeem grabbing him by the collar. "I will do nothing that endangers the life of my crew or the passengers of this ship. While I am alive it IS I who will remain in command Mr Hakeem and ... if you kill me or harm any officer or crew or any passenger, this ship will not sail. We have our engines idling, we are adrift and in no time, our status will be picked up in our Miami operations center who will alert the United States coastguard, that is, if they are not ALREADY underway...........we have been adrift for 30 minutes."

Hakeem smiled mischievously. The captain and deck officers were puzzled. Hakeem casually pushed back the Captain who then braced himself for a violent assault.

"Hamilton" Hakeem said politely, "Come with me to your Communications Center where we will arrange a special message for you. Come, the message will be here soon, it will create a better understanding between us and then maybe we will not see so much American blood washing over your nice blue decks and polluting God's oceans. You walk first, go on down the central passage, second door to the left, I know where everything is in MY new ship."

Hakeem walked a few paces behind Captain Hamilton until they reached the Communications Center. Brightly lit, the soundproofed room was full of noisy static interference and stray signals mixed with faint trawlermens conversations around the Caribbean; some words in drunken Spanish were voicing over a ship's transistor playing Mariachi. Some more whistling sounds interrupted Creole dialect in argument with an angry Russian, maybe a fish factory ship disturbed in laying a net in deep water or an old Cuban freighter carrying sugar cane or Russian milk powder.

Hakeem pushed the Captain back into a swivel chair at the Center's main console. He then grabbed the ship's phone and dialled out a long number. Both men then waited in silence, Hakeem's left hand holding the pistol pointing straight at Captain Hamilton. Hakeem spoke at length into the phone in Arabic, paused to listen and then began to get agitated, shouting loudly into the mouth piece "EL-AN, EL-AN!", Arabic for 'now'.

Hakeem slammed the phone down onto the cradle. "In a few minutes I will have a special fax message for you Hamilton and when you receive the fax message you will then power up the engines to Full Ahead and steer West 40 degrees. When I say so you will then slow the ship down to 15 knots. That is exactly what you will do Hamilton."

Captain Hamilton now sitting upright in the chair looked up at Hakeem defiantly. Hamilton was about to speak when the fax machine clicked and started to hum then stop. Then hum again. Both men looked at the fax machine as the top of a page appeared. Slowly in a stop-start drone a page with dark patches and the image of a figure appeared faintly. As it came out of the machine Captain Hamilton's eyes opened wide in horror as the patchy image revealed that to be his wife, seated, gagged and bound all over.

Hakeem snatched the page out of the machine and slammed it down face up on the desk. "Take a good look Mr Hamilton you will see your lovely wife is now our prisoner somewhere in England. We have wrapped her in barbed wire in her own little prison. And yes, look very carefully, the newspaper jammed into her wire prison is the Southampton Globe Newspaper from yesterday. But you cannot see the message clearly yet Hamilton, that message is coming next!"

As Hakeem spoke the sunburned colour drained from the Captain's face, his eyes staring at the fax on the desk. He picked it up and his hands began to shake. As the next page came out of the machine Captain Hamilton could only murmur to himself, "no, no, no" as the second patchy image revealed that to be an enlarged photograph of the face of his wife, like the shroud of Turin, but mouth gagged, eyes half closed. While the machine was still transmitting Hakeem ripped the sheet out of the machine, again slammed it down on top of the other page on the desk. "This is your special message. READ THAT, MR HAMILTON" roared Hakeem.

Captain Hamilton looked closely and across the top of her forehead were shakily written the words "Rod save me". As soon as he read the words Captain Hamilton leapt up at Hakeem knocking his pistol out of his hand. Hakeem in a second had picked up the gun again and began bashing the head of the Captain repeatedly until blood oozed in long dribbles down his face. Hakeem then heaved him, dizzy and groaning, out of the room into the passageway and dragged him back to the Bridge by his arms.

Captain Hamilton though half conscious realised that the hijacker was unaware of his shipboard girlfriend, Olga, the fitness instructor, who was asleep in his quarters just three doors away from the Communications Center.

Down below at Portside pilotage door number four, the trawler had come alongside and Zador together with Abdul and the rest of the brigade were busy unloading boxes containing the pistols, ammunition magazines, rocket launchers, tubes of Hexogen explosive, Zador's diesel cans and the 4 small red cylinders which would be critical to get the passengers out of their cabins.

As the Fantasea of the World continued to drift towards the outer marker of the shipping lane, Festival Cruise Lines WHQ in Miami were calling up the Bridge "Miami operations center calling. This is Festival Ops. Center Miami calling........Watch Officer, please respond. Miami Ops. calling." There was no response however. The only commands being obeyed on the

Bridge were the commands of Hakeem Belbachir. "Starboard 40 degrees all engines on Full Ahead"

Hakeem pointed the gun at the First Officer who refused to respond until Hamilton, slumped in a corner, drowsily slurred "Do as he says."

To starboard, four Sea Marshals were still patiently trying to talk Samia down from the lifeboat as, barebreasted, she continued to roar that Gino had tried to rape her.

Unknown to the Sea Marshals, some of the brigade from the trawler were scurrying up all the ship's stairwells, some taking the internal escalators leaping steps at a time. Any occasional wandering passenger unable to sleep or enjoying the hushed peacefulness of the closed shopping malls was ignored by the brigade. A chubby Philippino cleaning lady on her night shift continued the noisy vacuum cleaning of the deep marshy mallowsoft carpet in the Grand Foyer as a martyr hurdled over her machine's hose. As he ran past, neither person cared about the other. Each martyr was wholly focused on completing his individual task which together would mean complete control of the ship. Two martyrs each were assigned to the four entrances to the crews quarters. On the Bridge now were Zador, Khalil and Hakeem.

CHAPTER 7

"No Apostle should take captives until he has battled and subdued the country. You desire the vanities of this world but God wills for you the reward of the world to come; and God is almighty and all wise"
The Holy Qu'ran (Al-Anfal 8:66)

Suleyman and Amir would control the Passenger Activity Zones still open which were the Monte Carlo Piano Bar, the Klondike Casino and the 24 hour 'Pizza Planet' all on the same deck. Alif and Badshah would later work with Samia and Abdul in passenger screening.

Samia still on the ridge of the lifeboat, legs folded back like a camel jockey was relieved to finally hear a commotion on the deck below followed by several men rushing up the forward stairwell to the lifeboat deck. As the liner began to move, she looked toward the Bridge and quickly covered her breasts on seeing for the first time in six months since Yemen, the unmistakable bearded face of Hakeem waving to her indicating that all was going to plan. Hank and three other Sea Marshals still intent on distracting Samia and talking her down were unaware that the ship was almost completely taken over.

They turned to see what the arriving commotion was and before they had time to react they were all cut down in continuous bursts of gunfire from AK47s'. Samia rolled off the cover as shots and hot shell casings ricocheted around the deck, some shots going straight through the glass panes of the Bridge wing.

Down at the Klondike Casino all the passengers and the croupiers had fallen silent. No one moved, everyone frozen still with fear and in shock that they were hostages it seemed of a daring armed robbery of the casino's bank. Suleyman, in torn green fatigues was a balding overweight Yemeni, shining with sweat who concealed from Hakeem and the other martyrs his asthma, sneaking puffs of his medicinal inhaler during earlier assault course exercises. He was another loner like Zador but more controlled. He was edgy and trusted none of the brigade to support him in combat. He proudly displayed on his waist belt his curved Yemeni Jambiyya dagger which he liked to slice powerfully through watermelons; he was certain that the whoosh and dull plop sound was the same as the sound made by the executioner's sword blade at public decapitations which he never missed. He was proud to show his scarred forearms received from brawling with the Jambiyya blade following old Yemeni tradition.

Amir was also heavily bearded but Sudanese and distinguished himself with a matted nest of headhair bound inside a red headband. He wore a green combat T-shirt, the sleeves torn off to show his shouldercarved tattoo of a black crescent Khanjar knife underneath which poorly drawn crossed rifles were scarred into the skin. Both men quietly walked down the wide carpeted main aisle of the casino trying hard to conceal behind sullen faces their amazement at the glittering temple of mirrors, goldpaint, lights and flashing numbers. They could not understand what the entertainment was in the casino with it's deep green baize tables, sarcophagus like craps tables and row after row of slot machines. They both knew though that there was money stored somewhere in the room. Amir closely examined one of the machines and called over to Suleyman if he wanted some fruit. Before he could answer what he wanted Amir aimed his assault rifle at an aisle of machines whereupon the whole room full of passengers fell to the floor screaming as Amir fired off a full magazine, sending coins and metal splinters cascading onto the floor. Eyes agog at the hoard of treasure spilling out continually, he then reloaded to celebrate and fired upwards hitting the Waterford Crystal chandoliers raining prismatic slivers onto the passengers. Suleyman was spiked directly by a shard on his shiny scalp.

"STOP!" shouted Suleyman. "No wasting ammunition. Lets round up the passengers and put them all in the Piano Bar. EVERYONE TO YOUR

FEET NOW! START MARCHING!" The gamblers who had earlier been enjoying themselves were now sobbing and trembling with fear as Suleyman herded them onwards to the Piano Bar. The illiterate Amir brought up the rear of the group, filling his pockets as he did so with large chrome coin tokens marked 'FCL Casino 1$'.

Out on the lifeboat deck, was Hank 'The Tank' Kruger who now lay motionless on the deckfloor, playing dead, eyes open, uninjured as far as he could sense. Newly employed under strict probationer guidelines, this first assignment of Senior Sea Marshal on board a cruise ship was a first step in his adjustment to life as a civilian after 15 years military service. All around him now, the blood of his fellow sea marshals pooled, some moaning incoherently as life ebbed out of them. Kruger waited his moment before throwing himself over the deck rail and rolling under the same lifeboat number one that had been Samia's perch. Again he checked the patches of blood on his clothes; there was one seeping flesh wound in his shoulder. Otherwise uninjured he climbed in under the Lifeboat's cover to hide. He then quietly checked if his walkie talkie was operational.

Some months earlier Kruger had been dishonourably discharged from the U.S. Army's elite Delta force in Fort Bragg, North Carolina. He had been court-martialled and convicted of second degree murder of his wife, a drill sergeant at the base, during night combat exercises. He had refused to plea bargain and his hot tempered aggressive protest of his innocence during the trial was counterproductive. Adamant that someone had tampered with his ammunition magazine he was nevertheless found convicted of failing to load only bright tracer rounds into his weapon as required. The military tribunal refused to believe his vehement protests of accidentally mixing normal rounds with tracer rounds. Tracer bullets allowed the troops walk night-fire into moving night targets. At the time of his wife being shot, he was in the throes of being divorced by her for mental cruelty and abandonment. His baking platefuls of bugs for dinner was bad enough but his determination to sleep rough in bad weather as part of his own endurance fitness programme finished the relationship. The blazing rows overheard at the base on his return home at dawn was taken as evidence of both motive and unstable comradeship.

Hank was now going through the lifeboat supplies of flares, smoke floats and mercifully some canned water which he gulped down. Just metres away, on the Bridge, Samia had welcomed Hakeem, "Everything is good Hakeem. It is good to be with you again. God is good. I have the passenger list and I have at least twenty valuable passengers whom we must capture before they leave the cabins."

Hakeem held his hand up to her "No. Not just those twenty valuable passengers. Get me the full passenger list and scan the list for all passengers with American Jewish names and get them out of their cabins…..you have 30 minutes Samia, they are just as valuable to us.

You know the usual ones, the names that end with 'berg', 'mann', 'ein', and any ones you know yourself like Bloch............go now Samia! Take a martyr with you to drive the Zionist animals to the Sky deck pool, is that clear?.......the Sky deck pool..........not to drown them, we have the sea for that! Empty the pool first! Those Jews will be an even stronger shield from an air attack on us. Khalil, you round up the crew as they come out of the Crew Zones because soon I'm going to make an announcement to everyone over the ship's intercom. Zador you go down to the Engine Hall and let the engineers hear the sweet sounds of your Khalashnikov. But remember no killing engineers or any crew, the humble ones are the slaves of the Infidel....and we will need some of them too. No flame throwing either, the ship's fuel tanks are down there and still nearly full.

Zador grinned and quietly replied "with pleasure" as he turned to leave.

Samia on hearing the short time allowed to find targetted passengers, scanned the passengers lists instantly, marking off names quickly with a highlighter pen. With a few dozen names to start with she ran frantically through the passageways, in one hand torn sheets of passenger lists with Jewish names marked, and in the other her heavy assault rifle which she struggled with to bash in the stateroom doors with the butt yelling "UP, OUT, ...ALL JEWS OUT, JUIFS,........OUT OUT OUT, NOW OR DIE." She then fired off a couple of shots over beds where people were too stunned to move or who remained in a sleepy disbelieving torpor. With Badshah and Alif, she started on the lowest accommodation deck where she had gathered seven or eight elderly people. They then joined another group ordered out at gunpoint on the next upper deck. As she systematically went through the passageways rounding up Jews, other passengers not on her list peered briefly out of their rooms alarmed at the yelling, screaming and sounds of gunfire and quickly retreated into their cabins again. Samia was getting angrier as elderly passengers pleaded to return to get their medications. Those cries also jogged her memory of her parents anguish in failing to receive medicine for her during the Ethiopian famines. She answered their pleas with punches forcing them back, careful not to disable them and become helpless obstructions in the passageways.

However, only twenty minutes into her mission, Hakeem spoke into his radio to Samia "I'm getting all the passengers outside now Samia, I cannot wait longer, some passengers will have called America on their cell phones……………. Alif, go now to release the Mercaptan cylinders into the ventilation shafts, do you hear me."   A few seconds passed and then the animated voice of Alif blurted loudly over the radio. "Yes Hakeem I am on my way. I have three of the four cylinders already at the ventilation intake ducts. In a moment I can release the smell". Alif opened a packet of bubblegum he had in his pocket and began chewing all of it vigorously. He then pulled some out of his mouth and moulded two large lumps of pink goo which he stuffed up his nose. Unscrewing the cylinder heads he poured some of the noxious liquid into the huge air intake cowls. The violet coloured liquid flowed on down to the air and heat exchangers throughout the hull.

Samia having finally arrived at the small Sky Pool had begun shouting at the Jews to climb down into it as it was emptying. The water soon came up to the waists of those first in who had to wade down to the deep end to make way for others. More than one person was shaking their head in disbelief, having been asleep in bed 30 minutes earlier to find themselves at the mercy of Islamic extremists, climbing into a cold pool in the middle of the night; a tiled pool that suddenly had taken on other possible functions as a clinical abattoir and mass gravepit.

Hakeem looked at his watch which showed 03:00 hours. It was time to "awake Satan's fat American friends from their deep sleep". He walked over to the ships intercom, turning the dial to 'Ship Systemwide Public Address'……… "Ladies and Gentlemen attention please, ….attention all passengers and all crew. This is Officer Hakeem speaking. Listen carefully. This is not a drill. Due to a dangerous leak from the ship's gas storage tanks, repeat, gas storage tanks, I require EVERYONE,…… REPEAT EVERYONE to come up onto the open decks IMMEDIATELY. I repeat this is not a drill. Could all passengers please come up onto the open decks immediately. You do NOT have time to dress. Please come up immediately to the open decks for your own safety. This is NOT a drill." Hakeem switched off the intercom and calmly spoke over the radio to Alif. " Let the idolators think of death now. All praise be to Allah, Lord of all the World." Hakeem then approached the Bridge console and sounded 6 long bilious resonating blasts on the ship's horn.

He then listened over the ship's intercom to the sounds of people beginning to come out and talk in the passageways. He could hear some voices saying that it was just a hoax. Another man loudly declared "I'm just gonna sit out on my balcony, gas leak or no gas leak. There is plenty of fresh air in my back yard."

As the smelling marker agent began to seep widely throughout all ventilators soon the voices became louder, breaking in to shouts "COME ON, LETS GET OUT OF HERE, I CAN SMELL THE GAS, FOR GOD'S SAKE DON'T LIGHT ANYTHING, DON'T EVEN TURN ON YOUR CABIN LIGHT OR A SPARK WILL BLOW THE SHIP CLEAN OUT OF THE WATER. I'M OUTTA HERE!"

A broad smile broke across Hakeem's face as he listened to the gathering stampede of feet mingled with the roaring of people calling out for family and friends and high pitched screeching of terrified children. Hakeem's voice came back over the intercom: "Thank you for co-operating ladies and gentleman. Please come to the open decks where you will be quite safe. There is no need to wear life jackets. All that you need will be fresh air. Everyone onto the Lifeboat decks port and starboard ……..follow the signs please….to the Lifeboat decks, …you are not allowed use the elevators….use the stairs only." . Hakeem then activated the Fire Sirens throughout the ship.

As the crew also came rushing out of their quarters they were met by Khalil, and the seven other armed martyrs with machine guns at the ready. Khalil ordered "Everyone into the Broadway Theatre NOW, do as I order and your life will be saved. Anyone who disobeys will be shot or…………. thrown over the side…instead of wasting bullets. Maybe you would like to be breakfast for the sharks? HANDS BEHIND YOUR HEADS NOW." he shouted.

Hakeem had carefully studied the ship's passageways and planned that the movement of the crew into the theatre would not cross with the panicking passengers coming out of their cabins heading to the Upper decks.

As the crew were led into the theatre, holding clothing against their faces to avoid what they thought was gas, they were ordered to take seats. As they did so the plush red theatre curtain lifted up to reveal the heavy bipod mounted M60 machine gun on a table. It was pointed at the centre of the auditorium. A bullet belt led from it into a large green ammunition chest. From the left wing Ahmed walked lazily across the stage and as the people filed silently into the semi circle rows, he turned to them and roared in broken English "ANY CREW PEOPLE WHO MOVES OUT OF SEAT

IS SHOT AND MAYBE SOME MORE PEOPLE SITTING BESIDE. I NOT CARE WHO DIES, I CARE WHO MOVES. ANYONE TALKS I SHOOT YOU. NO MOVES. YOU SIT AND YOU SHIT WHERE YOU SIT." Ahmed was otherwise a surly tour guide on a rusting unreliable river boat cruising the Nile. There he was unable to depend on the passengers rare tips to survive, and refusing to bring beer to passengers from the boat's bar didn't help. Sacked for theft he left for Syria where he received food and shelter with an Islamic fundamentalist cleric. Later he dreamt up for himself a lone suicidal mission if he had found employment as a baggage handler in Paris Charles de Gaulle airport. He would await the opportunity to drive a luggage loader into a fully laden American airline taxiing for take off. For months he was steeling himself for instantaneous death by incineration as he was certain he would be engulfed in the fireball of fuel as the loaders raised conveyor ruptured the plane's tanks mid fuselage. Deported from France however for falsifying a work permit, Hakeem had little trouble persuading him to join this meticulously planned mission; Hakeem demanded an intense commitment from his chosen martyrs: living in the confined quarters of a ship for days on end with no place to hide from the attacking infidel would test the nerve of every one of them, and more and more as time passed, waiting for a counterattack.

Soon after all crew had been ordered in to the auditorium, Abdul appeared walking up and down each aisle looking for the American Chef who called him a 'deadbeat sandnigger' just hours earlier. Anyone who slumped away from Abdul's view was ordered to stand up to face his pistol. That got the undivided attention of everyone in the room.

"ALL CHEFS AND KITCHEN WORKERS STAND UP NOW" Abdul demanded at the top his voice. Almost 60 crewmen and women stood up in various poses, some leaning on the seatback in front of them, others leaning back, most standing erect, arms down. In an instant Abdul had recognised the Chef, no longer the arrogant kitchen general but a young petrified crewman, standing up, paleface forward, eyes looking straight ahead at Ahmed's heavy gun barrel on the stage. As Ahmed waved him out of his seat row, the Chef's white trousers greyed around the crotch as he pissed in his pants, a prelude to a more pungent abdominal torrent following instantly.

"So I'm a deadbeat sandnigger, Mr Chef, would you like to say it again to me?

Am I dead, or beaten or a nigger? I don't like the sand....isn't it you and filthy American people that like sand, where you and your women display your infidel bodies and pollute God's oceans?"

The Chef remained silent, but began shaking with fear.

"Mr Chef, I am going to make sure you will never say such things again". Abdul pushed the Chef head of him and up onto the stage.

"Ahmed, I will need your help but watch the rest of the crew. This Chef will not be tasting food again............hold him down on the ground. Now Mr Chef, you have a choice to give up your life or your tongue, what is more important to you?"

Some crew in the audience began to break down, sobbing.

"Good Mr Chef, stick out that foolish red tongue, MOUTH OPEN FULLY, NOW! The chef was lying in his back with Ahmed kneeling on his shoulders, with some difficulty.

Abdul then lay down his pistol and reached down into the chefs dry mouth and in one jerking left hand movement seized the fat rear dorsum of his tongue as far back as the epiglottis; Abdul with the other hand then grabbed out of his kitchen jacket a handful of the knives he had taken earlier from the kitchen. Choosing the smaller tomato slicing knife, he slid the serrated blade under the tongue through the black veins and stretched ligament. Blood gushed around the Chef's mouth who began choking as he tried to roar in agony; Abdul worked fast sawing through the thick sulcus packed with nerves and taste buds. In a minute, Abdul victoriously held up the Chef's tongue for all the crew to see. As Abdul stood up the Chef rolled over onto his front, coughing and vomiting to clear his throat, leaving lush red liquid falling down in streams off the stage front. Only then after clearing his windpipe could the chef with one deep breath, release one long scream of pain. Abdul dragged him to his feet and put him on Ahmed's chair. Grabbing the Chef's head by the hair, Abdul pulled his head back to see his handy work, and marvelled at the wild fibrillations of the severed tongue stem. Abdul then walked forward with the chunk of tongue skewered on to the tip of a long carving knife, the sight causing several of the crew to puke forcefully between their legs.

"Later, ladies and gentlemen, I will let the Chef have his tongue back, cooked in the microwave for his dinner. He should be thankful, that he still lives and eats and eats well"! Abdul ordered two crew to come up and take the Chef to the back of the theatre while Ahmed played with diverting the red streams, seemingly attempting to shape a word in Arabic with the heel of his boot.

Meanwhile the upper decks to windward quickly filled up with the passengers scrambling over stacked deck chairs and sun loungers, racing to get to the deck rails to breath in the warm fresh Caribbean airs brushing that side of the ship. Some adults hyperventilated while some who had small children carried them shoulder high to catch the cleanest night air. Other passengers threw up, some continuing to retch in convulsions afterwards, as they inhaled the odour.

Hakeem spoke to Captain Hamilton. "Now Hamilton you will order the deck officers to come out of the Broadway Theatre where they are my prisoners also and you will command them to prepare the lifeboats for launch. You will be glad to hear that I have no need for your cargo of shameful women or their children. Every lifeboat will be launched except the Bridge boat. Any MAN boarding will be shot either getting into the life boat or IN the life boat if he gets that far." Hamilton turned away defiantly from Hakeem whereupon Hakeem waved the copy of the fax showing Gwendolen Hamilton. "Hamilton…….. it is time to command your collaborator crew over the intercom."

Hamilton staggered to his feet, still dizzy from the blow to his skull and in a slurred voice spoke slowly over the deck tannoy:

"Ladies and gentleman as a precautionary measure I am asking all women and children only, repeat women and children only to take to the lifeboats in an orderly fashion. This is for your own safety. The lifeboats will be lowered into the water when they are full. Please follow my instructions exactly as I have said. This is not a drill. Attention All Lifeboat Crews. To the Boat Stations. All Crews to the Boat stations. Stand by to operate davits. Davits can be operated at will. Repeat, davits can be operated at will."

Before the Captain had finished, wailing had started amongst women clutching their husbands concerned for their safety on the ship supposedly filling with gas. As yet many of the passengers coming up from the cabins had not been alerted to the presence of the armed gang on board. The male passengers on board were puzzled as to why they were excluded from the command and the lifeboats began to fill with families including mothers and fathers. Hakeem handed the ship's open intercom microphone to Hamilton. "This is a warning to the men folk on board the ship. Remember it is women and children first. Only women and children. Any man found on board a lifeboat will ....face the gravest consequences." At that point Zador appeared at the base of the ship's funnel. "FIRE! FIRE! FIRE! he roared wildly at the crowds below. His voice was not carrying and he tried to address the fleeing passengers as loudly as he could. "Good morning fat sea rats! You heard your Captain, only women and children first! Go now before the whole ship goes up like a bomb. Look! Do you see this?" Suddenly Zador triggered a projectile flame burst from his flame thrower, sending a corona-like arch of flame into the air, over the lifeboats and pouring on down into the water below. As the hissing of steam died away, Zador ranted hoarsely again "I will help you all arrive back in your big American houses in a couple of seconds but one piece of you arriving later than another piece! Get on the boats NOW." At that Zador started laughing menacingly as he pretended to ready the flame thrower for a second 20 metre burst. The decks below him were packed with hysterical passengers. He then called out "Any Jews, you stay HERE, enjoy once again the smell of gas, go on! BREATH IN THE AIR OF DEATH! The good news is ...there are no showers for you JUST A NICE DEEP POOL!

Zador was working himself up uncontrollably. He then took his assault rifle from his back and started shooting wildly in the air roaring "GET INTO THE BOATS, GET INTO THE BOATS....NO JEWS ....JUST

THE CRUSADERS BITCHES". In no time women, half dressed, were scrambling into the boats pulling the younger children by their pyjamas in on top of them. As Hakeem stood on the Bridge wing surveying the chaos he caught a glimpse of what appeared to be an exceptionally strong passenger clambering over womens heads. The passenger's head was hidden by a lifejacket. Hakeem unholstered his pistol, took aim and in a single shot blew the man over the deck rail, somersaulting like a high diver into the water below. The responding howls of the passengers sounded inhuman and the further mayhem delayed the deck officers trying to get to the winding gear of the lifeboat davits, even with each crewman pushed ahead at gunpoint by a martyr.

Husbands violently pushed their wives into the lifeboats and threw small children bodily into the boats as it rapidly became clear that what was afoot was an organised hijack of the liner by crazed killers. In the melee, one passenger, middle aged, tanned and fit, called out to Zador in Russian:

"Hey, vodkanik, yeh, you the mad spineless retard, having fun up there? Easy to scare women and kids eh? you want a real fight, come on down, lets see how brave you are without your firework. C'mon, meet a Russian soldier, unlike you, a piece of doorway dogshit!"

Zador's glee faded off his face, as his expression changed to an ugly scowl, though partly intrigued "well what have we here, a rich Russian fuck? Maybe a rich Russian fuck friendly with the Russian holy Onion heads too and….. the Kremlin Gas troops who killed my Chechen comrades eh?" Zador was becoming angry and building up into another rage "And you dare call me a coward? spineless? I'll show you! I'll stick you head in one of the ship's gas ovens………………………yes, wait there!"

No sooner than Zador had finished speaking he lost sight of the Russian who ducked in to the tumult of passengers running into one another. Some passengers fell underfoot only to be trampled on by more panicking passengers seeing Zador drop his flame thrower and bound along the Funnel deck making for the nearest stairwell down. Zador passed Suleyman as he made his way further down and along the boat deck, grabbing the curved dagger out of Suleyman's belt on the way, "I'll give it back to you nice and clean," Zador promised. "We have a rich Russian commissar on board who wants to give me a souvenir"!

Zador continued along the Boat deck, knocking people out of his way until he realised they would jump clear if he held high the dagger. He was sure he had caught up with the Russian, when he hooked a fleeing passenger by the top of the shoulder with the curved tip of the blade. The man groaned as the hook sunk deeper pulling him backwards to the ground. Zador immediately rolled him over onto his stomach, and kneeling on his lower back, he plunged the knife deep between the man's shoulder blades dragging it down vertically, slicing through his clothes and cleanly cut open his girdle muscles. The man roared in agony as Zador thrust the blade on through the fascia muscle sheath of his back. He stopped momentarily and then set about a frenzied filleting of his spine, carving in long downwards scythes. "Call me spineless, then I'll try out yours!" The curving blade cut clean through ligament and fibrous cartilage in single thrusts but Zador was slowed by the slippery pasta like strands wrapped around the vertebrae.

As he sawed hurriedly at one rib, the knife kept slipping onto the next one. He was impatient to finish his task and grabbed the yellow fibres by his fingers, fumbling about in streams of hot blood pouring out of the torso. Zador was tiring of the fiddly dissection and paused, inhaling deeply the pungent smell of fresh iron coming from the welling blood. He then hacked wildly at the base of each disc to break off the ribs much as he would sever and trim branches off a sapling. What he wanted, now that he had started, was a mission trophy unimaginable to his comrades. Finally after twenty minutes of exhausting cutting and sawing, Zador emerged onto the boat deck, the curved spine of his victim around his neck, a mess of rootlets, ganglion, chopped rib ends, and shredded artery. Dripping gluteous tissue slid down his jacket front like melting butter. Hakeem had to look twice before realising what he had been up to and called up Zador on his radio.

"I have not ordered any ritual slaughter....and mutilation of the dead is against God's law! Keep your strength Zador." Zador replied that only now was the man dead and he would not mutilate him.

The First Officer on the Bridge, at first disbelieving his eyes until he saw discs falling from Zador's bony scarf, vomited a warm projectile gush across the console, splashing Hakeem's front with clotted stinking béchamel.

Hamilton spoke again "Well Mr Hakeem are you satisfied, you succeeded in terrifying hundreds of women and children and now you are going to let them off in lifeboats without a crew member to be left at the mercy of the open seas? The only punishment fit for you and your butchering thugs is the keel haul....you will rot in hell!"

Hakeem looked at Hamilton and replied "Don't worry, as you said, your headquarters know there is something wrong. They should live. Hamilton, we will give them a good start in the water too: this ship is not stopping to lower the life boats.... you just pray to your idol that the lifeboats don't capsize as they hit the water at 20 knots. Those that survive will soon be picked up by your friendly coastguard!" Hakeem handed the Captain Hamilton the ship's intercom microphone without saying a word. Hamilton spoke in a firm voice "Attention again all lifeboat crews, the ship will maintain speed while the lifeboats are being lowered. As soon as the lifeboats are in the water release the lifeboat stern cable first, repeat stern davit cable first and then the bow davit spring. Repeat, the ship is maintaining speed while lifeboats are lowered and released. Use all your skill in this difficult operation. Thank you men. God bless you and all our passengers." Hakeem snatched back the microphone and switched it off.

Hamilton's thoughts turned to his new partner, the fit gymnast Olga who to his relief had not come up into the Bridge from his quarters. Maybe she had followed events from the monitors above his chart desk and was one of the women clambering, he imagined with agility, into one of the lifeboats. Alif and Khalil appeared on the Sky deck behind the Bridge shouting "Hakeem, Hakeem, what would you like, a watch? Diamonds? Take a look!" Covering the lower arms of both men were at least a dozen watches and around their necks were stacked necklaces of pearls and diamonds. In their combat jacket pockets they had stuffed cigars while Khalil had a full roast chicken spiked on top of a bayonet. Zador, back again half way up the ship's funnel hanging onto the ladder, cheered and hastily began to climb down. Throwing the last spinal vertebra off his neck, he ran off down several flights of outer stairs knocking women and men out of his path. Turning a corner his body collided head on with an enormous black passenger with the appearance of a body builder, muscle bound and dressed in vest and shorts. The slim framed Zador, covered in blood, bounced back onto the deck floor and as soon as the body builder saw the assault rifle he jumped on top of Zador. The body builder grabbed Zador by the collars of his jacket but Zador was first to speak into his face. "Why don't you look where you are going, American pig?"

The body builder's face came down nose to nose with Zador's and he spoke slowly and clearly into Zador's face, looking into his squinted eyeball, "you've just walked into the Titan, King of the World's Wrestlers. Little fella, why don't YOU go where you're LOOKING? Are you one of these stinking brain dead asshole gunmen wanting to rob little old ladies?"

Zador lying flat under the heavy weight of the body builder began to squirm. "Okay yankee gorilla you want a fair fight? I give you a fair fight. You might have a fat black neck but I can get my hands around it and choke the air going into your big American mouth. The Titan got up, lifting Zador bodily with one hand by the jacket lapels, ripped the assault rifle off Zador's back with the other and flung him into an empty life jacket trunk. As he then reached for the lid of the trunk to slam it down, Zador had already taken a pistol from his coat and fired 2 shots straight into him at point blank range, before the gun jammed. The Titan collapsed in heavily back on top of Zador. Zador heaved him off him, clambered out and slammed the lid closed.

CHAPTER 8

This temporary set back had delayed Zador by a couple of minutes in his mission which was to get to the casino and fill his pockets with as many dollars as he could squash into them. He arrived at the door of the casino, combat jacket now almost saturated with blood and flecked with clinging threads of tissue. He stalled to recover his breath. He surveyed the scene of smashed casino machines and the marble floor littered with shards of glass from the chandoliers, themselves reduced to canopies of tangled cord and wire hung with icycle like crystal slivers. As he stood there quietly in the doorway he could hear sobbing from somebody evidently hiding under one of the casino tables. Zador took his pistol out of his pocket and very silently walked along the carpet in the direction of the sounds, stepping delicately on broken glass crunching underfoot like the frozen snow of home. He went down onto his knees and looked under a roulette table to find a girl croupier cowering and sobbing quietly. Zador took off the safety clip and with a wave of his gun ordered her to stand up. He grabbed her by her hair and brought her over to the roulette wheel. He then spun the wheel. He whispered quietly in her ear "Red, you live. Black, you die."

Tears streaked down the face of the croupier, her heavy mascara beginning to drop black lines down her cheeks. Zador pushed her head forward to look at the spinning wheel as the roulette ball hopped from black to red to black to red, to red again and then to black. Finally the ball settled on a black number. The croupier started to moan and Zador pushed her head down into the wheel. With a flick of his finger he pushed the ball from the black into the red slot. Zador looked at her and said "this time you live. There is a better place in the next world. I am not afraid to go there unlike you, infidel." At that Zador emptied out into his hand all the bullet chambers in his pistol. He then picked one bullet and put it back in a chamber. " I will live with the glorious." Zador then with the palm of his hand spun the chamber and, playing Russian Roulette, held the barrel to his head. He then pulled her head up against his blood spattered cheek,"who knows how far a bullet travels through one head? Maybe it goes through......... two heads? Lets find out?"

Still pressing her head hard against his, he then pointed the pistol at his own right temple and pulled the trigger:- 'CLICK'. The girl screamed as he let her go, slumping to the floor. Zador then walked over to the casino bank turned around and ordered the girl to go to the theatre in the next five seconds or be shot "There you will find the rest of your filthy friends." The girl ran out of the casino screeching fitfully. Zador began to stuff hundred dollar bills into plastic packets taping them to make them waterproof. When all his pockets were full he returned to the Bridge.

One by one the lifeboats were lowered then let go with precision coordination by two crew men controlling the bow and stern davit release cable. Some boats were half empty, others overcrowded. Men, left behind, began throwing life jackets down; most of them missed the boats and ended up in the water. Some men then jumped overboard hoping to join their family if they survived. The incessant calls of women in the lowering boats to the men on deck receded as the boats dropped away to water level. On hitting the water at speed, the cables were released and recoiled like whips; some lifeboats submarined bow first into the sea then sprang back, rocking wildly as the boats buoyancy tossed them about in the ship's side wake; one boat slowly capsized inwards towards the ship then turned turtle, coffining its passengers while its small propeller spun uselessly like a wind vane.

Rounded up in the now empty Sky pool were a total of sixty hostages, men, women and children with Jewish names which had been traced by Samia from their cabin numbers. Hakeem was disappointed to hear over the radio that no more than sixty had been found and asked that Samia find out if any of the crew had Jewish names.

Hakeem knew that soon the American coastguard would be appearing at much the same time as the sun rose over the calm horizon. Over the radio he ordered all elevators to be shut down, outer deck doors locked and all passengers confined to the upper deck. He then ordered all canopied inflateable life rafts to be thrown overboard. This would keep the U.S. coastguard and Guantanamo patrol boats busy checking life rafts for more passengers. Most of the brigade then took positions on the upper decks mingling amongst the passengers lying around the decks. "Prepare now to defend the ship from attack." Hakeem commanded over the radio to his fellow martyrs.

Ahmed remained on stage at the Broadway Theatre sitting behind the heavy gun, bored. He knew from a close look at the floor that the stage either moved in a circle or came out of the ground. When another martyr joined him he planned to find the controls and amuse himself.

Festival Cruise Lines Operations Center, Miami

Unknown to Hakeem an engineer in the Engine Hall had telephoned Fantasea Cruise Lines WHQ in Miami to advise that the ship had been attacked by an armed gang and called for immediate assistance. Minutes later, the few Directors of Fantasea Cruise Lines not on the maiden voyage had been awoken at their homes and were arriving for an emergency briefing in the headquarters. The City of Miami Police Chief had alerted the coastguard who then called the Department of the Navy at the Pentagon. A conference call had been arranged by the Police Chief between the Directors of Fantasea Cruiselines and the Secretary for Homeland Security who joined in Admiral Burbridge of the U.S. Navy Atlantic Fleet. The President himself was then awoken and informed of an American registered cruise ship hijacked off the Haitian coast. He requested an immediate cabinet meeting on the situation with a briefing for the media arranged for midday no matter how events unfolded. He also wanted to personally read through the passenger list as soon as it was faxed in from Miami. He needed a headcount of politians, military, judges and other Americans associated with organs of Government or National Security. He approved the eavesdrop and recording of all cellphone calls or text messages to and from the ship and authorised the interception of all email fax and marine communications with immediate effect.

A conference call was arranged for 07:30 Eastern Standard Time. As the Directors of Festival Cruise Lines arrived at their WHQ, refreshments were being served in the boardroom, now renamed the 'Emergency Response Center'. Several executives paced up and down silently, every now and again going over to look at the boardroom radar repeater screen to see the position of the liner. It was very slowly tracking towards Cuban waters which were strictly out of bounds without pre-clearance from both the governments of the United States and the Republic of Cuba.

MacDill Airforce Base, Florida

On the orders of Homeland Security, six F-15 fighter jets took off from MacDill Airforce base in Florida. Within twenty minutes they radioed for massive and immediate coastguard and naval assistance to pick up hundreds of passengers seen adrift in the lifeboats. By personal order of the President the rescue was to be a complete triumph. He required the deployment of all available high speed naval craft and the requisition of all large high speed leisure craft on the Florida Keys to recover alive every passenger released from the hijacked liner.

The F-15s had flown past the lifeboats and rolled and dipped their wings to acknowledge the frantic waving and cheering of the women and children. He also ordered an emergency reception facility to be set up at MacDill Airforce base for all passengers needing immediate medical and psychological care, using army medical personnel. Counsellors were assigned to calm hundreds of distraught women separated from their husbands and partners demanding explanation and reassurance about the mens safety on the ship. Debriefing specialists were flown in to listen to and correlate all the accounts of the womens experiences. Police artists, criminologists and FBI psychological profilers were drafted in from all over Dade County to write up reports on each terrorist described by passengers. Each passenger's story was then cross referenced with others in a database networked with CIA headquarters at Langley, Virginia. Interpol was faxed visual reconstructions of those terrorists that made a lasting impression on passengers, Zador the most terrifyingly memorable.

On the pretext of national security and despite protests from the television news networks, all international and domestic airports including all airfields and helipads in the State of Florida were closed until further instructions from the Federal Aviation Authority. Florida airspace was declared off-limits for all civilian overflying; any transgressors would be escorted by fighter jets to the nearest military airfield for investigation and later escorted out of U.S. airspace back to country of origin.

The President hastily made another four executive orders. Firstly, all passenger ship sailings from American ports were immediately cancelled with ships confined to port until further order. Secondly all American registered cruise ships currently in foreign ports were forbidden to sail until further order. Thirdly all American registered cruise ships currently at sea were to return to the nearest port subject to the destination port being approved by the Department of the Navy. Lastly all American registered cruise ships currently at sea were also to receive a platoon of marines, dropped by helicopter and deployed throughout the ship with a mandatory guard placed permanently on the Bridge.

Miami Festival Lines Ops. Center

In WHQ phones were now ringing incessantly throughout the entire office building as families became aware of the plight of the ship on the early morning American news flashes. One of the Directors watching television was drawn to the fax machine in the boardroom as it clicked and an incoming sheet began to appear. Slowly a handwritten message was appearing on the ship's note paper which read as follows:

"Message for the Infidel Zionist President Sherman Grattan of the USA from the Commander of the Holy Warship, the Jihad of the World now under the full control of the Guantanamo Martyrs Brigade.

We have 700 American passengers on this ship who, except for Jews, will be freed, in exchange for the 601 prisoners in Camp Delta Prison in Guantanamo. If you attack the ship we will kill everyone and blow up the ship. Death is Glorious. There is no surrender. No

negotiation. The time of sending this fax is now 07:00. At 15:00 the prisoners must come by boat to the Holy Warship. We will allow one representative of the United Nations and one representative of the Red Crescent to witness that we will exchange the prisoners one for one. If the prisoners are not released by 15:00 then 10 passengers will be beheaded every hour. Death to America.
Commander Hakeem Belbachir."

The White House

As soon as the fax was received it was transmitted onwards to the White House and the Pentagon in advance of the conference call. President Grattan called in his Defence Secretary and requested both Admiral Burbridge of the U.S. Navy Atlantic Fleet and Major General Kirwan the Commander of Camp Delta in Guantanamo to join in the call. Grattan was agitated, gulping cups of coffee. "Get me the Israeli Premier on a line and keep him on hold during the conference call. Where is the ship now?" A call was put through to the Joint Special Operations Command at the Pentagon. It was confirmed that the ship was half a mile inside Cuban territorial waters. After a few moments of quiet reflection the President snapped at an aide "Get me Castro on the line".

Fantasea of the World

Back on the liner the total head count of the male passengers was finalised at 709. The crew, including the engineers in the Engine Hall, the deck officers on the Bridge and the crew in the Broadway Theatre amounted to 615, with 17 unaccounted for. With the smell of the gas marking agent clearing, conditions were nonetheless worsening for the crew, all crammed into the 600 seat theatre. Some of the crew in the aisles had slouched into sleep while others were quietly saying prayers. On stage Ahmed sat on a deckchair, feet up on the table, behind the heavy machine gun. Every now and then he would walk the stage, stop, and make a pistol shape with his hand, point it at someone, and walk back. Other times he would walk out to the very edge of the stage, clear his throat and launch a glob of spit as far as he could; he demanded to know what seat row he had reached and then demanded applause. If he hit anyone, that person had to stand and applaud as well as any other person Ahmed pointed to, as he strutted along the stage front.

Eventually Samia arrived in the theatre with the crew name list, on which she had circled names likely to belong to Jews. Samia went to the front of the stage and called out as aggressively as she could. "Everyone, you listen to me! We are breaking up the crew into smaller groups and you will all be more comfortable in other places on the ship. When I call out your name, you are to stand up and come forward to me. UNDERSTOOD?" With this there was a murmur around the hall as there was nothing reassuring in her angry face or in the voice tone of this pretty girl carrying an AK-47 on her back. Some girls recognised her as the friendly child counsellor now dressed in fatigues. Samia's room mate Bonnie bravely put her hand up ."Samy it's me……. Bonnie, your room mate, what's wrong….. what have we done?……please don't hurt us." Samia was taken aback for a second, at this nice girl's question. Samia looked at Ahmed who loudly unhooked the safety catch of his M60. "Shut up bitch" Samia replied but not loudly enough and then yelled "SHUT THAT MOUTH! OR I WILL HAVE YOUR AMERICAN HEAD CUT OFF…SLOWLY!" Bonnie burst into tears, sliding off her seat to the floor. Samia ignored her and read on through the crew list. Calling out the names it was soon obvious who was being selected as all the last names ended in 'berg, stein and mann'. After 20 minutes there was an unlikely group of crew, young and old, of different nationalities and colour lined up on the stage. She then walked slowly up and down the full length of the stage front, looking at each row of crew. She then shouted "I WANT ANYONE CALLED 'JANICE' TO STAND UP NOW! NOW! JANICE, WHERE ARE YOU?

A mournful moan was heard followed by some movement in the middle of the room and Janice, the Bankteller stood up. Samia called Janice to come up to the stage and then asked Ahmed to call another martyr to bring the woman up to Hakeem on the Bridge. Hakeem who proclaimed no attachment to money for pleasure use had told Samia that large amounts of dollars must be seized as that was treasure craved by the Infidel. Who Janice was remained a mystery to Ahmed; later Hakeem would personally escort her to the Bank where he would empty the safe of the larger denominations of dollar bills before the prisoners were running loose about the ship. While Janice stayed behind awaiting her escort to the Bridge, Samia commanded the rest of the crew on stage to walk in front of her in the direction of the Sky deck.

Outside, the decks were crowded with passengers lying close together in groups, most still in night clothes. Some were huddled together, just holding hands. Others sat in circles talking quietly. As the procession of crew walked through them the passengers fell silent and cleared a path wondering what would happen next.

All of a sudden before Samia had time to react one of the crew had leapt over the deck rail and disappeared into the foamy water at the speeding ship's waterline. Momentarily his head appeared on the surface before disappearing again in the ship's wake. Samia lost her tough composure for a second, looking anxiously over the rail before she began shouting at passengers lying around her on the deck to clear the way for her column of prisoners. Some passengers had dared to fall asleep on the sunloungers and whom she kicked angrily in passing. As she moved through she noticed a bowed head which looked away from her. She went over and pulled the head back by the hair. It was Gino, still in the Sea Marshal's handcuffs. Samia pulled him up painfully onto his feet by his ears.

"Greetings again, Infidel filth. Now it's your turn to risk your life...get up on the rail. Sit up on the rail, face out and look down at the sharks drinking poisoned blood! Gino began to plead with her.

"No Samia, please I have a family and wife, I didn't know .....I didn't mean to offend you, I'm only a man, you are a lovely girl........" Samia belted him on his mouth with the pistol telling him to shut up. With another martyr she then hoisted Gino up onto the rail, holding him by his shirt, his back to the water. "Face the other way and look down..NOW! Monsieur G."

Gino manoeuvred his legs one by one slowly over the rail and wedged his feet between the bars beneath him to secure himself.

"You are an insult to the human race...there is not enough water in the whole Caribbean to clean me after your hands touched me. Sit and do not move! Contemplate death. Any Jew passenger that pushes you over will live"! Samia had radioed ahead to Hakeem about the arrival of more Jewish prisoners for the emptying pool. Hakeem ordered her to go and select some Jews to be tied to the liner's communications tower as a shield against attack. Before doing so, she tied two Jewish crew to the rail close to Gino. "Remember," she said to the two crew, "any Jew who pushes him in will live! If he escapes then you all die!" Gino began to shake on the rail then cry as he looked at both young crewmen. Both crewmen glanced at Gino uncomfortably and then looked longer at each other, pondering survival and death.

As the temperature rose with the morning sun Samia ordered that bottles of water be thrown amongst the passengers. Hakeem then spoke over the ship's intercom: "this is Commander Hakeem I am now in charge of this ship. It is now a ship of Jihad. From now on anyone using a cell phone will be thrown overboard. You will soon be free in exchange for the prisoners of Guantanamo prison camp. Be patient. You will be exchanged one for one from boats that will come alongside the ship and the prisoner exchange will be supervised by the United Nations. Until you are free anyone who disobeys any order will be thrown overboard or decapitated...we need to save our bullets in case of attack. But as prisoners of war we will treat you with more respect than your government treats the prisoners in Guantanamo prison. Stay where you are until you have an order to move down to the doors at sea level for the prisoner transfer. If you think you can trust your government then you will not be afraid. We do not trust your government, but we have no fear and we are prepared for death!"

CHAPTER 9

The White House

"Please Mr President, Presidente Castro is on the line" advised the presidential aide.

"Good Morning Presidente Castro, Sherman Grattan here. As you have heard, terrorists have hijacked an American cruise liner and we believe it is now inside Cuban territorial waters. They demand the release of our prisoners at Camp Delta in Guantanamo in exchange for the passengers on board the cruise ship. This is a security situation where we would look to you, Presidente Castro, and your security forces for full cooperation which will be in both our interests. I trust that your government, no more than any other country claiming a civilised society will NOT tolerate the presence of terrorists either on Cuban land or in Cuban territorial waters?"

"Good morning President Grattan. I have learned of your problem and I am checking with our Revolutionary War Marine the exact position of the cruise ship. Firstly let me say that we Cubans have had to tolerate the presence of terrorists on Cuban land, terrorists brought by you onto Cuban soil at Guantanamo, to your Camp Delta, rented to you. Obviously under that unjust Treaty of Relations signed between your President Roosevelt and the Cuban criminal Battista seventy years ago, the Cuban government has no control over anything that happens at Guantanamo Naval Base."

"Presidente Castro, this situation could become another crisis between us which neither you nor I need at this time." interrupted the U.S. president.

"President Grattan, for a long time we have wished to be a good neighbour of the United States but it is your government that has embargoed our country, starved Cuban babies of powdered milk and forbidden the medicine factories ofAmerica to supply our Cuban hospitals with cures for our sick children. However, do not underestimate the resourcefulness of the

Revolutionary Armed Forces to protect Cuba and the interests of the Cuban people. If, President Grattan, it is in the interests of the Cuban people to assist the United States government with your crisis then we will offer such assistance.

It is NOT my wish that the Republic of Cuba OR Cuban land rented to America become a shelter for the enemies of America no more than we expect you will shelter enemies of Cuba in Florida? However, you can expect me to show more respect for you than you show me President Grattan. Do you think it is just to pay only $4,085 dollars annually to rent Guantanamo Bay from the Cuban people? Why do you also make those cheques for rent out to the Treasurer General of the Republic of Cuba when that institution has disappeared many decades ago? Let us therefore talk about realism and a new cooperation between us, which can help rid the world of this terrible disease of terrorism."

"Presidente Castro, I have listened to what you say and will be back to you within 30 minutes to take our discussions further. Let us look to the future and not the past. Thank you. That's all for now, goodbye."

President Grattan instantly picked up the red telephone unit and threw it as far as he could before the phone cable pulled it crashing down onto an Oval office side table. "God damn that son of a bitch. I won't be held to ransom by anyone. Terrorists or Castro! Let's go to conference call now!

"Good Morning everyone, everyone tuned in?" Several

voices affirmed participation in the call. "As President I am conscious that the eyes of not just this great nation but of all nations of the world are on us, watching how we deal with this crisis.

This crisis can be solved successfully using a combination of measured but well timed force used tactically; the objective gentlemen is to save lives and we have a special burden to save the lives of US citizens; lets be blunt, we know that Americans are first in line for execution after any Jews. Don't know if there are many American Jews yet. So...... let's hear some options for my consideration right away, simultaneous with an accurate assessment of the facts of the situation as they are now."

The commander of MacDill Airforce base spoke first. "Mr President we have a pinpoint of the ship's position, it is definitely inside Cuban waters but only by 350 metres or so, in my latest briefing. This Sir, I believe is intentional. Even so, we could mount a heliborne attack using Chinooks, fast-roping special forces onto the decks. The problem is, that there are hundreds of passengers crowding the upper decks, all held hostage at gunpoint. One of the crew has called us on a cell phone also stating that almost the entire crew are held captive in an interior auditorium. The auditorium is overcrowded and we are informed by the company that there are over 600 crew on board. In terms of destination?......no idea, the ship seems to be near full power, speed estimated at a good 20-25 knots, and definitely shadowing the Cuban coastline."

President Grattan interrupted "Admiral Burbridge,

any suggestions?"

"I've discussed options with the Joint Special Operations Command here at the Pentagon Sir and we remain available to advise you constantly as envisaged in this type of evolving crisis. We've activated our Naval Special Warfare Command to execute any order you may choose to make whenever necessary. The NSWC can deploy Sea Air Land forces Sir. Those navy SEALS have available in Guantanamo a Special Boat Squadron with four medium range special ops. craft. If the ship is doing 20 to 25 knots however, there is no way we can mount a seaborne ambush with any sort of special ops. or amphibious craft even at night."

The Admiral paused for a moment then went on "We do have a submarine close by, returning to Guantanamo, she's the 705 City of Corpus Christi, a fast attack Los Angeles class Sir and we can shadow the ship's movements as long as the depth isn't a problem. The onboard sonar systems in the submarine can pick up and filter conversations on board the ship's decks if there aren't a couple of hundred people talking at the same time. We can of course pick up and amplify all conversations on the liner's Bridge. We can also jam all communications and even better, knock out the ship's radar and 'Comms.' tower with a missile but you may want to keep lines of communication open Sir?"

Yes, yes Admiral, good," replied President Grattan. "Get that submarine right under the ship and give me an intelligence feed as soon as you have anything worthwhile to report...............Major General Kirwan in Guantanamo can you hear me?"

"Yes Mr President."

"General let me know what the situation is regarding those prisoners. In principle get them ready to embark on whatever you have down there. It has to be an unarmed civilian vessel or something with no obvious attack capability but that can take all your prisoners. I don't care if it's a floating rust heap. At least for now we can go through the motions of getting the prisoners ready to board some sort of large craft to sail out to meet the liner. Use your brains General....I don't need another ship hijacked, courtesy of the Navy. By the way how many prisoners, sorry Illegal Combatants, do you have in total at this time?"

"Mr President, we have got 595 illegal combatants in total."

"Hold it there, General." the President said. Reflecting for a moment, he rotated a coffee cup in his hand and continued:

"General, the terrorists on the ship believe that there are 601 prisoners. Can we get some special forces dressed up in the prisoners kit and maybe get them out on to the liner mixed in with prisoners?"

"Mr President that could be problem. Offhand I'm not sure we have anyone that might pass as one of these lowlifes, they are a pretty unique bunch....toothless mountainmen, scrawny peasants, most of 'em don't even speak Arabic properly...your talking apples and oranges and a lot of nuts Mr President. Some of the Camp Guards have picked up some pidgin Arabic and Afghan words. The guards would be instantly recognisable and we're probably talking about a painful death for them...sort of payback and revenge...big time..... Mr President. Wouldn't want any U.S. forces becoming hostage either, if they were let live. That for sure wouldn't do much for morale in Camp America here in Gitmo Sir."

"Okay General. Thanks everyone ....end of conference call."

The President's aide handed him another phone, with the Israeli Premier waiting on the line.

"Good morning Premier Bloch, are you up to date on the terrorists hijacking of the liner which is currently in Cuban waters?"

"Yes President Grattan, good morning to you. I understand there are some Jewish people who are being singled out for execution."

"Premier Bloch we have a deadline of 15:00 hours Eastern time here to begin the exchange of prisoners for passengers. Jews are excluded from the exchange which is of course unacceptable. If we had more time we would ask you Premier for a detachment of Arabic speaking commandos whom we would like to pass off as prisoners from Camp Delta in Guantanamo. Admittedly it would of course be a pretty risky mission for your guys. Right now even if you were to offer such we don't have enough time to get them over here from Israel by 1500....don't know if we can get a delay from these terrorist sons of bitches".

"It may be some help to you Mr President that we do have at your Delta Forces Training Center some elite Israeli cracktroops. Though the Jews may not be Israeli citizens which would be a worse problem for me, I am always available to help you, our greatest ally. My Defence Minister tells me that there are about five Israeli Sayamet commandos in your Fort Bragg and some of them may have knowledge of Arabic. Sherman, I should say that I offer you my full support in whatever action you take and if it leads to casualties that is unfortunate but you must NOT collaborate with terrorists."

"Premier Bloch I appreciate your support and will take up your offer of Israeli soldiers if the plan's a Go. I believe that if they speak Arabic they should be of assistance. I'll have the Vice Pres. update you every hour. Thank you and good day."

The President was then briefed by the Chief of the United States Coastguard that the operation to rescue the passengers adrift on the lifeboats was almost complete without any casualties. It was planned to airlift the women and children from Guantanamo base straight to Miami. "There is something else Mr President," added the Chief. "It appears that an unauthorised light aircraft, possibly from the media, was shot down or maybe hit by a missile fired from the cruise ship. There are no survivors." The President looked down shaking his head uttering the word "Idiots." The Coast Guard Chief continued, "if these hijackers have a shoulder fired Surface to Air capability Sir, our fighter jets should use diversionary heat flares as a matter of form." The President ordered his Chief of Staff to contact Admiral Burbridge and get an exclusion zone around the ship. "Keep those F-15's flying and get it out there that any sightseeing small boats as well as aircraft will be destroyed. We don't know who is doing what right now and any unauthorised sea or air movement will be treated as a threat to national security. We shoot first and ask questions later. Get those Israeli officers down to Guantanamo to mix in with the prisoners. Maybe make sure everybody is wearing the orange prison overalls and those goggles or blindfolds and ear things. One other thing, tell the Vice President to talk to that UN representative and that Red Moon guy, or Red Crescent guy whatever he is, what the hell is wrong with the Red Cross anyway? In fact, no, I will deal with the negotiations myself personally through the Commander of Guantanamo base. I don't mind if everyone calls me Commander in Chief from now on......or President as you wish."

> "Remember when the Infidels contrive to make you a prisoner or to murder or expel you, they plot but God also plans; and God's plan is best."
>
> The Holy Qu'ran (Al-Anfal 8:30)

Camp Delta, Guantanamo Naval Base

By 11:00 hours the Commander of Guantanamo base Major General Lindie 'Chuck' Kirwan was in conference with the UN representative and the representative from the Red Crescent. All of them were eager to prepare the prisoners for the transfer to the liner in time before the 15:00 hours deadline. General Kirwan addressed the two representatives while he stared out his office window across Guantanamo Bay. To his left were the cages of Camps 1, 2 and 3 where the prisoners were housed in solitary confinement spending long hours in stifling humidity. On the right of his quarters, were Camp Echo and the disused Camp X ray. Furthest away and the camp with the best views of the bay was Camp Iguana holding the child prisoners.

"I have orders from the President that this operation is not an exchange of one Illegal Combatant for one passenger. It will be an exchange of one I.C. for one passenger AND one crew member. That is two for one. Between the three of us, if you think that the President is going to allow a bunch of terrorists sail freely back to Libya, Sudan or some goddam State in the Gulf while 600 enemies of the United States military enjoy fine dining and the luxury of a U.S. registered cruise ship you're very much mistaken. In fact you can take it that unless this exchange of I.C.s' goes to plan this crisis will end in a bloody mess with a $2 billion dollar liner renamed 'Titanic II' lying on the ocean floor. The only difference will be that there won't be an iceberg hitting the ship but a salvo of torpedoes courtesy of the United States Navy. The terrorists wanted you guys but you act on OUR terms. No side deals, nods, winks, and if I hear that either of you even smile or shake hands with one of these hijacking bastards then I will personally rip your scalps off." The General walked over to the table and leaned over, within inches of the nose of the Red Crescent representative, and glancing briefly at the UN representative, whispered "put it this way if I lose my scalp then you both lose yours for real. Now get over to that marine radio over there in the corner and call up that psycho war priest Mr Holy Haykeem. You tell him we will have two self propelled pontoon barges one carrying the prisoners and the other motherfucker of a motorised platform barge plenty big for all passengers AND crew. Get this straight: the crewman driving each pontoon barge is a volunteer sailor, unarmed and their safety is your direct responsibility, do I make myself clear? secondly, remember what I just said that there will be two passengers or crew exchanged for one and nothing less! Now get your red crescent flag of Islam and your United Nations little boy blue beret offa my base and start kissing those hairy Ayrab asses out in 'Gitmo' bay, GO! get outta heeyah"!

The White House Press Room

Back in the Press room of the White House, the President entered at 12:00 sharp for a Press Statement which he decided as more appropriate than a televised address to the Nation. That might have been an option later in the evening Eastern time but events were moving fast and he had to calm the clamour for reaction followed by a plan for action.

"Good Morning Ladies and Gentlemen, please be seated. As your President, it is in times of crisis in

which American interests are at stake, that you expect of me, candour, strategy and wisdom and above all humanity. That, as your leader I promise to deliver to you.

Today, a small group of cowardly terrorists are holding as hostages many hundreds of innocent people, men women and children in an act of terrorism that challenges the very values upon which we have built our stable and prosperous civilisation. Those innocent people were on vacation when not long out of sight of America, they found themselves at the mercy of barbaric thugs and in whom their safety and welfare is now entrusted. However, as your President, I will not be held to ransom by anyone at any time. I repeat I will not be held to ransom nor have anyone other than the government that you the people of this free land have elected, determine our domestic or foreign policies.

This morning I have instructed my Secretary of State to work with the United Nations and with our neighbours, the people of Cuba to see to the release, unharmed, of those men women and children on board that ship, God bless them. As for the illegal combatants at Guantanamo, they should not look forward to liberation and even though they may, if circumstances require, be removed from Guantanamo to another place under a different authority, they should never call themselves free men. We will hunt down the terrorists and their conspirators relentlessly, as long as it takes, and strike at the earliest moment but, at the moment of *our own choosing. If any country, large or small, seeks to interfere in what is a matter of domestic policy within the territory of the United States, then I will declare that country an enemy of the American people and they must expect to pay a very very heavy price. To those countries, both allies and those with whom we have disagreements, who sought the release of their nationals held in Guantanamo, I now forgive you your misjudgement. I trust that I have your unwavering support in what is a challenge not just to America but to all civilised nations in the world. Thank you. God bless America".*

Camp Delta, Guantanamo

With two hours to go to the deadline for the prisoner exchange, the Fantasea of the World had slowed to fifteen knots, holding a position of two nautical miles inside Cuban territorial waters. From the prison watch towers of Camp Delta in Guantanamo the gleaming white liner was easily visible through the guards binoculars as it approached Guantanamo Bay. Admiral Burbridge of the Atlantic Fleet called up Major General Kirwan.

"General, you have an Underwater Delivery Vehicle on your base that can take up to 8 Navy SEALS. Let's look at some covert underwater actions here. The Corpus Christi itself is no use unless we're going to send the ship into orbit in a million pieces. What can we do with a UDV?"

"Admiral, I can have that UDV operational immediately and I suggest we use it as an underwater escort for the platform pontoon barges we intend to use to transfer the prisoners to the ship if that's the President's Order. The SEALS can also attach limpet mines to the pontoons for later detonation as desired."

"Good. Get that submersible operational and staffed. Advise the SEALS to expect combat and combat on an opportunist basis but I need to be consulted."

The Admiral ended the call and briefed the President and his Cabinet in the White House on speaker phone.

Guantanamo Bay

Underneath the liner, in the Sonar Center of the submarine three officers were seated with eyes closed listening through headphones to garbled conversation picked up from a needle antenna, sticking nine feet above the surface, all but invisible. After filtering all noises, sounds coming through to the Sonar Center consisted of some clear words but not enough to make any intelligible sentence.

On board the ship, passengers on the open decks were beginning to scald red as the midday sun beat down. They had had no food since the day before and occasionally passengers, all men and teenage boys, shouted for water.

Down below in the Broadway Theatre the crew were also suffering in the cramped conditions. Samia ordered the kitchen staff at gunpoint to distribute whatever food was available in the kitchens to the crew in the theatre. This consisted of stale bread rolls, fruit and cartons of juice or milk. She had warned any of the kitchen staff that any ideas of concealing a knife or sharp metal objects would mean execution without questions.

Hakeem staying on the Bridge, surveyed the deserted Cuban beaches leading to Guantanamo Bay's headland. Astern, he had noticed a small navy ship in Cuban territorial waters about one mile off which bore the Cuban flag and kept it's distance. Hakeem wasn't concerned about being shadowed by the Cuban Marine forces most of whose surface fleet was tied up in need of essential spare parts and repairs. He was more concerned about two larger and faster U.S. Navy coastal patrol boats further out in international waters one of which had slowly come closer. On the foredeck of both, he could see through his binoculars a swivel mounted gun, firing he suspected 5mm or even 10mm rounds, which could spray the liner's Bridge by the hundred in a matter of seconds. One of the US patrol boats continued edging closer to the ship, a couple of metres every few minutes or so. Hakeem grabbed the liner's Bridge VHF radio and switched it to Channel 16 reserved for 'Distress and Urgent Messages'.

"This is Commander Hakeem of the Holy Warship of Islamic Jihad. I have a message for the American Navy Warship that is coming up on our starboard. Unless you change course immediately we will begin executing passengers, do you hear me?"

Silence followed and Hakeem spoke again repeating

the same message. There was no response and Hakeem looked over to Captain Hamilton. Hakeem asked if the Navy ship had heard his message. Hamilton shrugged his shoulders. At that point Hakeem looked up at the mast flags and thought about hoisting a passenger by the neck up a halyard followed by the yellow marine flag of a ship in quarantine. As he looked at the liner's full dress of decorative triangular flags from bow to stern he lingered on the large billowing stars and stripes, the red stripes he counted at seven in total.

Hakeem spoke into his radio "Zador get me seven passengers. No more than seven. Pick them at random, big and fat and bring them down to the Promenade deck." Shortly afterwards Zador had rounded up seven terrified passengers, some old, some young all standing in a cluster in front of Zador's AK-47. Zador spoke into his radio. "What next Hakeem?" Hakeem took up his binoculars and looked at the American gunboat still approaching directly.

"Zador its time for blood. Sacrifice those men. I want you to tie each one of the seven bodies onto the deck rail about two or three metres apart. I want seven big red stripes down the side of this ship for our American friends to see."

Zador yelled at the passengers to turn away from him and face the oncoming US navy gunboat "Start waving to your American friends to stay away, to go away, shout, ………..shout as loudly as you can 'go home American scum, and friends of Satan, go back to hell."

Without hesitation the seven men obeyed and began desperately roaring and waving as ordered. Zador quietly stepped back, took aim and fired rounds continually at the heads of the group, the last to be hit being shot in the face as he turned around to lunge at Zador. The men fell about against each other, dead as they hit the deck, showing neat facial exit wounds. Zador had avoided puncturing the torsos of the men to avoid immediate blood loss. He then cut lengths of lifebuoy rope and began the process of tying together the feet of each corpse. Spreading the corpses along the deck, he then tied the bound feet to the top wooden banister rail, then heaved each one onto the rail, balanced belly up, arms outstretched.

Taking Suleyman's dagger out again he plunged the blade into each throat slicing deeply into the left vertebral artery then dragged it across through the longtitudinal ligament to the right artery. Most heads quivered as cervical nerves were severed which Zador had waited to happen. However one head startled Zador as it jerked up to stare wide eyed directly at him before he quickly tipped the body over the rail. All seven cadavers dangled at different levels, like bloated side fenders, limp, upside down, arms gently swinging, blood freeflowing downwards, human scarecrows to ward off the foolish crusader. Zador leaned out eagerly over the side, seeing the streams of crimson cross the goldpainted band and on down over the white hull of the ship to the waterline. He walked away disappointed that the ship's foamy wake kept it's fresh creamy tint and did not bleed a wake of red threshing turbulence.

At that point Hakeem picked up the radio again. "This is another message to the Commander of the American warship. Please take a close look at the stripes at the side of our ship. The stripes are in blood. Just like the stripes of your American flag. Unless you change course immediately there will be more stripes. Look closely through your binoculars. Seven people are dead, change course immediately. If you don't this ship will no longer be a palace of the ocean but a ship of Satan, a funeral ship carrying a cargo of the dead". Hakeem turned off the radio and picked up his binoculars again. Moments passed. Very slowly the gunboat turned away and began following a parallel course to the liner keeping its distance to about a mile.

Zador turned to Captain Hamilton with a smile. "Now it is time for this warship to use its bigger guns." Hakeem spoke into his radio ordering Suleyman to fire a rocket propelled grenade at the gunboat from his shoulder held launcher. Cheers went up from the brigade having heard the command over their open radio channel. Suleyman chose the highest point on the ship and rested the launch tube on his right shoulder aiming for the boat's wheelhouse. A jolting thud followed by a swishing sound and the grenade shot way, again to cheers from the brigade. It landed in the water well short of the U.S. gunboat but the explosion and the upward cascade of water had the brigade chanting together, "Death to America, death to the infidel".

Zador turned again to Hamilton "well, now I go to use

my water gun in the big jewish piss-house, I will cool them down since there is no water left in the pool, you can too Captain, you have my permission!"

Hamilton replied in a flash "that'll make the Jews laugh for a couple of hours seeing your little hooded snake"! Zador's good humoured expression dropped at the mention of 'jews laughing' and 'little snake'. He hadn't understood the word 'hooded' but he guessed what it meant. Zador immediately left and returned later, loudly sighing, feigning great relief but showing a less than convincing smile of satisfaction.

Moments later two F-15's swooped down out of the sky and each one flew past the ship at Bridge level in a deafening roar. The martyrs hadn't time to aim their guns at the fighter jets flying past at MACH 1 and then soaring vertically up into the blue until out of sight. Each left a trail of aluminium diversionary chaff sparkling in the sunlight like glittering firework stars. Hakeem looked at his watch and the time showed 13.30. He continued to scan the land horizon with his binoculars.

Bunker De La Comandancia
De Las Fuerzas Armadas Revolucionarias De Cuba
Havana

In the Comandancia in Havana Comandante Castro called a meeting with his brother Raul, General of all Cuban forces, the Fuerzas Armadas Revolucionarias. Also brought together in Soviet Zil limousines speeding down Miramar's 6th Avenue in Havana were members of the military command council of the Cuban Eastern Army. The council were meeting in the Comandante's bunker in Vedado, Havana, allowing everyone to speak freely knowing that the room was impenetrable to CIA listening systems.

Fidel opened the meeting. "Comrades let us review the situation facing our forces at this time. We have a hijacked liner inside our territorial waters which we are following with a Yevgenya mine sweeper. There has been some killing of passengers but the main objective of the Jihadistas seems to be to liberate the prisoners in the U.S. Naval base at Guantanamo. If the Americans release the captives in exchange for the passengers let's all think where the ship will then go. Let me have your ideas in a moment. Then we have some more problems. I have no doubt the Cubano locos in Florida and their friends in the American congress will look for any excuse to invade Cuban territory again if the ship stays in Cuban waters with the freed prisoners on board. We all know the state of our ships in the Marina de Guerra Revolucionaria. We don't have anything more than another operational mine sweeper and at this moment we cannot defend our territory from an amphibious assault by American forces."

Raul Castro interrupted Fidel, "we have taken the artillery platforms off the old ships and we can have on the beaches near Guantanamo two mobile Bandera IV missile batteries within an hour. We also have two rolling platforms with Russian SS-N-2 styx missiles that we can also show as evidence of our intention to defend our homeland."

"That's not enough" replied Fidel.

"Let's see if we can help the Americans in return for getting rid of this treaty of relations where we get a miserable $4,000 dollars from the US Government every year, the amount a Canadian tourist spends in Varadero! Compañeros, Guantanamo Naval Station belongs to the people of Cuba and we are never going to recognise this Treaty of Relations made between that mafioso Battista and Roosevelt. So the first thing to do is to bring units of the Eastern Army up to the perimeter of Guantanamo…which is 24.6 km in total. We will also mobilise Especiales and any other commandos we have on the pretext that we will not let any prisoners escape into Cuba from Guantanamo. That will of course sound cooperative but also make the Americans think twice if they intend to come into Cuban territory in hot pursuit of escaped prisoners. They invade Cuba, we invade Guantanamo, it could be as simple as that; they don't belong in Cuba and they will find that out the hard way but we belong in Guantanamo! Commanders, who do you think the nations of the world will support in that case?" Fidel sat down and hailed an aide to get a call through to President Grattan.

"Good afternoon President Grattan. We have been watching the developments on board the cruiseship and we are sorry to learn now of the killings of passengers on board. As the situation is worsening let me assure you that we intend to offer our full support to the American Government to ensure that this cruiseship is not run aground or sunk in shallow Cuban waters. For us too it is important that your prisoners do not break through the Guantanamo frontier to escape into Cuban territory. We will be stepping up our security presence with specialist units to secure the border from the Cuban side. Of course it is all Cuban territory and I said earlier to you that it is an annual insult to the people of Cuba and to me personally that you send me a cheque for a couple of thousand dollars every year for occupying Cuban territory. Therefore while helping the American Government we believe this is also a good time to focus on normalising the situation with regard to Guantanamo. You President Grattan and I know that a naval base in Cuba is not essential to the defence of America."

President Grattan replied "Presidente I fully expect your co-operation in this crisis and we don't have the time to start renegotiating a new treaty of relations about Guantanamo Bay Naval Base! Let me say to you Presidente that allowing us to enter Cuban Territorial Waters in the name of civilisation to arrest these terrorists will be applauded around the world and it would hugely strengthen our ties of friendship."

"President Grattan I AM aware that an American submarine is in Cuban waters right at this minute and I am offended you did not ask my permission before this act. Given the state of relations between Cuba and the

American Government this is a deliberate provocation and a violation of our sovereignty. It could be a matter for the security council of the United Nations."

"Presidente Castro we intend to do everything that is reasonable to find a quick solution to this crisis and if there is or is not an American submarine in your territorial waters, I ask your permission now to allow our submarines enter Cuban waters in the vicinity of Guantanamo during this crisis."

"President Grattan that sounds again like the problem with Guantanamo. You enter Cuban waters first and then talk later."

President Grattan was getting agitated by the issue of Guantanamo Bay returning to the conversation. "Look Castro, sorry ...Presidente what do you want? $4 million dollars a year for Guantanamo? You do realise that it is a legally binding international treaty? Remember you cashed in one of our cheques...and that seals a deal in any language".

Castro replied "for now, we will observe and offer assistance ......we will not detain the ship entering Cuban waters illegally without a permit. I will call you again later."

The White House

Both men put down the phone simultaneously President Grattan resuming "What does he want? $4 million dollars? $40 million bucks? If he thinks he's going to get back Guantanamo Bay forget it." President Grattan had an aide call up Admiral Burbridge at Joint Special Operations Command at the Pentagon to find out if there was any carrier battle group in the vicinity. "Mr President we have 'Big John' that's the aircraft carrier 'John F. Kennedy' in Guantanamo Harbour for crew change and resupply. Before you called I've ordered her disembarked crew to return to stand-by status. The carrier has fuel and can sail immediately Sir....next best thing to a fleet display. It won't be a battle group but if you need to show the Cubans some marine muscle in a sail-past, that's the floating fortress for it. She has a full air wing compliment and would otherwise be ready to sail in three days time for the Gulf."

"Good" responded Grattan "get the carrier out and show it off to the Cubans and if she edges inside Cuban territorial waters well that's just too bad."

Guantanamo Bay Naval Base

The time was coming up to 14.00 hours and two huge motorised platform pontoon barges were started up pierside. One pontoon would take all 595 prisoners on board, it's flat metal surface sections now as hot as roasting tins in the afternoon sun. The second pontoon would take the passengers as well as the crew off the liner back to the Naval base. At 14.00 the Commander of Camp Delta, Major General Kirwan ordered all prisoners to be dressed in orange prison suits, blind folded and wrists tied with plastic strips before boarding army trucks and driven to the gangway and the moored pontoon. In an orderly line all the prisoners including the juveniles from Camp Iguana were led onto the pontoon. Amongst the blind folded prisoners were the five Israeli commandos of the elite Sayeret Matkal combat team also wearing the orange prison suits but more loosely blindfolded and with hands bound in weaker plastic strapping. They were led by an American special forces veteran Jack Branagan, an instructor in Military Sabotage and Psychological Warfare. Branagan worked in covert missions in Afghanistan, Pakistan and in Iraq before the downfall of Saddam Hussein. He had some Arabic but was not proficient to the same degree as the five Israeli commandos who had been flown in from Fort Bragg where they were training with him.

Branagan, before joining the prisoners on the pontoon had spent the previous hours feverishly studying the layout of the ship including the services ducts and air vents to the Broadway Theatre on board. He was to lead the team of Israeli commandos, concealing in orange overalls their weaponry of several pistols, ammunition magazines and small flash bombs. Around their legs were strapped hand grenades and smoke canisters. For stealth killing, each had pocketed lengths of choke wire and long titanium needle spikes for keyhole killing through the heart. Each commando was prepared for immediate action if necessary either on the pontoon itself if they were discovered by other prisoners or later as they boarded the ship when they might be searched.

The commandos and Branagan positioned themselves around the edges of the floating pontoon so that they wouldn't be pushed up against prisoners who might be suspicious of their lumpy bulk or the feel of pistols and grenades concealed in the overalls. Branagan had picked up some words of Russian on covert missions in Chechnya working with Russian militia. He had just turned fifty years but with his shaved head, and pumped up body muscles, he could have been twenty years younger save for his face. Deep wrinkles lined a taut leathery face which was cut through on the left cheek with a hot pink scar. It crossed his cheek from earlobe to nostril, a souvenir of hand to hand fighting at an Afghan mountain pass roadblock.

  Since he had joined the marines he quickly rose through the ranks, obsessed as he was with perfection and carrying out missions exactly according to strategies and battle plans. He and the Israeli commandos, all lightly blindfolded could still see in the distance the Fantasea of the World's upper decks rising above the headland which divided Guantanamo Naval Base from Cuban territory. Once the pontoon was loaded with all 601 figures on the platform, legs folded, hands tied, they were ordered to remain silent. Some prisoners wept at the prospect of possible freedom or maybe in fear of what might happen next. The exchange of prisoners for passengers could be an excuse for a shoot out between U.S. Forces and the martyrs brigade on the ship when they might be conveniently shot by the Americans in the targeted cross fire. As the minutes went by in the baking heat the pontoon barges cable hawsers remained firmly attached to the pier stanchions. The operation to manoeuvre the pontoon of prisoners out to the ship awaited an executive order from President Grattan.

Guantanamo Harbour

Less than 300 metres away on the quayside where the aircraft carrier John F Kennedy was tied up, bus loads of sailors were arriving and running up the gantries in response to Admiral Burbridge's sudden order to set sail. It would still be an hour before the carrier would be ready to leave Guantanamo Harbour.

The last people to board the prisoner pontoon barge were the United Nations representative carrying a white flag emblazoned with the black letters **UN** and he was followed by a representative from the Red Crescent carrying another larger white flag with red crescent moon. Each representative was given a bulky marine telephone into which only two numbers had been programmed, the number of the Fantasea of the World and General Kirwan's number at Guantanamo Naval base. Kirwan called the President confirming that the Pontoon barge had been loaded, engines were running and was ready to advance out to the open sea upon an executive order.

Bunker De La Comandancia, Havana

From an observation tower on a ridge high in the hills behind Guantanamo Bay officers of Cuba's Eastern Army were reporting directly back to Comandante Fidel in the bunker in Havana. They confirmed that the prisoners had been released from Camp Delta and looked ready to be towed out to the liner.

Fidel, on receiving the latest information addressed again the military council. "We are now approaching a moment which could be the greatest threat to the Cuban Revolution since the Bay of Pigs invasion. If these prisoners end up on Cuban territory it will give America the perfect excuse to send in it's forces in hot pursuit of the prisoners. We may end up losing more land than just Guantanamo. Raul get those missile batteries onto the beaches beside Guantanamo. We must be prepared to use them not only against US Forces but against that pontoon of prisoners if it makes landfall on our coast. I think I can say to you all that if we were to sink the pontoon and lose the lives of the prisoners we cannot expect a hostile response from President Grattan and his Government in Washington...and, maybe not immediately, but the embargo would seem in the eyes of the American people as being more cruel than ever! We would have done Grattan a favour and solved the problem of court marshalling 600 prisoners and also the problem of Camp Delta being an increasing embarrassment for the American Government."

Raul put his hand up half way through his Fidel's address to the council and received a nod to go ahead and speak. "Fidel, that is a high risk strategy where after an act of aggression by Cuban forces against a pontoon full of unarmed prisoners, nothing will have changed. The embargo will be in place, Guantanamo will still be in the hands of America and might fill up again with more prisoners in the years ahead. Worse, the Cuban people will still be insulted annually with the cheque from President Grattan or whoever for the rent of Guantanamo Bay of $4,085 dollars. I say we should not be the first ones to try and make friends with President Grattan. Up to know we have told them we will return any escaped prisoner to Guantanamo and we will secure the border from the Cuban side. We must get something from this crisis. I think if we can save the lives of the passengers and crew as well as the prisoners and oppose American aggression as a means of solving the problem then Cuba's standing in the world will be even greater. Maybe we could consider joint sovereignty with America over Guantanamo and we could propose to share some of the facilities including a ship repair yard and spare parts for our navy?

At this time Fidel most of our ships and our three submarines are not just non-operational, they are rusting in the sun and badly need replacements. Cuba can never match U.S. air power but for an island a navy is critical and more critical than the army. If ever the locos in Florida invade again our first defence must be the navy and then afterwards the army. The people will take care of any surviving Florida mafia arriving on Cuban territory."

Fidel thanked Raul and asked General Arroyo, Commander of the Eastern Army what he thought would happen to the liner if the exchange of prisoners for passengers went ahead. "Comandante there are a couple of options, the first one being most unlikely that it will sail for a Muslim country, somewhere maybe on the West African coast....Nigeria maybe. That would be too long a voyage and the Americans could not resist the opportunity to attack the target even if it is a moving one and whatever hostages on board are killed, then so what? It would be somewhere in the mid-Atlantic, unseen by anyone. I don't believe the Israelis either would resist an attack once the ship came within range of it's airforce. Remember the rescue by their Matkal commandos of the hostages at Entebbe airport in Uganda in 1976?....that shows you the range the Israeli special forces have when necessary.

The second option might be that the Jihadistas have an arrangement with guerrillas in Colombia or Nicaragua where helicopters will land on the ship and take off the prisoners to land somewhere in the central American jungle. Again I think the American forces would intercept and anyway we have no intelligence from our Latin comrades that they have found religion and joined up with a holy Islamic militia. Another option might be that the ship will be deliberately run up on rocks somewhere along our Southern coastal flank with the prisoners believing they could escape into our Southern provinces. This I believe should be prevented by our forces at all costs. As I said there is a high risk that American forces will pursue the prisoners into the jungle and we could have months of jungle warfare between armed prisoners, American forces and Cuban infantry caught in the middle fighting both. As for other possibilities, the ship could sail for Haiti or Grenada but American forces on those islands will be waiting for the prisoners. What else?.........well the Jihadistas could blow up the liner in deep water and hope they all get a lift to paradise on a magic carpet!!" The military chiefs broke into raucous laughter releasing the tension that had built up in a gloomy assessment of the situation so far.

Fidel put up his hand to stop the laughter. "Comrades there is no time for hours of negotiations between us and the American Government. The Cuban people are not going to be bribed by any amount of millions of dollars for the rent of Guantanamo Naval base from Cuba. It is Cuban territory and must return to the Cuban people! Let us look for the support of the United Nations and the people of America to demilitarise Guantanamo as the beginning of a process to reclaim it. Cuba is no Devils Island,............... this cruise ship hijack has shown that the safest place for these so called prisoners is on American territory and not Cuban territory. Grattan has learned now that Guantanamo naval base is too remote to be an American jail. Do you think Comrades that this crisis would have happened if the prisoners were on the island of Alcatraz in San Francisco bay and not the island of Cuba? The American government needs our co-operation to stop these terrorists moving freely inside Cuban territorial waters. Let us leave aside any talk about money in our discussion with Grattan. Let us forget about the embargo in the negotiations, instead let the situation bring about the support of the

United Nations to de-militarise Guantanamo naval base!

Do you think then in a year or two there will be any protests from the American people if we take back our land at Guantanamo by force when it is no longer useful to the American people. An empty no man's land and we'll let them refuel their fleet there still! Come to Cuba, Uncle Sam, for your oil"! There won't be any shooting and if there is we won't start it first. What do you think Raul?"

Raul and the rest of the military commanders were nodding in agreement at the idea to recover the valuable naval facilities at Guantanamo. Fidel asked that a call be put through to President Grattan again:

"Good afternoon Mr President. I see that the prisoners are ready to be released and brought out to the cruise ship. Let me say that America has our full support in this attempt by these Jihadistas to embarrass you and the American military."

"Thank you Presidente Castro. The support we want from you is to not interfere with our plan and if it means that our forces attack the liner to rescue the passengers and if that liner is in Cuban territorial waters I ask you for your agreement to pursue the terrorists even if they are inside Cuban territorial waters-if there are casualties they will not be Cuban"

"Let me say this President Grattan: Camp Delta has become a problem for you and for me. Every year you humiliate the Cuban people by offering an insulting cheque under that worthless lease signed by the mafioso Battista and your Roosevelt. The rent of $4,085 dollars is only realistic if there was nothing in Guantanamo. If it was demilitarised then there is no issue between you and the Cuban people renting what will become a piece of useless neutralised territory and not an embarrassment to you..... and a provocation and embarrassment to us. We will not have the indignity of a big American naval presence on the island of Cuba. Yes, we will acknowledge our obligations under the International Treaty of Relations where you can continue to rent the base if it is demilitarised, say for shelter and refuelling which will keep the lease in existence. But never again must it be used as a prison camp. This crisis has come about only because you have selected Guantanamo as a prison camp and now you can see the result of what clearly has been some careful planning by terrorists who seek to exploit relations between you and I."

The White House

President Grattan had his phone on speaker and around the room he could see the Chief of Staff and the Admirals of the Atlantic and Pacific fleets gesturing that demilitarising Guantanamo would not diminish the strength of the American influence in the Caribbean. The Treaty of Relations which gave Guantanamo naval base to the Americans was now an embarrassment, not only in itself but more so now that there was a real possibility of prisoners landing on Cuban territory and outside the control of the American government unless it intervened militarily.

Grattan replied after a moment of silence.

"Presidente Castro, we are prepared to remove our fleet from Guantanamo if it is excess to our fleet requirements which looking around the cabinet table here my cabinet indicate it just might be. Put it this way, if you let me have your full cooperation in relation to this matter then you can take it that we will very favourably not only consider your request to turn our naval base into a demilitarised zone, instead of ………………….lifting the embargo… which I had thought of recommending to Congress".

Comandante Castro replied in a sarcastic tone, "unfortunately while I appreciate your good thoughts about lifting the embargo, I understand Congress has a mind of it's own, no? So we agree in principle to cooperate fully but you must phone me in advance of any plans to enter Cuban territorial waters…other than your submarine now in our waters due to 'faulty navigation equipment', eh?..... so that I can advise our naval commanders accordingly that any increased presence is not a hostile act against Cuba. For now we will continue to shadow the cruise liner and let the United Nations find a solution that is acceptable to both you and the people of Cuba."

"Thank you Presidente Castro" replied Grattan as he ended the call. "Okay, Gentlemen, fellow commanders, I am making an executive order to release the pontoon of prisoners out to the cruise liner and let the exchange of prisoners for passengers begin. Lets get all American passengers and crew off safely as a matter of priority and let the Israeli commandos take care of the Jews retained on board, I've enough to be going on with. May God bless the commandos on their mission to take control of the ship and extinguish those blackmailing Godless sons of bitches".

Guantanamo Bay

The time was 14.30 and as the hawser cables were winched back around the pier capstans the huge pontoon barges were propelled away from the quay slowly out in the direction of the harbour mouth. It was clear that they were not going to reach the cruise liner by 15.00 and the UN representative called up the ship.

"Commander Hakeem, this is the United Nations representative, we have the ship in sight. Two pontoons are on the way to the ship, one carrying the prisoners and one to receive the passenger hostages at the same time. We need all the hostages, we must have all the crew most of whom have nothing to do with America or Israel. We are on our way; we will try and reach the ship by 15.00. You must wait. The pontoon is full of prisoners and our speed is only six or seven kilometres per hour."

As the box like pontoon platforms rounded the headland to the exposed sea they started to yaw and roll in the swell while the prisoners at the front of their pontoon turned their heads away from spray that was thrown off the top of the waves by the strong breeze. The pontoons had no rail and the bound prisoners and disguised Israeli commandos around the edges rolled themselves inwards as they felt the water hit the sides of the pontoons and splash onto the metal plating of the floor. Every couple of minutes, the pontoon was slapped broadside by a wave, echoing with the deep thunderous resonance of a metal drum. When the pontoons were outside the harbour mouth, the UN and Red Crescent representatives were permitted to cut the plastic wrist bindings and blindfolds on the prisoners. Just a couple of metres underneath the prisoner's pontoon, eight Navy Seals were in the Underwater Delivery Vehicle awaiting combat instructions from Naval Special Warfare Command.

The leading pontoon of prisoners slowed a little to allow the larger empty one behind catch up with the intention that both pontoons could come alongside the ship which now appeared to be slowing down to a speed of approximately five knots. On the ship the first pilotage door nearest the bow had opened and Hakeem was at the entrance signalling that the leading prisoner pontoon come alongside that door where the prisoners would enter the ship. As it neared the ship the prisoners and disguised commandos began to stand up and to shouts of 'ALLAH AKBAR' continuous cheering began as their bindings and blindfolds were thrown aside. At the rear of the ship the second pontoon was coming alongside pilotage door number six which had opened and which would become the exit point for the crew and passengers in exchange for the prisoners.

Overhead USAF jets screamed down out of the sky

and swooped low over the ship releasing bursts of silver chaff as they did so against possible surface to air missile launch from the ship. Hakeem was aware that if the prisoners entered the ship first without the exchange of passengers the fighter jets could have the excuse to open fire on the prisoners pontoon, shooting as many as possible. Hakeem waved his hand to the prisoners and called on them to stop cheering. He wanted to speak to the prisoners to remind them that they were not yet free.

Eventually the prisoners became quiet as Hakeem addressed them against a strong Caribbean breeze:
" Welcome to the Ship of Jihad! Welcome warriors of Islam, Liberated by the will of Allah from the land of the Infidel! By the grace of Allah we will return to our places of birth. Let us not forget that we are free of the great Satan of America but we must escape through the island of Cuba, not just a land of false Gods but a land of people with no God and no hope. This is now a very dangerous time in our mission when the passengers will be led from the upper decks down to the rear of the ship to board the empty pontoon. This will leave the upper decks exposed to a possible helicopter attack by American Marines. Arm yourselves immediately you come on board and go to the top deck". Hakeem knew that this was the mission's most vulnerable moment as he released all 700 passengers and crew of 616 for the 601 prisoners. He would need the smaller but still significant shield of the Jewish hostages more than ever. After a moment's pause Hakeem spoke over his

radio to Zador to start transferring the passengers and crew to the rear pontoon platform. After about a dozen passengers were on board the rear pontoon Hakeem with his pistol waved in the first of the Guantanamo prisoners who began cheering jubilantly again, some turning East facing Mecca in thanks. As these first prisoners in their baggy orange overalls came on board Hakeem ordered Suleyman to get each prisoner to recite a verse of the Holy Qu'ran as they came on board. He suspected the Americans might try and infiltrate the prisoners with marines and he didn't have time to frisk each prisoner coming into the ship. He needed these freed fighters on board and armed as quickly as possible.

At the same time at the rear of the ship the male passengers were tumbling out onto the pontoon, some being pushed by Zador as the pontoon heaved up against the ship and then pulled away again with the gulf widening up to three or four feet. Some passengers just about reached the pontoon as it drifted away from the ship momentarily. Through binoculars the scene was being surveyed by the U.S. Special Ops. Craft. Zador spoke over his radio to Ahmed sitting in the Broadway Theatre, the heavy machine gun facing the captive crew. "Ahmed, get the crew down to pilotage door number 6 at the rear of the ship to release them onto the pontoon." Hakeem's words were overheard on Suleyman's radio by the passengers who were waiting to board the pontoon. Hakeem continued "Samia, get the Jews out of the pool and tie them to the Sky deck rails, around the pool, a few metres separating each Jew. That will be our defence to an attack on the ship until we land in Cuba."

At the front pilotage doorway the jubilant prisoners were reciting the Holy Qu'ran as required and once in, picked up pistols and ammunition. Some loaded their pistols immediately and began shooting aimlessly at the ships light fittings chanting jubilantly as they ran throughout the ship. The first of the Israeli commandos leapt off the prisoner pontoon helped in by Hakeem's outstretched hand. Suleyman asked him to recite a verse. The commando who had been cheering went silent. Suleyman looked him in the eye and asked him again to recite a verse of the Holy Qu'ran again. Suddenly the commando reached inside his overall at which point Suleyman grabbed him and pushed him out the door where he fell between the pontoon and the ship. Suleyman took out his pistol and fired into the gap but the orange overall never surfaced. Suleyman roared at Hakeem "THE AMERICAN INFIDEL IS TRYING TO TRICK US, SOME OF THESE ARE NOT PRISONERS". "Anyone we suspect not being a prisoner will be shot without question" assured Hakeem. The remaining prisoners on board the pontoon cheered but boarded less excitedly unsure how Suleyman determined who was or was not a prisoner.

The Israeli commandos led by Branagan knew that something was going wrong and readied themselves for action once they were on board. Suleyman now had his pistol drawn and every prisoner coming on board came face to face with the pistol as he was asked to recite any verse. The next Israeli commando climbing on board was surprised by the request and as he hesitated, Suleyman fired point blank into the commando's face. Hakeem then dumped his body over the side of the ship onto the pontoon. The prisoners then rolled it off into the water as soon as a gap opened between the pontoon and the ship. Hakeem warned. "There are traitors amongst you. We know who you are."

Ten minutes passed before the next Israeli commando was pulled on board the ship and as soon as he saw Suleyman's gun he lunged at Suleyman. In an instant Hakeem had shot the commando several times and his body was heaved overboard. Observed by the remainder of the Israeli commandos on the pontoon they saw that they had been discovered somehow. As Hakeem surveyed the hundreds of prisoners crowding the front of the pontoon to board the ship two figures in orange overalls dived off the windward side of the pontoon, one shortly after the other, throwing pistols and knives out as they hit the water. Badshah who was surveying the scene from above on the Promenade deck opened fire at the spot until it receded too far astern of the moving ship.

Still looking for the distinctive orange clothing surfacing in the wake, Badshah couldn't believe his eyes as he saw a small Dolphin shaped object surface and divers leap out. Badshah aimed his AK-47 and opened fire hitting the water in front of the receding creature-like craft which then submerged seconds later. Hakeem angrily remonstrated with the UN official that the Americans had planted enemies amongst the prisoners and warned the remaining prisoners: "We know all of you. We know which of you are prisoners and which of you are spies and traitors. Any traitors will be shot immediately".

At the same time the pontoon tied up to the pilotage door at the rear of the ship was filling up quickly as passengers fell over one another in their anxiety to get on board. The passengers already on board dived flat as they heard the zing of Badshah's bullets whizz past. It was clear jumping off the moving ship onto a pontoon was much easier than the prisoners task of jumping up and in to the ship. In a hurry to complete the discharge of all male passengers and also all crew, Hakeem gave an order: "all crew are to be pushed out as the second pontoon is more than big enough for 700 passengers and over 600 crew. It doesn't matter if people fall in to the water, the operation must be hurried." The order wasn't needed as passengers and crew fought savagely to get off the ship. Once on the platform however they remained fearful that the blood spilling down the side of the ship had brought an escort of hungry sharks to attack them if they rolled overboard. The passengers and crew on the heaving pontoon sat down in small groups and linked arms for greater stability.

Hakeem called out to the UN official, "these are my new instructions. Tonight at 21.00 hours you must have two C130 United Nations transport planes in Santiago de Cuba Airport and the United Nations will fly our liberated comrades back to our homelands from Cuba. We will tell you later about the destination. Remember we need two C130 transports. You must also arrange with the Cuban government safe passage for the prisoners travelling from the ship at Santiago Port to Antonio Maceo Airport in Santiago. These prisoners are not prisoners of war recognised by the United Nations, they are innocent muslims. Do as I command or the United Nations will pay the price of being a collaborator with the great Satan. Did you hear what I said?" The UN official nodded and repeated back to Hakeem what he had heard. Below the ship a fresh surveillance crew in the submarine's Sonar Center had picked up the conversation, the duty officer rushing to the submarine's Command Center with a written note of the conversation. In a matter of minutes the conversation notes were passed to the Pentagon and had arrived in the cabinet room of the Whitehouse.

On board the prisoners pontoon, one of the last to be pulled in to the ship was Jack Branagan who leapt on board and stood up behind a line of three other prisoners who were each being asked the same thing. Branagan caught the word 'Qu'ran' followed by the prisoner's chant like recitation; Branagan had less than 60 seconds to work out a strategy. The two prisoners ahead of him recited verses jubilantly and armed themselves with pistols before running off down a passageway. Branagan, his six foot four inch frame, towered over Suleyman whose pistol was pointing into his face. Suleyman asked him in Arabic to recite a verse from the Qu'ran. Branagan pointed to himself angrily shouting "CHECHNYA" and then excitedly garbled out loudly what sounded like Russian interspersed with the word "Allah". Suleyman paused for a second and looked at the size of the agitated prisoner. He gave him a friendly slap on the shoulder and waved him through. Branagan, duly grabbed a pistol and a ammunition clip and ran down the nearest passageway but ducked into a stores room instead of going on to the upper decks.

CHAPTER 10

In the stores room, Branagan pocketed the Glock pistol and took out his own Smith & Wesson fitted with a silencer. He had to revise his strategy. He was uncertain if he could mingle amongst the freed prisoners and get to the ship's Security Center while at the same time be ready for instant combat in case of discovery. He knew there were Chechen prisoners on board who had come to know one another in Guantanamo. He only had a limited amount of grenades and ammunition which wouldn't hold off dozens of suicidal prisoners attacking him. He decided against mixing with the prisoners but would instead remain in orange overalls to avoid immediate suspicion if he was seen skulking in passageways.

He had to assume he was the only commando to have successfully boarded the ship but he also knew the hijackers could not be sure if several others had infiltrated on board. He decided to set off a series of random explosions around the ship. He also needed to arouse suspicion and hostility between the different nationalities which he had been briefed about in Guantanamo; he was told how the Saudis despised the illiterate Yemenis and how the Iraqi Fedayeen refused to eat with Turks. The Egyptians were hated by the Syrians while no one had any time for the Hamas Palestinians who were considered a spent force reduced to stone throwing at Israeli heavy armour. His main objective after the Security Center was to reach the Bridge, taking back control of the ship and arming whatever Bridge officers were held captive. He pulled out a paper layout of the ship and reckoned he was directly under the Bridge, 17 decks above. The best and quickest way up was by elevator; Suleyman had by now closed the pilotage door. The exchange was over. Branagan looking out of the storeroom could faintly hear the rapid sequences of 6 shots from the prisoners pistols, fired off in celebration. Slowly he walked out of the storeroom, gun in hand, walking casually and calmly in the direction of the forward starboard service elevator. He could hear the whirring of the elevators busy with freed prisoners enjoying the sensation and novelty only otherwise seen in movies.

Arriving quietly he pressed the call button and after an agonising wait, the doors opened, elevator car empty except for one teenage prisoner. Branagan barked angrily at him in fake Russian and pulled him out by the collar. Once inside he closed the doors and pressed the button 'C deck'. As the elevator ascended, the sweat rolled down his cheeks from his forehead. He briefly raised his face into the cool air of the roof fan. The elevator slowed and he fingered the trigger of his pistol, ready for the unexpected. Suddenly an automated voice announced cheerfully "C Deck" unnerving him for a second. Then the doors opened and he was facing a service passage way with an arrow directed left with the words 'Grand Foyer and Reception' underneath.

Quietly walking along he arrived at the service entrance to the Grand Foyer, standing before a vast carpeted space where passengers first embarked. Standing inside the entrance he could hear cutting and then some tearing sounds. There were then some gasps, groans and more cutting. He then heard a ripping sound. It was time to move. Branagan leapt out of the entrance, pistol held in both hands, arms outsretched. In front of him was a prisoner, crouched on the carpet, yanking up a rectangular piece of it. It was only then that Branagan noticed other sections of carpet cut out, as makeshift prayer mats. Branagan got to work cutting out a small piece for himself, knowing that he would not be disturbed at prayer. He looked at his watch with the compass set into it, showing East, which was directly opposite to the ships forward movement. Looking out a large lounge window he saw land less than a mile away he reckoned; the ship was well inside Cuban Waters. At that point he noticed a smell coming through the airvents; something was burning and he needed to know if the ship was being set ablaze; he guessed it wouldn't take more than 15 minutes sailing before the the burning liner would be aground on the Cuban coast where he imagined the prisoners would abandon ship leaving the Jewish hostages to die in an inferno.

Branagan walked up the broad sweeping staircase to the Promenade deck. Outside he saw groups of prisoners standing around discarded orange overalls on fire; some of the prisoners were laughing at each other's new appearance; each had dressed himself in clothes from ransacked boutiques, some wearing illfitting sports jackets, designer blazers and slacks. One black prisoner, sported mirrored sunglasses under a new Panama hat, price tag fluttering in the breeze while another was wrapped in several colourful scarves and beachwraps.

Relieved that the ship was not ablaze Branagan continued on his way to the Security Center. Unnoticed he arrived at the smashed door, peered around the room and saw that the center was empty. Most of the monitors were on, giving him a chance to assess the location of the hijackers not on the Bridge and to see where most of the prisoners were. Some monitors had been shot at but his attention was drawn to the Sky deck where he could see the Jews tied to railings around the deck, facing seaward, heads bowed.

He observed on several monitors other groups of prisoners jubilantly throwing their prison overalls overboard while the main kitchens were full of prisoners scoffing food by the handful. Branagan could also see the Engine Hall manned by two crew, sitting in Pods on gantries high above the humming turbines. The birdseye camera on the ship's mast was focused on the stern which was cutting a wide frothy delta shaped wake indicating that the ship, Branagan estimated, was sailing at or close to, full cruising speed.

He went over to check the weapon's locker in the forlorn hope he might add to his own weaponry. Doors broken open, the only remotely useful items were distress flares, some hand held, others rocket flares which might disable any man at close range.

Branagan quickly filled his overalls to bulging point with flares. He then smashed all the remaining functioning monitors before he then interrupted the ships music with a back to back recording of the anthem of the United States broadcast over all speakers. Knowing it should attract several angry hijackers back to the Center, he then lit three red distress flares and threw them into the Center before leaving and closing the door after him. He took up a position out of view of the door and in less than 3 renditions of the anthem, a squad of men were heard running towards the Center. They burst in the door and were immediately engulfed in thick red smoke. As the last of the men entered the room, Branagan ran up to the door and lobbed in a hand grenade before making off down the passageway. The ship's interior fittings rattled as a muffled deep boom sounded inside the ship. On the Bridge Hakeem felt the shockwave underfoot.

"INFILTRATORS"! he shouted looking at Hamilton as if he had arranged it.

Hakeem grabbed the microphone for the ships public address speakers. In Arabic he warned all prisoners to be vigilant and demanded that every prisoner greet each other with any verse from the Holy Qu'ran. Mohamed would be their protector against the treachery of the Infidel.

Beneath the liner, the surveillance crew in the

submarine picked up the bomb blast. In seconds they had it's soundwave analysed on the their combat audio database and which came up as matching a grenade's soundwave spectrum. A report was filed directly to the Pentagon and the President updated by phone directly.

Branagan heard Hakeem's angry tones over the ship's speakers as he moved swiftly along the deserted passageways and through the passenger lounges, making his way to the Bridge. He passed by the door of the Broadway Theatre where he saw the unattended heavy machine gun mounted on stage facing the seating. He immediately made for the stage and wrapping bullet belts around him he lifted the gun up on his shoulder. He then headed for the galleried three storey shopping mall facing the theatre. Surveying the unattended boutiques, souvenir and jewellery stores he chose the ladies beauty salon as the safest place to hide the heavy gun he expected to use later in the mission. As he came out of the salon he startled two passing prisoners. Realising that they were now curious what he was doing in the salon he pulled out his Smith and Wesson pistol and in a series of rapid muffled shots at point blank, both prisoners fell backwards to the ground. He hauled both bodies into a Ladies clothes boutique and propped them up against the half dressed mannequins in the window. He then quietly walked up the plush carpeted central stairwell and heard sounds coming from the 3-D cinema room. He slowly opened the door and entered the darkened room where several prisoners were sitting wearing 3-D glasses and marvelling at the visual effects of a wildlife movie. The prisoners were laughing momentarily as they tried to reach out and grab some exotic birds; the next moment they were diving under their seats as a tiger appeared to leap out of the screen.

Branagan entered the seat row behind the prisoners crawling on his hands and knees. One by one he pierced each through the chest from behind using his titanium needle until all were slumped on the floor. He quickly exited and went up two more flights of stairs to arrive on the boat deck. He could see the Bridge wing windows while at the end of the deck in front of him was the small cordoned stairwell up to the Bridge deck and forebridge entrance door. He stooped as low as his bulging suit let him and moved as fast as he could along the deck. He stopped at the bottom of the stairwell, eyes fixed on the Bridge door with it's small window.

Suddenly he felt a heavy blow to the back of his head and the daylight faded as he blacked out.

CHAPTER 11

Fantasea of the World (Starboard Lifeboat no 1)
"Jack Branagan! Jack, Jack! wake up you mean bastard……..guess who has just just given you a tit of lump on your big know-all skull, wake up! It's me….Hank the Tank, you remember, ……Hank Kruger, your ex bad mad soldier………always obedient for you Jack, c'mon come around…..your skull's as thick as it's smart…..now you obey my command this time…..c'mon kick start those brain cells in there". Kruger was talking to Jack as he poured water over him, both men now under the tented cover of a lifeboat.

Branagan came around slowly, his vision clearing. "Who the hell is this I'm looking at?………is that…….. you..Kruger you son of a bitch, what the fuck are you now?….. a holy muslim soldier or what"?

Kruger covered Branagan's mouth as footsteps passed by. "Shut up Jack, if you don't mind me saying so and if someone lifts up that cover man, you know what you gotta do?

"What?" replied Branagan wearily.

"You, instructor Branagan is gonna give me a big cuddle and a kiss, we're gonna be two prisoner lover boys who don't like being disturbed!....how does that grab ya?, now shut up Jack."

Kruger continued in whispers to Branagan..."I am a Sea Marshal in the service of the United States government, and I get to wear some zappy tourist clothes......it's nice to hang out with the fatcats and the flash chicks for a living........and by the way before I forget, sorry about the bump, what the hell are you doing in that orange baby suit and what's with the piece of carpet sticking out?..... you collecting souvenirs of this tin whorehouse or just missing home comforts in your old age"?

"Okay that's enough Sergeant Kruger, we need to work as a team just like the old days in Fort Bragg. Sorry to disappoint you Kruger but there ain't no fatcats or flash chicks on board no more, they've been exchanged for 600 Guantanamo camel kissers. The mission you and I now have is to save a bunch of Jews still held hostage, and then we take control of this ship. We need a shot at sailing these prisoners out to sea for recapture or even better to sail it into the hands of Camp Delta's lonely prison wardens, waiting for us in 'Gitmo'. The Captain is held hostage still and probably on the Bridge or in his quarters behind the Bridge".

"OK Branagan, got the briefing but get your facts right......there IS a flash chick on board, one Ayrab babe who started off this bloody mess....I reckon she's top muslim brass.....hangs out on the Bridge, name of Samia, let me at her and I'll have her singing for her sweet little life in 5 minutes..or maybe 10, I might need more quality time Sir, if you know what I mean."

"Forget the chick for now Kruger, lets get the bastards on the Bridge believing we're a big posse and get these Jews safely hid around the ship ………. THEN we take the Bridge. Now here are some tools. Okay so you have your own lifeboat flares….. should be good for ramming into some hijackers ass but don't forget to light the fuse first. Save your bullets. Here's some grenades, and a loaded Glock for a present. One more thing, these desert sons o' bitches got hold somewhere of a Motherfucker 60 with ammo which I've hidden in a shop called 'Peaches and Cream'…………. a beauty salon, second level shopping mall….don't worry about CCTV, I knocked out the security monitors."

"Scarface Branagan?…. in the beauty saloon? oh that's touching! Well, I'd say you'd be the ugliest mug ever inside of that girlie paintshop!"

"Zip it Kruger, consider you've been called up for action as a reserve and that's official, got it"?

"Yes Sir"? whispered Kruger enthusiastically. "Let me get to the hostages on the top Sky deck".

Branagan agreed but only after a series of surprise attacks on the prisoners and hijackers throughout the ship. Branagan would deal with the ship aft of the funnel while Kruger would work through the forward sections of the main decks, concentrating on areas as near to the Bridge as possible. They agreed to meet up at 18.00hrs in the beauty parlour.

Both men climbed out of the lifeboat onto the deck, Branagan still with a thumping headache making for the rear of the liner; the time was 16.30 and there was ninety minutes daylight left.

The White House

President Grattan, the joint Chiefs of Staff and his cabinet each now had a copy of Hakeem's demands sent on to them from the submarine. Grattan halted the various private conversations going on in the room.

"Gentleman please, not for the first time has the Office of President become preoccupied with Cuba and the Cuban dictatorship. Let me put a couple of scenarios to you.

The first scenario is to put some faith in Castro and accept his full cooperation with the end result that Castro recaptures the prisoners for us and agrees to hand them back to us in Guantanamo. In return we give him an appropriately woolly-worded commitment to demilitarise the Naval base. Well gentlemen, that still sounds too much to me like blackmail and I am in no mood to have our defence policy hijacked by any senile tin pot Stalinist remnant of communism. What's your overview Admiral about Guantanamo Naval base as part of our strategic network?"

The Admiral resplendent in white uniform with gold epaulettes and buttons paused before speaking. " We did need Gitmo more when it was originally a navy coaling station in the 1930's. Mayport in Florida is a more up to date facility although it wouldn't have the Bay's shelter and deep water. If you ask me Mr

President, would I lose sleep if Gitmo was no longer part of our presence in the Caribbean?..... the answer Sir is 'no' strictly from a strategic viewpoint, speaking for the Atlantic fleet's requirements. However if at some future date we needed to sweep through Cuba, with a base already established at one end of the island, all we need to do is start a campaign at the other end and the Cubans would be caught in the middle fighting on two fronts."

"Thank you Admiral," replied the President. "Let's leave the status of Guantanamo Naval base on the agenda but take the focus off 'Dmil'. Instead let's talk through whether the United Nations can pressurize Cuba to offer full cooperation and recapture the prisoners en route from Santiago Harbour to the City's Airport. Don't we have a problem gentlemen with the UN not recognising the detention of these fanatics as legitimate? So maybe we don't want the 'Union of Numbskulls' involved in this at all. Hell will freeze over before I let these prisoners fall into the hands of the UN unless it first accepts that they are lawfully detained, right?" The military chiefs nodded, everyone knowing that that wasn't a likely prospect. "A different mood would prevail gentlemen, dare I say, if the UN building instead of the Pentagon got a bellyful of Boeing during 9/11. Those third world bums would now expect F15s escorting them back to their penthouse suites in the Waldorf Astoria! As for the grand old jelly-kneed Europeans, expect air space clearance for any UN plane bringing home these prisoners to whatever destination those planes are going to; except of course airspace over their pretty heritage cities but you can bet your bottom dollar these fanatical so called martyrs will again by targeting U.S. cities and interests in next to no time. Air Marshal Jansen, let me ask you a question...could you get me a couple of C130 transporters painted up in white for me immediately?"

Air Marshal Jansen stood up at the table and replied "Yes Commander in Chief, if you are proposing to send two U.S. Military planes posing as UN transporters that can be arranged. What's more Mr President if the UN already has its own C130s in the air we will order them to land under fighter escort at MacDill Air Force Base. We can use some pretext of ....say.. an inspection of the planes for security purposes en route to pick up the prisoners.......... to make sure there are no weapons on board. We could also order them to land for transgressing military flightpaths or something like that Sir."

The President didn't reply but paced up and down the room at the head of the table. "That's fine Air Marshal but all this is officially your idea ....well done, I....appreciate your creativity........it'll stand you in good stead in the future and that's between ourselves and the four walls of this cabinet room, clear gentlemen?" Everyone seated around the long mahogany table nodded though Air Marshal Jansen shifted a little uncomfortably in his seat. He was worrying about his career and possible appearances before Congressional committees investigating U.S.

airforce equipment posing as United Nations humanitarian transports; rather than express his reservations he thought quickly of an improvement to the idea:

"Might I suggest Mr President that we inaugurate immediately a new airline named 'United National' or 'United Nationwide' so that at least we can stand over the letters UN painted clearly on the transports?

"OK, do it," the President replied, "fastrack it through whatever hoops you need to but I need 100 percent secrecy, everyone, any 'admin.' staff involved are to be isolated fully and after this saga is over, sworn to secrecy …clear"?

"Of course Sir" responded the Air Marshal "I do have one concern with the C130s crewed by American pilots arriving in Cuba to load up with hundreds of fanatical passengers ready to slit their throats? …God knows, once those psychos get a bird's eye view of shining downtown Miami…with all respects Mr President we could be talking about Miami's 9/11 Sir!"

At this point General Hudsen of the Army asked permission to speak. "Mr President if I might suggest that we first request the full cooperation of the Cubans to escort the prisoners from the port in Santiago de Cuba to Antonio Maceo Airport in the city, just a coupla miles inland. We will fly in two white C130 transporters 'leased' from the Air Marshal's …ahem…..new airline,…. each one carrying a couple of hundred of our best marines who will be deployed for combat on arrival. With surprise on our side, that's the best start any military tactitian wants. If the going gets rough on the ground we could chopper in Blackhawks for precision strikes and for Chinook cover...we could have a couple of dozen Chinooks drop off enough marines to finish the job quickly before daybreak."

The president interrupted General Hudsen, "whether Castro's forces would intervene and attack the Marines, seeing them as invading Cuban soil...I don't know. Maybe if they want Guantanamo badly enough they might just back off hoping for that demilitarisation they want. I expect though you will hear a couple of angry speeches about a second Bay of Pigs ...... and for sure there will be lots of cheering and applause in his Plaza de la 'Revolooocion', but isn't that what he loves? Well, let's give the demogogue a dose of military might that'll cut short any 6 hour long antiamerican tirade of verbal dysentery!"

The President stopped pacing back and forth and sat down at the head of the table. "Okay, lets walk through this plan. We know there are Jews on board so we don't want to upset the Jewish lobby or the Israelis who already offered us and indeed sacrificed commandos in a failed attempt to infiltrate the ship. We don't need to see any Cuban blood on the streets of Cuba as an expectation nor for that matter do we have to have Cuban blood spilled on the tarmac of any Cuban Airport. I think gentlemen before we finalise any plan lets call up Castro to hear what he has to say about his country being a safe haven, for a bunch of fanatical hijackers and get this, devout religious ones at that! Lets see what an atheist he is and will he do any dirty work for us. Gentlemen, we're in for a long night. Let's get some grog shipped up from Housekeeping, pizzas and stuff and we'll get some caffeine pills or whatever does the trick from my physician".

CHAPTER 12

The White House Cabinet Room & Bunker De La Comandancia.

The President told his aide to call up Havana.

"Hello Presidente, this is Sherman again. As you can appreciate we are not very happy about the prospect of these prisoners prowling around in Cuban waters still holding, God knows, how many American citizens captive. We believe that they are captive because they are Jews and now we have this outrageous demand that these terrorists sail in like a bunch of tourists into your port of Santiago de Cuba. They then want a safe transfer from the port to Santiago Airport and probably looking for a guard of honour from the Cuban Army lining the highway"? The President finished his stream of conversation running out of the one breath he took at the start of the call.

"President Grattan, you will not direct or even influence Cuban foreign policy. This situation is a result of the American decision to establish a prison in Cuba for men that you call illegal combatants and which the world knows have no protection under the Geneva Convention. Your occupation of Cuban land at Guantanamo and your decision to use it as a detention centre has now resulted in severe difficulties between us for which you are entirely responsible. This is not a crisis caused by the Cuban government or the Cuban people. President Grattan…this crisis would not have happened if you had placed these prisoners on Alcatraz! Instead you have chosen Guantanamo and the result is the humiliation of the Cuban people. We didn't ask to be further humiliated by being asked by the UN to allow safe passage for criminal hijackers landing on Cuban soil and using our Cuban airport to escape. The hijackers are criminals and the Guantanamo prisoners are not. We do not want to stand by and we will not stand by and allow that situation to happen on our national territory unless we have your commitment that the American military machine will disengage from Guantanamo for good. Secondly the American Government must undertake never again to use Guantanamo to imprison anyone. This is a simple request which we make directly as a consequence of your actions President Grattan.

It is correct that the Armed Revolutionary Forces of Cuba will escort the prisoners from the cruise ship docked at Santiago to Antonio Maceo airport in the city At the airport we will detain the prisoners as having entered Cuba illegally and Mr President that will be the first time that these prisoners detention on the island of Cuba will be a legal detention. They will be in violation of Cuba's immigration laws. Of course Mr President it will take some time before the Cuban Courts can process each application and that should allow us plenty of time to agree a protocol to dismantle the Naval base at Guantanamo. I am sure that you will find another suitable prison on mainland America...that is before you imprison your entire black population! Any protocol should of course be registered with the UN. We will then deport the prisoners from Cuba through Miami where as transit deportees you can act in any way you wish Mr President."

President Grattan replied: "Presidente, I'll ignore the cheap shot at our great system of Justice; let me just say you have given us a lot to think about. Before we can reach an agreement on your suggestions it is important that you do nothing to interfere with the liner currently heading for the port of Santiago where it should be allowed to dock. I emphasise we don't have all the passengers liberated. We estimate there are over 60 Jews and still some crew on board that to the best of our intelligence are citizens of America and some of them may even be citizens of Israel, our strongest ally in the middle east. These captives have to be part of a solution that brings them home alive. Mr Presidente, stand by for a further call if you would."

President Grattan went to sit down at the large mahogany table in his cabinet office. Still present were the Joint Chiefs of Staff, the Admiral of the Atlantic Fleet and along with several officials from the Pentagon were both the Director of the CIA, the Secretary for Homeland Security and Director of the FBI. Grattan sitting at the head of the table looked around the table. "Gentlemen does it seem to all of you that the United States of America is being held to ransom on two fronts? We have been forced to release our prisoners from Camp Delta into the hands of terrorists on board a liner in Cuban waters and if I am not mistaken Mr Castro intends to oblige us by handing back the prisoners only if we yield to some bullshit notion of withdrawing the USN from Guantanamo. I think it is time gentlemen that we put the interests of this great nation first and foremost. We have an obligation in the first instance to save the lives of American citizens and those of our allies and second, not far behind that priority, is the need to recapture our prisoners from Camp Delta now enjoying themselves on an American registered cruise ship. THIS IS JUST NOT ACCEPTABLE! Guantanamo Bay is sovereign United States territory and if there are going be any negotiations about that base it will be from a position of equal strength. I will not tolerate our prisoners in Camp Delta being used by Castro, or anyone else as a bargaining card. Our ace card in this region is our military strength which we are going to use and use effectively………but with some discretion of course. I am making a second executive order that those repainted C130 transport planes arrive at Santiago Airport fully laden with our special forces. Gentlemen, let me introduce Operation …..Hurricane except spell it with a 'y'. There's a very unseasonal Hurrycane coming ashore at Castro and people are gonna get blown away when we're in a hurry!

On that very point General Hudsen, get the word out to our forces that they are not to get trigger happy…that I want prisoners captured alive if possible. But, anyone shoots at us …we shoot back, we don't shoot first. Whatever way this operation goes, our standing in the world couldn't get much worse so lets salvage the lives of those innocent hostages, then as many prisoners as we can; As for that the ship itself? I don't need an oceanic spectacular with a liner the length of a skyscraper nose up, disappearing under the waves and supplying Cuba's metal needs for the next ten years! Get me that Cuban cat's furball on the line for the Goddamn last time."

A few moments later Grattan was back on the line. "Presidente Castro we are interested in your idea having discussed the matter here with our Navy Chiefs. Guantanamo would be excess to our requirements if we upgraded Mayport Naval Base in Florida. As far as relocating the prisoners from Guantanamo we will avoid if we can, their return to Guantanamo. Their new location is still under consideration. Mr Presidente, all due regard must be had for the safety of the Jewish hostages and therefore no steps should be taken to interfere with the terrorists plans to dock the ship in Santiago Harbour and they should be escorted to the airport as they demand. Let the United Nations planes arrive and the UN representatives on board can negotiate the liberation of the Jewish prisoners into the safekeeping of your armed forces at the port. You will have a heavy burden of responsibility as Jewish or otherwise, those remaining hostages are mostly citizens of the United States. If you successfully recapture the prisoners we would agree to register an Exchange of Notes with the UN to neutralise Guantanamo as an offensive capability naval base at the earliest practical opportunity. The UN can talk if needs be, to the Israelis and Palestinians to hammer out a deal for the release of the Jewish hostages. So Mr Castro do we have a deal that the prisoners arrive safely, whether illegal migrants or not, in one piece at Santiago's Maceo Airport for onward travel?"

"President Grattan the Cuban forces will not attack the prisoners unless the Cuban military is attacked first. As illegal immigrants they will be escorted from the ship on the basis that they will be flying out as deported illegal immigrants on the United Nations planes. We must work towards something more concrete however than an Exchange of Notes, we should be able to agree a protocol annexed as an amendment to the 1936 Treaty and registered with the UN. That is our wish President Grattan, let us take this as the beginning of a new era of cooperation between the Cuban and American government with the objective some day of normalising trade relations."

"Leave these complex thoughts with me" replied President Grattan "...Hasta la vista Mr Castro."

Tel Aviv

Comandante Castro immediately ordered his aide to call up Premier Bloch of Israel.

"Greetings from the Republic of Cuba, Premier Bloch"!

"What a pleasant surprise to hear from you President Castro. Here in Israel we hope that Cuba will do everything it can to protect the rights of all people to live including the lives of both Jewish and non Jewish passengers on board the ship in your territory"?

"Of course Premier Bloch, we do not want to see the blood of more people spilled and we in Cuba can identify with the Israeli people who like Cubans have been living with the threat of constant attack from enemies at it's frontiers.

We have persuaded President Grattan that Guantanamo is no longer acceptable as a prison camp and Cuba must never become another Devil's Island to receive transported prisoners; that is an imperial concept long stopped by the Europeans in their colonies. Premier Bloch, we are happy to offer the Jewish hostages on board the Cruise ship the best of Cuban health care for which we are famous in the world. We will arrange food and medicine for them as a condition of the ship docking in any Cuban port, whether they are allowed off the ship or remain on board as prisoners of these terrorists. Our doctors and nurses are putting their lives in danger in their humanitarian mission-we will not tolerate suffering by any Jews on our land or in our territorial waters Premier Bloch.

Naturally we would hope that you and all Israelis and all Jews everywhere will have a greater understanding and sympathy for the plight of the Cuban people struggling against the vicious trade embargo which your great ally, America uses to strangle our survival. The greatest compliment from the Jewish people of the world will, I expect, be to support the rapid demilitarisation of Guantanamo and an end to the embargo and the persecution of the Cuban people, Premier."

There was a long silence at the other end of the line. Premier Bloch was heard to speak in Hebrew while he covered the mouthpiece before Bloch put the phone on mute.

Castro looked up at his Chief of Internal Security and rotated his forefinger gesturing if the call was being recorded. The Chief nodded anxiously to reassure his Comandante. Castro intended to hear a translation of those muffled Hebrew comments later.

Premier Bloch then returned and continued: "Yes, you have the support of the Israeli government if it is your view that Camp Delta prison camp in Guantanamo should close. As for demilitarisation of Guantanamo and the trade embargo, we cannot interfere in the affairs and treaties between nations but I firmly believe President Castro, that the standing of Cuba amongst all the nations of the world will be greatly improved if Cuba can help resolve this crisis without more killing or the spilling of Jewish blood."

"I appreciate your support Premier. Let me add that hijacking is a very serious criminal offence in Cuba and while we will agree to the UN arranging the transit of the prisoners via Cuba, the hijackers on the other hand can expect to spend a long long time in our harshest maximum security prison in Sancti Spiritus. If the Israeli police seek to extradite these criminals we would hope the Cuban Courts can assist them. Of course our Revolutionary War Marine would be more effective in battles against sea pirates in the future if we had coastal patrol craft similar to your excellent naval equipment. Let us advance this issue if we can by our Minister for the Navy meeting his Israeli counterpart……not a public or formal visit you understand."

"In principal President Castro we look at any export opportunities of certain weapons to countries that are the friends of Israel provided those weapons and equipment are to defend a country's legitimate Borders."

"Thank you Premier Bloch, it would seem we have an understanding about mutual but very different external threats to each of our country's survival. I will have our Foreign Ministry keep the Israeli Ambassador in Havana fully informed."

After the call ended Premier Bloch held up the telephone receiver and dropped it from a height, mimicking an aerial bomb drop on to the phone unit where it partially landed. "That communist geriatric compares the suffering of Cubans to the persecution of Jews and the State of Israel? That Caribbean cockroach persecutes his own people! Wipe the earpiece before I speak on this phone again!" Bloch ordered storming out of his Cabinet office.

Meanwhile the Cuban military chiefs seated around the table with El Comandante were openly cynical of Bloch's remarks "Israel makes its own mind up where it wants it's borders, legal or not", Raul Castro remarked.

Another Raulista, Aero-Mariscal Diego Figueroa of the Fuerza Aerea Revolucionaria added " the Israelis ignore not just Treaties and UN resolutions but any agreement made with anybody if it doesn't suit them".

Comandante Castro halted the conversations by raising his hand "Comrades, we will win the support of many millions of American Jews if we not just help the Jewish hostages but also rescue them! Raul, call up our best hand to hand combat medics, battle hardened from Ethiopia, Nicaragua and Angola; they may have to kill to save lives ……..absolutely no medical school conscripts or civilian surgeons are to board that Cruise ship. We meet again here in 1 hour!"

CHAPTER 13

The Fantasea of the World
On board several groups of prisoners had taken turns to demolish 'Macky Sullivan's Irish Tavern throwing most of the wood and brass fittings out through smashed lounge windows. Others fired off shots at the displayed bottles of alcohol behind the Bar and others pissed into the beer flooding the bar floor as the beer taps were opened and left running. The smaller Monte Carlo Piano bar and Cindy's Champagne Club were stripped down manually over several hours to a state that a bomb would have achieved in seconds; marble flooring was continually smashed into smaller fragments, ceilings were pulled down, fire axes were swung wildly in all directions smashing mirrored tiles

and restroom fittings. The bank however received most attention in an attempt to find undreamt of riches. Safety deposit boxes had been shot open and on the floor jewellery boxes lay strewn about. Unknown to the prisoners and most of the martyrs, Janice, the Bank teller and Hakeem had taken to the Bridge two heavy sacks containing uncounted millions of fresh dollars in neatly bound bundles. Despite repeated attacks on the bank by the prisoners, it still retained a semblance of a street bank until an explosive charge of 2 kilos of Hexogen was begged from Zador to use on the safe door. Not only did the explosion blow the safe open sending thousands of one dollar bills everywhere but it smashed every window in the vast 3 storey Bel Air Shopping Mall, carpeting the marble walkways with broken glass. The entire ship shuddered and threw Branagan off his feet on the Sky deck as the deck plating warped with the impact of the shock wave. The ship continued to vibrate from stem to stern for several minutes as the shock waves echoed back and forth within the structure. Kruger wasn't sure if Branagan had been attacked in the Beauty Salon but as the time was only 1700 he had yet to begin counter-terrorising the prisoners or hijackers. He wondered if Branagan intended to sabotage the turbines still driving the ship at near full speed; He meant to warn Branagan that the fuel reservoirs were unmarked and close by the turbines. Kruger remembered that sombre briefing dealing with vulnerable aspects of the new liner; if the vast reservoirs ignited, the blast would rupture the hull blowing the stern clean off and likely bring all 17 aft sections of stepped deck housing with it.

Branagan however was far from the Engine Hall and had just reached the highest deck of the ship, hidden inside slatted metal doors in the Aircon Center at the base of the ship's smokestack, sited amidships.

USS City of Corpus Christi

Below the liner, the submarine crew eavesdropping for conversations had screamed in pain as the sound of the Bank blast woofed through earphones, shattering their eardrums. Demented with the thundering blast magnified hundreds of times, it was as if a grenade had been hung from each earlobe and then both pins pulled simultaneously. Both crewmen rolled and squirmed on the floor, hands over their ears, each man witnessing the scrunched expressions on the other's face, mouths stretched open in agony, all in a complete deafened silence.

The captain of the submarine called off the sonar surveillance and angrily dialled up Admiral Burbridge for an authorisation to torpedo the ship's propellers; he assured the Admiral one torpedo programmed to home in on propeller vibration would disable all four props through collateral damage. The rudders however would need a separate strike but he argued that steerage wasn't an issue. The Admiral firmly denied the request as it would leave the ship adrift in Cuban waters; " the question of control over a two billion dollar hijacked ship whether it would stay in Cuban waters or eventually come out into international waters was not going to be handed on a plate to the God of Neptune and his unpredictable tidal currents and sea wind", concluded the Admiral. The Captain responded saying that the submarine's own engine power combined with the reinforced metal hull could take the job of nudging the liner broadside and push it out to international waters. He would have to surface however and neither he nor the Admiral could guess what the hijackers would throw at the submarine's conning tower and exposed hull plating while surfaced. Surface to air missiles and rocket propelled grenades could not be ruled in or out and there was a chance that the submarine's communications antennae would be knocked out. Contact needed to be maintained with the submarine and the Admiral confirmed that the submarine was to continue the covert escort but call off the listening surveillance. The Captain affirmed the order and reminded the Admiral that depth would soon be a problem as the liner entered the approaches to Santiago port where it could be within two hours.

The Fantasea of the World.

Branagan continued to peer through the slats of vent panelling and surveyed the coastline. Less than a mile off he could see the build up of housing and one or two large factory complexes. He took out of his pocket a map of Cuba and given that the ship was heading in a westerly direction along the coast he was sure the ship would be heading into the sheltered waters of Santiago's bay very shortly.

Branagan knew that when he met up with Kruger at 1800 hrs he would be much more effective. Knowing that the Cuban forces would be waiting at the quayside at Santiago as the ship docked he wasn't sure whether he could rely on them for support if he was to launch an attack on the prisoners at that time. He expected that the hijackers would mix the Jewish passengers amongst the Guantanamo prisoners as a defence against an attack on the prisoners by Cuban forces or even an attack from the air by American forces. The Jews had to be liberated soon.

In the Aircon Center while the room was still foul with the smell of mercaptan, Branagan began his first ship wide diversion, going outside for fresh air momentarily. Lighting all his flares, both handheld and rockets, he threw them down into all air intake ducts. In less than a minute the sound of the rockets exploding in the airshafts echoed around the ship, sending any prisoners indoors rushing outside to the decks. He had also started a coughing epidemic affecting everyone on board including Hakeem on the Bridge. Hakeem, in between bouts of throat clearing ordered all prisoners to be prepared for war on board the ship; the American infiltrators could attack before the ship docked in Cuba. As Hakeem spoke, red smoke and white smoke flowed out of the different ceiling vents, sometimes in thick puffs floating along the passageways at head height; other times it snaked out of the ceiling grills in wispy trails before falling to the ground much like dry ice. Some martyrs believed it was a knock out gas, launched before an imminent assault on the liner.

By the time two of the martyrs brigade had arrived at the Aircon Center, Branagan was well concealed in between high stacks of sunloungers. He then walked about the room casually. Inside, the martyrs gave him no more than a cursory glance in his orange jumpsuit and they went on looking between the machines. Branagan took care to bring his pistol up to a couple of inches behind the first martyr's head, and with one shot reserved for each man, both men were blown forward with the short range impact of the hushed bullets blasting through skull plate.

Branagan picked up the lighter of the two men and carried him outside on his shoulder. There was enough cover from the smoke drifting out of the extraction vents for him to climb the ladder up to the Radar unit in safety; there he unloaded the corpse onto the rotating radar scanner, slowing it down while the extra weight caused the bearings to squeak noisily. It would only be seconds before the radar repeater on the Bridge monitor would sound a malfunction alarm. Branagan jumped off the ladder and knew it was time to go back inside and take further advantage of the smoke cover while it lasted. Before going, he took a last look up at the communications tower, and the orange rotating body draped over the bar, hair smouldering around the gaping head wound from the gunpowder flash.

Suddenly he heard the deep groan of the ship's foghorns. Branagan threw himself on the flat of his stomach along the freshly painted French blue metal deck. Looking around the horizon quickly, he drew out a small scope and saw a small grey naval craft flying a huge Cuban flag. On both it's port and starboard deck he could see torpedo launch tubes. Judging by the wake of the motor torpedo boat it had been heading toward the ship but had now begun to turn and was seemingly guiding the liner through the deep channel into Santiago port.

On the Bridge Hakeem ordered Captain Hamilton into the Captain's chair Hakeem's pistol again pointed at the rear of the Captain's head. "Mr Hamilton I am sure Fantasea Cruise Lines would like you to guide safely their $2 billion dollar cruise ship into Santiago port. If you don't believe that then I command you as the supreme officer on this holy Islamic warship to guide this cruise ship into Santiago port and hold it successfully against the quay. There will be no ropes thrown nor will the anchor be dropped. There will be no harbour pilot to assist you Mr Hamilton so you will just have to rely on all those years spent playing war games at sea. If we have any bad luck Mr Hamilton, and this expensive liner runs aground then I will assume Mr Hamilton that you have done this deliberately and I personally will feed you in pieces to the hungry sharks that have been following this ship drinking the blood of your passengers hanging from the rails."

"Mr Hakeem I will guide this ship into Santiago port but you are mistaken if you think that you can escape into Cuba and live freely there. Mr Hakeem, Cuba does not recognise your God nor my God. You are now arriving at the land of the real infidel Mr Hakeem. There is no God in this land. Go ahead Mr Hakeem and make friends with the real infidels. Soon, you will be pointing your pistol, not at me, but in the direction of the hundreds of Cuban soldiers that are waiting for you at the quayside. Look Mr Hakeem."

Hakeem looked into the monitor on the left arm of the Captain's chair and ahead both men could see clear black and white images from the Bridge camera zoomed in on scores of Cuban infantry men and women fully armed, marching along the quayside. Hakeem ordered Captain Hamilton to slow the ship to four knots and Hakeem spoke over the ship's intercom.

"Liberated prisoners of Guantanamo and Guantanamo Martyrs Brigade, everyone must go to the top Sky deck, pistols loaded and ready. We are approaching the port of Santiago de Cuba where the Cuban army is waiting for us. Be prepared for battle. Neither the Cubans nor the Americans are allies with us in Jihad. We only know that the Americans and the Cubans are not allies and we must hope that they are still enemies and remain enemies today. Though you will leave the ship, we as martyrs will not, we will hold the Jewish passengers captive until we have no need for them. This is our only guarantee that both you and this ship will not be attacked by the Cubans or the Americans. Remember you will not be safe until you are on the United Nations planes waiting for us at Santiago Airport. If you are attacked then all the Jews and remaining crew will be executed. Liberated prisoners of

Guantanamo you will soon be free to return to the battle against the great Satan."

The prisoners on the ship had long ceased celebrating and had become very nervous of the bizarre deaths on board. They had discovered their fellow prisoners slumped in the shop window of the ladies boutique, in the presence of the half naked mannequins; the Americans would be avenged for this insult to those soldiers of Jihad.

The sudden blast of the ship's foghorn had drawn their eyes to the dead prisoner rotating on the squeaky radar scanner like a weak blood sprinkler. In the search for infiltrators, some of the martyrs had found a prisoner's head in the library, face down in a blood soaked Playbabe magazine opened out on reading table.

While over a hundred had been at prayer on the open Sky deck which they considered the safest place, Kruger had lobbed a Flash bomb up amongst the bowed prisoners. Kruger wasn't finished.

He had laid out a shot prisoner in one of the casino's sarcophagus-like craps tables. Incensing the prisoners further, Kruger had drenched the dead man in alcohol and bound the dead man's hands around the empty bottle of whisky held upright on his chest. Rammed into the dead man's throat was a full bottle of gin which engorged his mouth cavity to the extent that a stream of the clear spirit dribbled continuously from each nostril.

On his way to the beauty salon to meet up with

Branagan , Kruger had come across the Character Wardrobe stores. Kruger had called over a solitary prisoner seemingly lost and strangled him after which he dressed him in a full size gorilla suit. He then placed him in a crouching position in the centre of the Grand Foyer and threw his prayer carpet piece over him.

Before going into the salon, Kruger had drawn on walls around the mall with a red makeup stick, large crescent moons with an arrow through them. Now the prisoners were sailing into the jaws of a professional army on the quayside.

Kruger had returned to hide in the beauty salon and propped the M60 up on it's bipod on the salon's reception counter. He would be ready for prisoners or martyrs scouting for infiltrators or still searching for the heavy gun. In the near darkness of the mall, Kruger heard a faint crushing of glass underfoot and checked his watch almost at 18.00. Unsure, Kruger took off the safety catch but it was Branagan who appeared on time and relieved to see that the gun was combat ready.

"Kruger, you've got to draw the fighters down here and let me have a chance at freeing the Jews tied to the rails; all hell is going to break loose if someone hits a trigger..........it doesn't matter if it's a Cuban, a hijacker or one of the prisoners.

The safest place for these hostages is anywhere inside the ship; finding sixty people hidden on this monster would be a waste of time.....we've got these goons rattled, they want to get off this thing without searching for any Jews!

"No way" Kruger replied, "I'll cover you while you're cutting the Jews loose, first we neutralise the hijackers standing guard over them."

"I only saw two hijackers up there," Branagan replied, "I reckon there'll be no more than that if they have a couple of search parties out; they sure don't want American commandos messing up their Cuban welcome".

Branagan had read the situation well. The prisoners no longer felt safe on the ship. The ship had now become another prison and one where death could be expected at any time, and worse a dishonourable death, with the dead body humiliated and defiled, a deliberate insult to Islam. This was truly a ship of Satan and the prisoners had soon begun streaming towards the Grand Foyer with it's double embarkation doors hoping to walk across Santiago's new cruise terminal gantry and down onto dry land again.

CHAPTER 14

Cruiseship terminal, Santiago Harbour.
The light of the day was fading but clearly visible on the quayside were hundreds of Cuban troops standing to attention, their pistols holstered and rifles at their backs. Behind them were rows of Russian built Yak army trucks and several military ambulances. Behind the army trucks stood groups of white uniformed nurses and doctors.

Branagan looked at Kruger, as both men surveyed what was clearly a ceremonial guard on parade. The Cubans were taking a neutral stance; looking around at the warehouses and some of the higher cranes in the docks, no snipers were visible. Branagan had a choice to make. To free as many Jews quietly after killing their guards, again quietly, or open fire with the heavy gun on the prisoners disembarking and face an almighty firefight with the prisoners on the quay, the hijackers on board and hundreds of confused Cuban infantry; Branagan and Kruger would be lucky if they were captured alive by the Cuban army. Both discussed whether they should get off the boat mingling with the prisoners; it would depend on what would happen to the Jews; if the Jews stayed on the ship they would stay.

Slowly Captain Hamilton with Hakeem's pistol still pointed at him, manoeuvred the giant liner alongside the Cruise terminal wharf. With no crew reporting to him from the Bridge wing or by radio from the bow or stern, he misjudged the width of his new liner. As a result the starboard hull plating of the ship bumped hard against the huge tractor tyre fenders hung over the quay wall causing everyone on the ship to lose balance momentarily. The sun was setting rapidly, tinting the white paint of the liner's port side a rich peach colour. The city rose up on hills surrounding the harbour. The western facades of it's higher tower blocks caught the evening sunlight in checkerboard colour blocks of terracotta hues and faded yellows. Rust stained corrugated sheets covered balconies on which curious families had crowded.

Ahmed, having lost the heavy M60 gun was ordered

by Hakeem to remain on the Bridge to watch over the First Officer and Hamilton. Zador on the Bridge was told to go to the Grand Foyer and speak to the Cuban advance party in Russian to confirm the plan to transport all prisoners to the airport. Hakeem also left the Bridge to brief Khalil who along with Badshah would be the only martyrs travelling with the prisoners to the airport, unnoticed amongst them to avoid possible arrest by the Cubans who were known to jail plane hijackers for decades.

Ahmed had not got over Hakeem's severe reprimand about losing the heavy gun and was needling Samia with questions about how anyone with Jewish blood could ever be a true fundamentalist warrior for Islam. Ahmed then went over to bind Hamilton's hands to the Helm console, his ankles still bound as before. The First Officer remained bound hand and foot sitting on the Bridge floor below an instrument panel.

Ahmed then left the Bridge and wandered down the passageway, looking briefly in the communications room. He walked on and arrived at the Captains quarters.

He looked around inside and then called out to Samia.

"I have found the heavy gun! Come help me bring the ammunition box to the Bridge, I will radio Hakeem."

Samia was pleased and came straight to the room. Ahmed immediately grabbed her, covering her mouth as he fell on top of her pushing her face into the bed clothes. Samia's screams were almost completely muffled and as she tried to turn over he landed a rapid succession of punches on her head. He then paused saying quietly, "yes the blood of an infidel flows around that pretty face. You tried to go to Israel, didn't you?..you with your Jewish ancestry...have you killed any Jews yet?.....no!.......I will tame you, you mongrel convert"! Samia couldn't resist properly as Ahmed sat on the back of her legs. Samia was struggling for air, every time she lifted her head up for air, he pushed it back down though she had long enough to draw breath.

Suddenly there was a loud crack and Ahmed stopped, then fell down sideways, off the bed onto the floor unconscious. This was followed by the loud thump of a small decorative brass diving helmet falling beside him.

Samia turned around, still catching her breath; standing over her was the blond Olga, the Captain's girlfriend who had cracked the helmet off Ahmed's skull. He was out cold.

"Who are you" asked Samia, shaking, her sore head throbbing from the beating.

"I am crew, an innocent fitness instructor but guilty of saving you from that animal. My name is Olga. I heard this pig call you.... Sami,?

"Yes, it is Samia, thank you for helping me. He would have killed me and hidden my body somewhere."

Ahmed stirred a little, and groaned. Both girls looked at each other and then looked at the Captain's large hinged porthole, on the quiet portside of the ship. Samia sat up and with out a word exchanged between them, the girls grappled with the limp and semi conscious Ahmed. Once his head and shoulders were pushed through the porthole, it only took one concerted heave before Ahmed fell out, his legs striking some of the railings of the stateroom balconies on the way down causing him to hit the water in a spin.

"I was used to lifting up men in Kiev. In Russia women learn how to lift their men half dead with vodka all the time."

Samia smiled at her.

Olga then pleaded with Samia to let her escape. She wanted to start a new life.

"I have little money and depend on the Captain to support me. He got me this job but he does not want to work anymore. When he stops work, I will have no job, he will make sure. Let me get off here in Cuba if that is possible? I have a Russian passport".

Samia thought for a moment. "The prisoners are getting off now. Some of them are crazy and if they know you are Russian, you will be killed, even tortured first...as they have been tortured. Wait Olga." Samia then left the quarters and was gone for at least ten long minutes. When she returned, she handed Olga an orange overall, dark glasses, a baseball cap and a small but heavy trash bag.

"Olga, put these on, and take the bag, every prisoner has taken clothes and souvenirs. In your bag, I have put dollars, more dollars than you can imagine. You will not worry about food for a long long time.......go, now...to the Grand Foyer!"

Samia looked out the door and brought Olga out through the Bridge, head down. Hamilton turned his head to follow the orange figure whose soft hand came down supportively on his as the person walked around the Helm console and out the forebridge door. Hamilton thought little of this as he was busy adjusting power to the portside bow thruster to hold the ship fast against the wharf.

When Olga arrived at the Grand Foyer, hundreds of prisoners were standing ten or fifteen deep in a wide circle around the slumped gorilla in the centre of the floor. They were wary of the creature looking so real yet seemingly dead but without marks. It could be booby trapped, or contain an infiltrator or maybe a dying fellow prisoner in a crouched position of prayer. Zador arrived roaring at the prisoners to clear the way. He saw the gorilla holding the curious attention of everyone. Safety catch off, without hesitating he fired off a full AK 47 magazine into the figure which absorbed all traces of the shots. He then walked over and kicked it onto it's side. No one wanted to open the gorilla suit after that. Zador then opened up the double doors while the prisoners around him broke into relieved nervous chatter and laughter.

CHAPTER 15

Cubavision Television Studios, Havana
As dusk fell across Cuba white strip lights of the residential blocks flickered on gradually across the cities. After the ship had come into Santiago port El Comandante was going on television to address the nation. People were crowding into any apartment that had a television to hear why according to the anti Castro propaganda Radio Marti in Miami, Cuban troops were escorting terrorists illegally entering Cuba. Radio Marti had also broadcast across Cuba that the

United Nations were organising two chartered jets to fly the prisoners out of Cuba to a destination unknown.

At 19:00 exactly CubaVision broadcast the image of the Cuban flag to a rousing rendition of the anthem La Bayamesa, before Fidel appeared at his desk in green military fatigues and plain cap.

"My Cuban comrades, defenders of the Revolution, a new menace confronts Cuba as I speak to you. Like many threats we have faced before, it has it's miserable origins in Yanqui imperialist ambition to break the will of this great nation.

Tonight, the future of the last colonial outpost of Imperial America on this great island of Cuba, Guantanamo Bay Naval Base is at stake. After decades of this deliberate provocation of the Cuban people, the actions of a group of murdering pirates have shown the world the foolishness of American policy to rely on Cuban land as a place of exile. Pirates have hijacked a cruise ship and have forced the American government to surrender its illegal prisoners in Guantanamo in exchange for the passengers. Now, the freed prisoners demand transit through Cuba back to their Arab homelands. However, Cuba is not an escape route for convicted criminals. But, these prisoners are not criminals, they have never seen a courtroom! Therefore we will not, repeat not, oppose a transit of these captives through Cuba. They are just captives from a war zone which the Middle East has become thanks to a new imperialist agenda in Washington; a new agenda where they colonise a country's resources without claiming the country. This policy has led indirectly to the most daring act of so called holy war by Islamic militants since the conquest of Spain by the Moors over a thousand years ago!

As for the captives, they did not cause this crisis. Nor is this crisis the result of their presence in Guantanamo. It is the result of the American presence in Cuba!

The American base in Guantanamo has attracted a gang of cold blooded criminals to Cuban waters like sharks to a fat old sea lion, juicy and weak and too far from home.

Compatriots, the Cuban government now demands on your behalf that the American government begin the process of tearing up, page by page the disgraceful Treaty of Relations of 1936. The day must come soon when Guantanamo Bay naval base will cease to exist as a deliberate insult to the Cuban people. However, until that day comes, let us be alert, as today has been a day of significant humiliation in Yanqui imperial history.

As Cubans know from history an angry Yanqui is a dangerous Yanqui! Be vigilant! Our defences are ready because their military arrogance often replaces their common sense, intelligence and restraint which is always in short supply unlike their equipment and resources. If they attempt a recovery of the prisoners on Cuban soil before we deport them, we will resist! Cubans do not fear hostile actions! Strength is not defined in millions of hectares or

dollars or missiles; we know that nothing is or can ever be stronger than a united people's undying belief in victory. We have endured 40 years of hostility and will continue to endure through self belief and willpower for the greater glory of Cuba. We will confront our enemies fearlessly, proudly, on our feet, never on our knees, because as true revolutionaries we would sooner DIE on our feet than LIVE on our knees!
Viva la Revolucion! Viva Cuba!

As soon as the broadcast was over, the Comandante ordered that Santiago's Committees for the Defence of the Revolution in each tower block arrange a crowd to line the route from the harbour to the airport. Crowd assembly was an occasional duty of the C.D.R. in addition to maintaining one phone line in each block outside a Committee members tenement as well as generally taking the pulse of residents exasperation about frequent power and water cuts. This night, the committees also called up the slogan painters and muralists to get to work immediately on any lighted wall or hoarding on the five km route from the port to the airport. Existing slogans of 'Socialismo o Muerte' and 'Corraje (courage) Cuba!' or 'No al bloqeo' were repainted 'Si al Jihadismo, No al Imperialismo'! 'Viva los Jihadistas', 'Guantánamo es nuestro' and 'Prisioneros Libres-Guantanamo Libre!'; many of the slogans were finished with painted images of red crescent moons.

Cruiseship terminal, Santiago harbour.

Castro's speech had hardly finished when the crowds overlooking the port were back on the balconies witnessing the arrival of three sixty foot articulated trailer buses in the port. Every major Cuban city has a fleet of these homemade 18 wheel giants, capable of carrying 300 passengers in a stifling over packed crush. Known locally as camels or camellos, it was because of the centre dip in the trailers roof, creating a raised hump at either end of the trailer. The camellos drove along the quayside between the lines of soldiers and the liner.

250 soldiers in neat lines on the quayside presented arms, marching in full parade dress. In front of them were three white uniformed Officers of the 'Marina de Guerra Revolucionaria' who were led by a more senior Officer bearing a sheathed sword. All were nervous, having heard Zador's long fusillade against the crouched gorilla in the Grand Foyer. The senior officer stepped forward as the passenger embarkation gantry was lowered to the quay which would allow him walk up into a covered walkway and on into the centre of the ship through the double doors of the Grand Foyer.

Flocks of seagulls began fluttering around the corpses still hanging high up from the starboard deck rails. The senior officer drew his sword and pointed it upwards. In crisp Spanish he ordered some of the martyrs looking down from the Sky deck, in his angry parade ground bellow that all bodies were to be hauled back onto the ship's deck instantly. Without waiting for a response the officer then briskly walked up the gangway where he was met by Zador, Badshah and Alif at the head of a deck full of agitated prisoners all eager to get a glimpse of their walkway onto Cuban territory.

"Capitan Fernando Fernandez Hidalgo, cuartel de Santiago de Cuba" the officer announced brusquely as he stepped on board. Glancing sternfaced at Zador, he ignored Zador's outstretched hand and strode on past him. Zador was awestruck and humbled by the splendour of the officer's white uniform with gold epaulettes, sleeve bars, peaked white cap, white gloves and knee length black boots. Zador became conscious of his own crumpled jacket, foul smelling and almost fully bloodstained.

He followed the Capitan as he walked through the Grand Foyer, the prisoners making way, falling into respectful silence as he walked through them, sword in hand. Zador spoke some words of welcome in Russian believing the officer might understand, given the connections between the countries. The Capitan's face, divided in two halves across by an enormous wide black moustache, turned about, didn't acknowledge Zador's presence at all and walked back to the doors. The Capitan finally broke his silence with a loud command in Spanish simultaneously pointing his sword at the prisoners that they follow him after which he waved the sword out in the direction of the gantry.

Initially the prisoners filed down the corridor and sloping gantry in an orderly fashion following the officer, still with sword drawn. Along the quayside were parked the three articulated camellos ready to transport the prisoners. Several other Cuban officers stepped forward and directed them to each vehicle. Soon the hundreds waiting inside the ship surged forward and what was a hurried disembarkation became a wild charge of prisoners, falling over one another as they raced towards the camellos. Several prisoners inside the ship fired off their guns in desperation before fights began to break out. Scrambling out of the Grand Foyer doors they walked over others that had fallen beneath, celebrating defiantly with shouts of praise for Allah, Castro and the Cuban people. Among the crush to exit the ship was Olga, sprinting down the gantry, leaping over fallen prisoners, loosing her cap as she did so. Both hands firmly held on to her trashbag, heavy with her 'belongings'. As she continued running, her golden mane flared out and then she sprinted for her life. She had seen the conspicuous Capitan Hidalgo and kept him in sight until he also spotted her coming towards him at a nimble and frantic pace. He stepped out into the path of the stampede with sword raised to clear a way for himself and for her to clearly see him.

    She ran up to him, braking fully by grabbing his arm blurting in Russian, "I am an escaping passenger, a Russian, they will kill me any second, help me, I will show you my passport, I am not Chechen!" Olga threw down her dark sunglasses.

    Hidalgo didn't doubt her for one moment, her stunning sky blue eyes locked on his, this blond haired woman, trembling, now vicegripping his arm.

He replied in perfect Russian that she was safe "I'll take you to an ambulance now, welcome to Cuba!

The Capitan ordered another officer to accompany her off the quay. This conspicuous orange suited figure moving away from the parked camellos, through the lines of green uniforms caught the attention of both the hijackers and Captain Hamilton, who was watching from the starboard Bridge wing. Hamilton recognised Olga immediately. "Good girl, brilliant," he whispered to himself joyfully, "she's escaped". Hamilton followed her as she was led further away. As she stepped in to the back of a military ambulance, she paused for a moment, looking back at the Bridge, when Hamilton, distinctive in white uniform and peaked cap, raised his hand and gave one wave. She glimpsed his gesture and entered the ambulance.

A crush quickly developed to board the camellos. As with the chaos of the prisoners departure from the ship the Cuban army let them clamber aboard their camellos in whatever way these armed prisoners chose. The Cuban officers held off any attempt to control what was an over excited armed mob to avoid an accidental firefight. The Cuban soldiers were given no brief save a strict instruction not to engage these prisoners who were to be treated as neither enemies nor friends of Cuba. The parade of the army was a show of strength in a non menacing way. If the Cuban army had otherwise taken up combat positions behind the cover of the port's buildings and their own equipment, that might have led to an unnecessary standoff only resolved by negotiations. It took just ten minutes for all prisoners to exit the Grand Foyer through the large double doorway. The prisoners continued to cheer and shout inside the articulated camellos while Cuban soldiers went around the quayside collecting items of clothing, several split trash bags, some lost pistols, and loose bullets.

Southampton Port, Southern England, Midnight.

In the port of Southampton, the daylong search for Gwendolen Hamilton was continuing into the night. The entire Hampshire constabulary had been mobilised with all leave cancelled. The Chief Constable had the day before taken a call from the Home Secretary advising that Mrs Hamilton was more likely to be recovered alive if located within 24 hours. The Prime Minister was taking a personal interest and he was of the view after a number of conversations with President Grattan, that an attack on the ship by U.S. special forces was imminent. The Chief Constable also called up all volunteer special constables in Hampshire for door to door enquiries. Special police dogs primed with the scent of an item of Mrs Hamilton's clothing had been let loose in vast dockland warehouses while the keyholders of all commercial and rented properties had been requested to return to their premises as part of the search. All routes into and out of the city and surrounding area were manned with checkpoints in case she was being moved about. After nightfall, army helicopters with infrared detectors of body heat hovered over empty business parks and industrial zones of the city.

The muslim community appealed to it's members for information through the local ethnic radio station. At the same time the city's Jewish population filled the city synagogue opened for readings from the Torah, the worshippers maintaining a vigil through the night in solidarity with the plight of the liner's Jewish hostages.

Copies of all phone records of calls over the previous two days from landlines and cellphones to ships at sea were produced by the telecom companies to Hampshire police; they had the careful tedious task of marine telephone number analysis which was a slow operation in a major port city. M I 6 in London continued to work through the night with the CIA analysing hundreds of eavesdropped satellite phone communications concentrating on conversations of frequently dialled numbers the previous twenty four hours throughout the Straits of Florida and the Greater Antilles Sea. Two leads became available as to the movement of the UK based martyrs. The first arose from tracing the fax line to the sacristy at the back of a very old and disused Church of England. That led to a search of all Churches, still in use or shut down. The second was a description of a Russian sounding man buying a steak in a butcher shop on the Chichester side of Southampton. The butcher had remembered the customer as the customer had insulted him, his meat and all Christians, so he thought. The butcher when handing over the steak asked the Russian if it was for himself whereupon the Russian replied saying, "no not Halal, this meat only for dogs"

The meat was indeed for a dog if Mrs Hamilton had one. The police had a photofit broadcast on television of the customer whom the police were satisfied was a Chechen terrorist on Interpol's wanted list and a likely ringleader of the martyrs English cell.

Otherwise crews of ships in port were ordered to search all holds while ships in the repair yards were inspected by the harbour police. All suppliers of barbed wire in the entire Hampshire area were visited to see if any foreign accented person purchased a roll of wire or sought to buy a small amount only, in the past week, too little for a fence but enough to wrap around a person.

CHAPTER 16

Santiago Cruiseship terminal: Pierside
The cab of each camello had a Cuban soldier behind the steering wheel. In the passenger seat was another soldier. Under orders from Hakeem, Khalil and Badshah had to sit with the driver in the first and

second camello respectively. Any attempt to disarm them or the prisoners was to be resisted. Hakeem wanted to ensure that the prisoners remained armed right up to the moment of embarking on the United Nations planes. He was sure any pilot, whether a sympathiser or not would refuse to board hundreds of armed men, no matter how long or short the flight. Hakeem was also uneasy about how the Cubans had permitted the full disembarkation of the prisoners without any attempt to count them and was unimpressed that they did not interfere with the chaos on the quayside as the prisoners attempted to get on board the transport provided. As time passed the prisoners began to roar and shout as they were clearly impatient with the delay. The time was now 19.30 hours. The outside temperature was still over 30C with high humidity. Inside the camellos the heat even with the folding doors open, was a stifling ten or fifteen degrees higher in the calm darkness.

Khalil, after 30 minutes of frustrating discussions with Cuban officers had finally got himself into the passenger seat of the leading camello cab with Badshah replacing the Cuban soldier in the second camello front cab.
Badshah had been arguing with the driver of the second vehicle who feigned ignorance of whatever language Badshah tried whether it was English, Arabic, or French. Even shouting into his face 'RAPIDO, RAPIDO' and 'SCHNELL' failed to ruffle the driver's indifferent demeanour; the soldier at the wheel

remained oblivious, eyes to the front.

Suddenly over a dozen figures appeared from behind an armoured vehicle all dressed in white coats and wearing stethoscopes around their necks. They were led by Capitan Hidalgo, who had earlier busied himself walking up and down the wharf, inspecting the ship. The cowed figures of the Jewish hostages on the Sky deck had a full view of him and followed him hopefully. Higher still, he noticed the rotating orange suited prisoner draped on the radar scanner. Capitan Hidalgo showed no interest in the indiscipline of the ragbag army of freed prisoners but looked for signs of the hijackers presence on the ship. Now at the head of the line of white coated men and women the Capitan came up face to face again with Zador at the entrance to the Grand Foyer. Zador immediately barred the Capitan's way shouting loudly in Russian that nobody was allowed back on the ship. The Capitan warned Zador in Russian that prisoners in the camellos would not leave the quayside unless the remaining hostages on board were examined by his medical team. He assured Zador the team consisted only of doctors, surgeons and two nurses.

Zador radioed Hakeem, who was observing the situation from the starboard Bridge wing. He ordered Abdul to join Zador and frisk the medical crew for any weapons. Zador began explaining to a doctor that the only hostages on board the ship were two Indian engineers in the Engine Hall, plus the ships captain, three Bridge deck officers and sixty Jews on the Sky deck. The crew did not need medical help. The doctor insisted everyone on board would be examined, including 'any martyrs'. The Capitan turned around to the doctor adding sarcastically in Spanish that unless the doctor was also a veterinary surgeon, he was over-qualified to treat any injured martyr. Just as the Capitan was about to address Zador, the ship lurched and moved away from the wharf, fully extending the telescopic walkway. Without waiting for Zador's invitation, the Capitan and the medical team rushed on board.

Hakeem was increasingly nervous with the delay in letting the camellos go to the airport and also unhappy with Hamilton's apparent incompetence to hold the liner fast against the wharf without being tied up to stanchions. After telling Zador to let the doctors attend everyone on board, he ordered him to disconnect the walkway as the ship would now set sail with the Cuban medical team on board and with the Capitan if he was still on board.

The First Officer progammed the engines into reverse propulsion to leave the harbour, then triggered three short blasts on the ship's foghorn indicating her movement astern. Cheers rose up from the apartment blocks with a view of the harbour. In the steaming hot camellos the prisoners also cheered briefly. The military drivers then heard the order to start up the engines and fronted by Cuban armoured personnel carriers, at the head of which were Lada police cars the convoy moved off. Flickering police lights and flashing headlights lit up the dark harbour complex.

Outside the gates of the port the first camello was met by subdued crowds politely clapping and waving small Cuban flags without too much exertion. Little children were held shoulder high to catch a glimpse of the prisoners waving to the crowd. Some women ran out to collect pieces of makeshift prayer mat thrown out by the prisoners. Others ran up to the camellos and threw in handfuls of rice and black beans, to much laughter amongst the Cubans but to the prisoners bafflement, not knowing that it was the staple of the Cuban diet, aptly nicknamed 'Moors and Christians'.

The convoy maintained a low speed of 15 kilometres per hour as it climbed the steep hill out of the port. To Khalil and Badshah, each gear change was painfully slow and over-laboured by the drivers who seemed intent on allowing the gathering crowd gape at the heavily bearded men inside; the men who had been prisoners of the mighty U.S.A. in Guantanamo just hours earlier were now shoulder to shoulder on board three of the city's public transports which some in the crowd had used earlier in the day. The prisoners cheered again when one read out and translated a slogan freshly painted on a billboard. 'Si al Jihadismo – No al Imperialismo!'

Fantasea of the World
From the ship Hakeem could see with his binoculars

the slow pace of the convoy snaking up the dimly lit roads out of Santiago Port. He tried to stay in radio contact with Khalil in the first camello cab but the reception was interrupted continually by interference. Hakeem endlessly turned the dial on his radio trying to improve the reception; Hakeem began to wonder whether his plan to communicate with the convoy might be caught up in Cuba's programme of jamming all radio communications from Miami or whether it could be a deliberate Cuban tactic to isolate the prisoners from him. He would try calling Khalil again in 20 minutes when the convoy should be approaching Antonio Maceo airport. If that failed he would take one of the doctor's cellphones hoping that the local Cubacel network coverage would be better than elsewhere on the island. He would demand that the Cuban army put him in direct contact with Khalil.

Zador brought the medical team led by the Capitan to the Bridge, where he saluted Hakeem, Captain Hamilton and the First Officer on arrival. "Capitan Fernando Fernandez Hidalgo", he announced, unsmiling and then sheathed his ceremonial sword. Hakeem did not return the salute; he instead drew his pistol and pointed it at him while he grabbed the Capitan's pistol out of its holster, the Capitan returning Hakeem's shifty stare, unblinking. The medical team were sent off to see the Jews; some of the elderly had long slumped to the deck, arms held up tied by the wrists to the deck rail, and were semi conscious, without any food, water or their prescribed medication since the previous day. Capitan Hidalgo mounted the communications tower ladder and pulled the prisoner's body off the rotating radar scanner, sending the stiff statuesque figure crashing onto the deck below. He then went off down to the Promenade deck and sliced his sword blade through the ropes tying the corpses to the ship, knowing they would be picked up in the harbour waters later.

Under the watchful eye of Alif, the medical team set to work connecting drips of saline solution and reviving one or two passengers with injections. The two women orderlies untied the hands of two Bridge officers and ordered them in English to bring supplies of water and soft drinks to the Jews; the women then went off to the accomodation deck to bring blankets and bedding outside. Most of the martyrs visited the Sky deck briefly to see what was going on and quickly left disgusted with the intense and coordinated busy work of the medical team reviving the Jews. The team had totally ignored Alif's repeated shouts of "NO" as the soft drinks and blankets arrived.

On the Bridge Hakeem was at the Helm console and was watching closely the fully functioning radar repeater seeing if any large moving echo was visible within radar range. Suddenly, with a deafening scream piercing the quiet calm of the sleepy harbour a fighter jet streaked overhead, seemingly just metres above the liner's masthead. Hakeem thought a missile had been fired at the Bridge. The Capitan then entered the Bridge, finding Hakeem on the deck floor. For the first time the Capitan smiled at everyone.

"No problema,………. Mig 29 Fulcrum Interceptor, terror Cubano!" he spoke proudly, offering some reassurance.

CHAPTER 17

MacDill Airforce Base

Two C130 transports in new white livery with two large black letters 'UN' painted on each fuselage behind the cockpit had emerged from the hangars.

The Ops. room on the base had been advised that Strategic Air Command had picked up the flight paths of not just one Cuban Mig but two Migs criss crossing Santiago City and peeling off to skirt in darkness the Guantanamo air exclusion zone. This was the routine for Cuban interceptor jets, well practiced in tailing U.S. Air Force craft flying in and out of Guantanamo. At MacDill, in the pilots briefing room, both planes crews were waiting nervously, ready to board. Most were chewing vigorously on gum, having earlier spent hours walking about, playing pinball in the canteen, filling up on coffee. Some chain smoked quietly reflecting on anything to distract them, counting the number of 'drags' from each cigarette or drawing shapes with stubs in the ashtrays. The pilots had been selected from a volunteer corps drawn from bases all over Florida for

'Cubacentric missions' and all were the sons or grandsons of Cuban exiles. All had inherited a fierce sense of belonging to a place where not just their families property but freedom itself had been appropriated in a campaign of terror. These aviators had pledged to rescue their motherland whenever commanded to do so, supported by their own families and Hispanic communities.

Their dangerous mission was made clear in the pre-mission address given by the Commander of MacDill base to the pilots and to several platoons of both Delta special forces and of marines gathered in the hangar:

"Men, in the hours ahead you will be taking part in a mission critical to the standing and stature of the United States of America as the greatest military power on this planet. This assignment without doubt will be a heroic episode in the great history of the Airforce and of MacDill base. In every airborne operation since aircraft became weapons of war, American pilots, marines and special forces have served their country with the greatest distinction, and made the ultimate sacrifice for their country which we never forget. Today gentlemen, you are following in that great American tradition of selfless courage and valour to rescue the honour and prestige of the United States. Let the Stars and Stripes forever fly high and proudly as you do gentlemen, in the blue skies above your fellow citizens, the men, women and children in this great land of the free. Good luck and God bless you all."

The flying time was one hour twenty minutes to Santiago. President Grattan wanted the planes airborne as soon as loaded but he accepted the Joint Chiefs advice to delay the departure time until 02:00 as the prisoners and Cuban soldiers would be weary and less reactive to a later night ambush.

Naval Special Warfare Operations were working on a plan to retake the cruise liner soon after sunrise, after 'Operation Hurrycane' was over.

Also being tracked by Strategic Air Command were two United Nations C130 transports seconded by the United Nations from the Royal Canadian Airforce, flying at 39,000 feet over Northern Florida. Two F-117 stealth hawks flew up to meet them and ordered them to land at an obscure airforce base named Calhoun's Field, sixty miles south of Naples, Florida. The pretext was one of a routine inspection of non-American military aircraft overflying US air space. Despite protests of incredulity from the Royal Canadian Airforce crew both planes touched down as ordered.

Bunker De La Comandancia & The Oval Office

Just after 20.15 President Castro called the White House and confirmed that the prisoners had arrived safely at Maceo Airport, Santiago.

"President Grattan I can also confirm that a full team of army medics and nurses is now on board the liner tending to the needs of the Jewish hostages. By cellphone, the medical team reports to my officers that although some of the hostages are unwell they will survive with treatment. The ship has now left Santiago harbour and our minesweeper is tracking the movement of the liner heading south, southeast. The prisoners are on Cuban land and we are processing these former captives who have arrived without any papers and are effectively illegal immigrants. Although they are in transit, nonetheless they have entered the Republic of Cuba without proper documentation. You will appreciate that processing this documentation will take some time and I suggest we also take the time that this allows us to finalise the agreement we discussed earlier in relation to the demilitarisation of Guantanamo naval base".

Grattan was not in his cabinet room but back in the Oval Office and was in the company of the Joint Chiefs. He was already aware from local intelligence that the prisoners had left the ship and had a full report about the action and inaction of the Cuban military at the Cruise terminal.

"Presidente, we appreciate all your doing to see that the lives of the remaining hostages are spared and indeed improved with the help of your medical staff. It is imperative that those prisoners are put on those United Nations planes which we will divert once airborne. Presidente we really don't have time to get involved in legalities to do with this longstanding Guantanamo treaty between our two nations."

"President Grattan these are matters where we can arrive at an agreement quickly if there is a will on the part of the government of the United States and of

Cuba. I have discussed this situation with our President of Judicial Power. The Treaty of Relations signed in 1936 and registered with the League of Nations states that the naval base is a coaling station. So Mr President, strictly speaking it should only be a base for refuelling your ships and in fact refuelling your ships with coal! The United Nations of course inherited this ridiculous treaty where the lease payment is wholly unrealistic as indeed is mention of any naval station in the 21st century being used to refuel with coal. I suggest, President Grattan that the need of the U.S. Government to maintain a presence on the island of Cuba is a political need unrelated to the needs of the United States Navy to pick up coal supplies!"

Fidel was raising his voice, becoming agitated. " Let me finish Mr President. You have mentioned an Exchange of Notes as being the only legal formality that we have time to complete given the crisis that both our governments face. Of course Mr President the Exchange of Notes between us is not something that requires registration with the United Nations. In fact my President of Judicial Power tells me it is not binding at all. Let us use the focus on Guantanamo that we both have tonight, to update this multi-lateral treaty with a protocol to be attached and registered with the United Nations under Article 102."

Back in the Oval Office the President had his phone on speaker and during President Castro's conversation there was much shaking of heads, part in anger, part in disbelief. At one point the President raised his hand in a pistol like shape and jerked it upwards as if he had fired off a shot at the telephone.

"Mr Presidente lets be quite blunt about this. There is an international treaty between us that may only be out of date if at all, in relation to the yearly rent of $4,085 dollars. At this point what I WILL do is disturb my Attorney General at home and have him get to work on a supplemental agreement in relation to our presence in Guantanamo. Hopefully in a matter of say four, five maybe six hours in communications through the night between our Attorney General and your Judicial Power guy something can be agreed. Listen, these things take time and the last thing we want to do is to register any agreement that is cobbled together in haste and afterwards we all repent about it at our leisure. For the moment Presidente I suggest the full involvement of the United Nations to work for the release of the 60 American citizens of Jewish religion, currently held on board the ship which is shortly going to be in international waters, if it isn't already. As for the Illegal Combatants roaming free in Cuba, I will tolerate a role for the United Nations to get them off your hands. But, as I said earlier, God help any country permitting these two transporters full of those fighters to land and then offer them asylum……… we will then deal with that third country in our own appropriate way! For now Presidente lets continue with both our low key positions and inaction which so far has saved any further lives being lost."

Comandante Castro replied "While your Attorney General and the President of Judicial Power are discussing the terms of an American presence in Guantanamo it will take us quite some hours to process all these prisoners before we will let them embark on the United Nations planes when they arrive. I have no idea how long but at least in the interim we are providing assistance to the Jews still held on the ship. You will of course understand President Grattan that we have no intention of being accused by anybody of allowing any of these freed captives to remain here and accordingly our military will cross check with your military the identity and nationality of each prisoner. We have more problems: our Foreign Ministry has had visits this evening from Ambassadors of different countries seeking the release of their nationals who were detained at Guantanamo. These countries believe, now that these men are on Cuban territory that we have a legal obligation to deport them to their country of citizenship. I don't think I need to mention to you President Grattan which countries have made representations to the Foreign Ministry. Strictly speaking as these captives were not recognised by the United Nations as prisoners of war, Cuba could find itself before the International Courts of Human Rights if we detained them. Imagine! Cuba and America sharing the same prison cell waiting for a sentence from the Court of Human Rights!

President Grattan, this chaos has its origins in your foreign policy towards Islamic nations and towards the heroic people of Cuba. Not only do I expect progress on

Guantanamo before sunrise tomorrow but I expect to see and I think the world will expect to see progress on lifting the blockade of Cuba immediately after this crisis is over."

President Grattan simply replied, "Leave it to the legal people for now. Goodnight Presidente."

Grattan turned to the Joint Chiefs slamming his hand down on the table, "This is the gameplan gentlemen. I want to see our two transporters touchdown, fill up with the bodies of those prisoners, more alive than dead and I want to see those planes landing within 15 minutes or whatever, in Guantanamo Naval base. I want to see those prisoners re-caged and waiting for breakfast tomorrow morning! Lets flex a little military muscle at the Guantanamo perimeter fence and eyeball the Cuban army without blinking. Guantanamo being demilitarised?....MY AAHSS!" General Hudsen, let me have the Cuban military picture in Santiago, what are we talking about?

"Mr President, as bad luck would have it Santiago de Cuba has the largest concentration of helicopters in the Cuban Airforce, all Soviet stuff but still packing a punch as we estimate they may get 20 helicopter gunships airborne. Santiago is part of the Zona Aerea Oriental, or Eastern zone, which is the third part of the 3 military zones in Cuba, the others being the Middle and the Western zones.

As far as ground forces go, our local intelligence is reporting that they are currently deploying their entire

Eastern Army in the direction of Guantanamo with several columns being diverted to strategic locations in Santiago city including the harbour and the city's airfield. We would expect the best of the Cuban soldiers, the Especiales, the battle hardened elite………. Castro's 'Republican Guard' if you will, to be mobilised; these are no part time 'bacco farmers Sir. We're talking about cracktroops who rightly got the credit for crushing the South African army in one hell of a tactical battle in Angola; these 'nasties' could well be deployed at Santiago airport too Sir."

"Thanks General, …..doesn't sound like an army of conscript hillbillies to me either. Give me another update in an hour", the President concluded wearily.

CHAPTER 18

Antonio Maceo Airport, Santiago

As the prisoners waited restlessly on board the camellos, crates of bottled water arrived and were distributed. Many prisoners passed the time reading or reciting the Holy Qu'ran. From time to time, a Cuban officer came aboard and leafed through the worn books, some small and ornate, others missing any cover. Nothing could have interested the Cubans less, no images, totally incomprehensible Arabic script, they were presumed to be survival manuals of some sort that the prisoners seemed determined to learn off by heart.

In Havana General Arroyo of the Eastern Army waited in the Bunker, walking back and forth along the huge wall map of Cuba that stretched the entire length of the Salon de Operaciones. Two women officers attended him, taking minutes of his coded radio commands to the different Brigadas and the Estaciones de Radar along the northern coast. The rotund General Raul Castro was in the next room, getting through a box of his favourite 'Trinidad' cigars supplied only to the Government and the Diplomatic Corps in Havana. His reading materials were the most recent reports on the useable combat aircraft available, of whatever vintage and their whereabouts.

Fidel had earlier gone to his sleeping quarters in the Bunker with instructions to be woken only by Raul or if a call came from the President of Judicial Power to advise on progress or lack of it in the negotiations with the Americans about the future of Guantanamo.

Straits of Florida

Approaching Antonio Maceo Airport at Santiago de Cuba two incoming C130 air transports called up the tower. As the airport wasn't capable of taking night flights Santiago tower ordered assistance from the Cuban military to light up the runway with headlights of Cuban military vehicles, and the airport's two elderly fire tenders. The pilot of the first aircraft spoke to the tower to explain his requirements for his own safety and that of his flight crew. He wanted a holding position over Santiago and would only land when the tower confirmed the passenger load had abandoned their weapons. Further confirmation of this was required from a senior Cuban military officer. The pilot continued "the prisoners must be disarmed by the Cuban military in accordance with UN policy and civil aviation practice. This is a designated peace keeping mission. If I land and they try to board bearing weapons, find me a good Hotel for the night. Tell them if they shoot me they're definitely staying in Cuba forever! I am not prepared to fly with a planeload of untrained armed militia on a 14 hour trans-oceanic routing regardless of destination. A flight path taking the polar route via the east coast of the United States is not available. So, not only is it my personal demand, it is a condition of refuelling in the Azores and a condition for overflying all African airspace that all passengers be unarmed."

Santiago's tower relayed the conditions to the Cuban military who briefed Khalil just as the C130s came into view for a low 'recon' flypast of the airport. The planes held a steady 200ft altitude as both flight crews assessed the runway lit up by two lines of military vehicles, headlights on. The ghostly white windowless planes, wheels up, came and went in seconds, the huge black letters **UN** lit up by their bright wing lights as they flew past the waiting prisoners.

Each pilot then throttled up his four engines to a screaming whine and banked sharply to begin the climb to 5,000 feet and level off; a holding pattern was given north of Santiago city pending the prisoners being disarmed by the Cuban military. The planes caught the first pink hue of the dawn sunrise as they slowly circled at 5000ft in the dark blue of the northern sky; the time was 0400.

Maceo Airport Apron

Khalil climbed up on the roof of one of the camellos to address all prisoners who were now milling round anxiously awaiting the arrival of the cargo planes they had seen flying past. Fatigue was setting in and their last meal had been anything edible they found hours earlier in the ship's galleys. Some had feasted and left convinced they had eaten enough for days ahead while others had stored some fruit and balls of pizza dough in their trash bags, which they were slow to share.

The Cuban officers stood by as Khalil then spoke to the prisoners: "Warriors of Jihad the moment of your true freedom comes nearer. You have seen the planes fly past. They will only land and fly us back to the Sudan if we lay down our weapons. We will only do so when the planes have landed and when we will have no need for assault rifles, rocket launchers or machine guns. But remember we are soldiers and a soldier without any gun is no longer a soldier. I do not ask you to lay down your small arms! Like our knives and daggers they are a symbol of the power of Islam on this unholy island! Conceal them until our destination. You must never again find yourselves at the mercy of an Infidel, abused and shamed. We are God's soldiers still on this strange island, where God is a fugitive. But tonight God is with us and as God's men we remain ready to fight and die for him.

Now we will throw down our bigger weapons which our Cuban friends will be glad to receive. Some day those same guns may be used against the great Satan that tries to starve our Cuban hosts of food and medicine."

Both Badshah and Khalil then tried to call up Hakeem on their radios but again there was only static interference broken up by whistling noises as they turned the dials. As a pile of weapons began to grow the Tower alerted the pilots that the prisoners were disarming and required the planes to come out of the holding pattern and land immediately.

As the first plane landed, the prisoners clustered in groups around the apron marvelling at the size of the craft as it roared to a halt at the end of the runway. Within fifteen minutes both giant aircraft were on the ground and taxiing to the far end of the airfield. The second plane to land turned a full circle to position for take off while the first one taxied off the runway to avoid the other's jet blast on later take off. After hours of waiting, there was a renewed sense of anticipation amongst the prisoners for the first time they could look into the future with some certainty. It looked like that they would now be leaving this island in much the same way they came in; in the hold of a aircraft, sitting for hours on a metal floor but this time with the huge comfort that they were free men again after years of indefinite isolation and idleness. Some prisoners began to break away from the main group gathered around the first camello. Cuban soldiers rushed forward and demanded in Spanish that the prisoners line up in an orderly fashion. Badshah approached one of the officers to ask what was happening. He explained that having arrived in Cuba illegally it was a requirement that every prisoner's identity and nationality be confirmed and the number counted out of the ship would now be counted out of Cuba.

Meantime another group of soldiers had moved the prisoners away from the pile of arms. Over in the centre of the floodlit apron in front of the terminal building several desks were being set up with a chair on either side. Again Khalil tried his radio to speak to Hakeem on the ship and then went to discuss with Badshah his concern about more delays. Hours had been spent waiting and only now had the Cubans decided to process the prisoners.

The prisoners began to get unruly with the Cuban guards until Badshah roared at them that the Cubans needed to identify each prisoner and his nationality and that they were to give their details to the Cuban officers as quickly as possible. It wasn't long however before Khalil was exasperated at the slow pace of the first interviews with a prisoner seated at each little table. He could see that the Cubans were having great difficulty writing phonetically the Arabic name of the prisoners, or even pronouncing it. Khalil was anxious to get the next prisoner seated and interviewed and was becoming visibly impatient with the Cuban officers antics of hand signals and gestures. Finally one of the Cuban officer's stood up to explain a date of birth and gestured to his abdominal area between his legs which he opened wide. He then made a pained face, protruded his behind, slapped it and then tapped a finger on his watch. The prisoner sitting opposite him stood up and stepped back, noisily siphoned snot into his throat and spat it directly at the Cuban officer's peaked cap. Immediately the officer drew his pistol and aimed it straight at the rebellious prisoner's chest.

Badshah quickly intervened asking the prisoner for his date of birth. He then addressed the hundreds of impatiently waiting prisoners explaining that he and Khalil will give their details on each prisoner's behalf to each officer as the prisoners came forward. This however was unacceptable to the Cubans who insisted that Badshah and Khalil stand back. As soon as each interview was complete, the prisoner ran straight back to the camello as ordered by the Cubans Only when all the interviews were over would the camellos be driven in convoy to the planes, waiting in silence, lights on, 400 metres away.

Maceo Airport: Airfield

Shortly after the interviewing began a military jeep sped out to the planes towing a stairway. Arriving at the plane, the stairway was brought up against the front door. An officer ran up the stairway and knocked on the door.

There was no response and no sound of any activity. The cockpit was in darkness. Despite several more knocks on the door, it remained closed as did the cockpit window. The tower observing what was happening requested the pilots to allow access. The pilots answered that any person, Cuban or otherwise would be denied access if armed. The Cuban officers radios then came alive with snappy commands and in a moment, the Cubans laid down their guns in full view of the cockpit. As the 4 newly disarmed officers walked back up the stairway, the door opened for them without further request. As each one walked into the dark interior, he was coshed on the back of the head and tied up by a U.S. commando dressed in Cuban fatigues and ready to take the place of their unconscious Cuban counterparts. The four marines briefly compared uniform insignia with the prostrate Cubans, then gave each other a joined fourhanded shake, picked up the Cuban radios and ran out of the plane down the steps to the jeep. They sat into it and waited for a call over the radio. In a few moments the U.S. marines, all Spanish speakers chosen from Little Havana in Miami replied that they had met with the pilot and requested the prisoners to come over and board the plane.

The Cuban Officer in charge of the prisoners deportation at the airport looked through his binoculars at the jeep and commanded the men to return as the prisoners would not be boarding without the personal command of General Arroyo. He then ordered all other Suzuki jeeps lining the runway to remain in position, lights off.

The marines looked at one another and realised that the only way they could progress the matter was by calling over the prisoners to the plane. They promptly jumped out of the jeep and fired several shots in the air to draw the attention of the prisoners, most of whom were still queuing up to be interviewed. Then in the glare of the plane's lights they waved at the prisoners to come on over to the plane.

CHAPTER 19

Maceo Airport Airfield
In seconds the orderly lines of prisoners queuing up became an unruly charging mass stampeding their way

in near darkness across the airfield, cheering and shouting with delight at the opportunity finally to board the waiting planes. The Cuban army reacted immediately, drawing pistols and firing shots over the heads of the prisoners hoping they would dive for cover in the grass where they could be encircled and rounded up again. The Cubans continued firing over the heads of the prisoners without any reaction from the running prisoners while the four marines took cover behind the Cuban army jeep. Some prisoners ran into one another, others stumbled and fell, then hobbled on, some making for the nearest transporter while some had already decided to run further for the second transporter.

As the crowd approached the planes the huge rear cargo ramp at the back of each jet began to open down simultaneously in giant inviting gestures of welcome. As they opened down fully, the first prisoners to arrive halted and looked in to the vast pitchblack tunnel of the cargo hold. Suddenly they heard loud echoes of engines starting up and a line of blinding headlights came on. With a screech of tyres, Humvees and armoured personnel carriers surged toward them, rattling over chains and floor plating, bouncing over the ramp hump and down around them at speed, missing them by inches before driving on out across the airfield. The APCs further back in the holds were gathering speeds up to 40 mph coming down the ramps until both transporters were disgorging lines of military vehicles, each one tailgating the other. These lines of motorised cargo sped in two different directions in a clear pincer movement to surround the hundreds of prisoners that had charged out to the airfield.

From the roof of the terminal the senior Cuban officers looked on in complete disbelief as a swarm of military vehicles bearing U.S. Military markings spread out across the airfield. The prisoners scattered around the airfield began to slow down their pace soon stopping where they were, trying to comprehend, confused and unsure of what was happening; unsure if this was a UN protection unit to receive them or whether they had mistaken the planes for Cuban army transporters delivering more equipment to line the runway as opposed to United Nations planes bringing them home.

Badshah and Khalil quickly realised however that it was a trap. Out on the apron Khalil finally managed to get a clear signal on his radio to Hakeem on board the liner. As soon as he heard Hakeem's voice Khalil jabbered hysterically "It's an ambush…… there are American forces coming out of the United Nations planes and we are being surrounded by speeding vehicles. They have guns but they are not firing. This is not what you said………… it must be a trap, do you hear me Hakeem"?

"Yes I hear you Khalil, are you sure they are American and not United Nations?"

"Yes they have the white American star, I know the Humvees of Satan anywhere, I know the sound, this is an American trick."

Hakeem paused for a moment and shouted angrily into his radio "KHALIL YOU HAVE AN ARMY OF YOUR OWN WITH YOU, TAKE OVER THE TERMINAL AND ATTACK THE PLANES NOW!"

Hakeem turned to Zador who was with him on the bridge, "It seems the Americans have forgotten about our Jew hostages. The sun will be up soon, may it's light shine brightly on the greatest confrontation between the forces of Satan and the Mudjahadeen. Bring anything that burns and build a great pyre at the front of the ship. Zador, now is your moment of glory. I want the bow filled with any plastics and wood, chairs, tables, anything that burns but not too quickly. The Fantasea of the World will be a morning star, a white morning Star of David that we will then melt, becoming a glowing red funeral pyre before sinking like a setting sun. Full speed to Guantanamo Bay! Full speed to the deepwater tomb of the Star of David! "

At the airfield, Khalil was now shouting orders to everyone to grab a weapon and take the terminal. "DO NOT LET THE INFIDELS SURROUND YOU, WHETHER THEY ARE AMERICANS OR CUBANS, PREPARE TO FIGHT! TAKE POSITIONS IN THE TERMINAL AND SHOOT AT THE PLANES IF THEY START MOVING."

On top of the terminal building senior Cuban officers

radioed to their men in the airfield not to open fire on the prisoners or the military vehicles rushing out of the transporters. When the officers saw the prisoners make for the stacks of weapons to arm themselves General Arroyo was asked for instructions. More and more prisoners began to grab guns, some of them immediately heading for the terminal while others had regrouped and decided to re-enter the first camello.

Out in the airfield scores of the unarmed prisoners had fallen to the ground and attempted to hide in the long grass. American marines on foot with infrared nightscopes fixed to their helmets were running in teams of threes grabbing prisoners bodily and dragging them to waiting APCs, rear doors open, roof gunner providing covering fire. Suddenly the message came back from General Arroyo that the prisoners were forbidden to re-arm and that there was just one army, the Revolutionary Army, in the Republic of Cuba. He warned his officers that marines coming out of the planes could be another invasion of 'contra locos' from Miami and ordered a full scale offensive and the capture of both C130 transporters.

The senior officers now lying flat on the terminal roof ordered their troops into action. Conscript reinforcements were called up from Santiago. Ten brigades of professional troops that had not yet arrived at the Guantanamo perimeter were recalled.

The U.S. forces were to be captured if at all possible

or shot by Cuban forces only in self defence. Immediately however the Cuban troops using the cover of their jeeps lining the runway opened fire at will at the American APCs racing around the airfield. The Cubans could see the helmeted figures of the US marines running for cover between lines of slower APCs which were filling up with prisoners. Some prisoners still in orange prison suits got up and with pistols firing made a dash for the airport perimeter. They were shot down instantly by both U.S. and Cuban forces.

Those Cubans forces ordered to stay in position were machine gunning anyone while the prisoners fired shots at anyone approaching themselves. The Marines returned fire at both the Cubans and the prisoners. From inside the terminal, several prisoners fired out at Cubans who had also taken cover from the marines out on the airfield. An hour into the mission, the first lustrous rays of sunrise filtered through the royal palms at the airport perimeter. The marines responded with smoke grenades thrown randomly around the field for more cover. The air was still, but filled with the crack of repeating rifles or pistols and answering short staccatos of machine gun fire.

The marines coming upon clusters of crouching prisoners riflebutted any protesters. Once inside the cramped APCs any further revolt was answered with a prolonged beating and hands and legs were bound again with plastic ties.

The laden APCs shuttled back up the cargo ramps of the transporters to unload recaptured prisoners who were dragged out and hooded again. The APCs then returned to the airfield. The recaptured prisoners heard for the first time in 24 hours the familiar accented shouting of Americans ordering them again, this time to lie flat on the metal roadway of the cargo hold.

Out on the airfield those marines still engaged in intense combat kept an eye on the aircraft. They had been briefed before their mission that in the event of the pilots throttling up the engines that it was a signal to retreat to the plane for take off. Any marines pinned down by gunfire were briefed to crawl to the deep gulleys at the far side of the airfield and await rescue by Chinooks which were already in the air from MacDill. Protecting the Chinooks were Black Hawk attack helicopters and F-17 fighters, all of which had now been picked up by the Cuban air defence radar system and the information relayed to General Raul.

Bunker De La Comandancia

It was 05.00 and a bleary eyed Fidel was in urgent conference with Raul, and General Arroyo of the Eastern Army. Raul was gulping a supply of espressos. After his fourth he spoke. "Reports from Santiago suggest to me that this is likely a decoy mission ahead of a full US invasion. Our radar is picking up intense enemy air activity incoming from Florida. Right now the Americans have 16 fighter jets heading for Cuban air space and I suggest we send up four more Mig-29s to shoot down the incoming slower aircraft, probably troop carrier helicopters. The Migs should avoid dog fights."

Fidel had his hands over his face and dragged them down slowly as if to wake himself from a nightmare. What was unfolding was as a result of his political miscalculation and he now had a military confrontation on Cuban soil. Fidel replied to Raul slowly. "They have…deceived us,… as usual. Should we surprise them? What looks like an invasion by U.S. forces using the prisoners as an excuse could just be an attempt to recover the prisoners- that bastard Grattan trying to save his tanned thick skin for re-election." Fidel paused to drink his own coffee, put the small cup down and rubbed his hands together suggesting he was back in combative mood and ready for a challenge.

"Did you know Raul that Grattan hasn't a tan at all!" Fidel asked Raul cheerfully. "One of our friends in the CIA reports he is a bronze diabetic….something to do with…… iron…. too much in his blood. When he dies Raul, they won't have to cast a statue in bronze, just stick him up on a pedestal maybe" Fidel's voice trailed off, lost in thought for a moment. Raul still sensed a note of despair in his brother's black humour.

"A man of iron?…Grattan?…Fidel, he needs to see a real iron fist, a real Cuban one! He needs prestige and it looks like he wants to get prestige at the expense of you and me, our military and our people!

Fidel interrupted Raul, recovering his focused

composure.

"No! I cannot see this as an invasion! Too little preparation!..and then fight us for a thousand kilometres through the whole length of the island from Santiago? No. This is NOT an invasion", Fidel asserted again more emphatically. "They're too stretched in the 'War on Terror', Iraq, Afghanistan, Pakistan. We're off the agenda unless we convert to Islam! Then, as new converts bending over for our first prayer we'll have UN weapons inpectors shining flashlights up our holes looking for plutonium! Be thankful for the Spanish missionaries Raul!

Raul, what U.S. forces are in Guantanamo Bay at the moment?"

"Other than the one submarine at sea we know about and shadowing the passenger liner, they are parading the carrier, John F Kennedy just outside our territorial waters trying to worry us. On her deck we can see four helicopter gun ships, twelve F-16's and two Harrier jump jets. No idea what's in the hangars below. Further out in the bay they have a Fuel Supply Tanker at anchor and in the harbour two frigates are tied up. In her dry dock the one hospital ship that has been there for years isn't yet decommissioned.

Around the harbour, the usual air defence systems. As for the total men who are combat ready?….probably a thousand sailors and a few hundred base guards……. it's not a big barracks. A lot of personnel would be support and administrative staff. If you want a comparison Fidel….by how much do we outnumber the forces at Guantanamo man for man right now? We have 9,000 professionals in the Eastern Army now in the vicinity of Guantanamo. That includes not just everyone from Santiago's Barracks but also the 3rd Corps from Holguin and the 5th from Camaguey. As for the conscipts on 'mili' this year, we've 60,000 with 20,000 in the Eastern Army but they'd be a liability....the only fighting they've done is in the queue for rations. If you are asking can we take Guantanamo back? Then the answer is yes but not for long. You are only talking about a matter of minutes before the planes on the John F Kennedy are airborne and playing target practice with our infantry."

Fidel was silent drumming his fingers off the top of the conference table. "Let's remember that we must keep the support of the international community on our side. We are the victim of an American deception where they have entered Cuban air space without permission. They have a submarine in Cuban waters without permission. They have held 600 men without trial who are not prisoners of war under the Geneva Convention. Years ago they bribed Battista for a little piece of Cuba and now dare use it as an isolation cell like they try to isolate us from the world. In effect comrades this latest military action further provokes not just the Cuban people but the international community to condemn America. We are dealing with a government that has no principles but is based on a dollar fascism. Did you know Raul that with a couple of signatures, I don't know how many exactly, that people in America can nominate an orang-utan for president? Grattan, though he looks human has the brain of an orang-utan and a greedy one who thinks he can help himself to Cuban bananas! I think Raul, I agree with you it is time to surprise the slimy Grattan. However we don't need to lose six Mig-29s which we cannot replace, we might need them another day when another horde of Miami locos tries to invade us on luxury power boats. Give me some ideas about how we can use whatever forces we have available to maximum effect."

Raul immediately called into the room Aero Mariscal Diego Figueroa of the Cuban Air force and Air Defence Command and repeated the question.

The air marshal replied without hesitation. "I can recommend that we use the surface to air missile battery at Antonio Maceo itself to bring down the two C 130s if they get airborne. As for the incoming aircraft currently heading along our Northern coast we also have a SAM battery at Puerto Padre and at Punta Guarico. I expect that all incoming aircraft will have diversionary flares and chaff to deflect these missiles but we will instruct our units to fire full salvos of missiles at a time which gives us a better chance of a hit."

Fidel then asked Figueroa if he thought the Americans knew about these missile batteries. He replied with some reassurance. "These are mobile batteries that we place in a different location every month and I don't think monitoring our surface to air missile batteries has been on the top of the Pentagon's list of worries."

Fidel looked up to the ceiling and nodded his head. "Yes you're right, they spend $80 billion dollars invading Iraq and they still can't deal with donkey and cart bombs at road blocks. Raul, send up two Mig-29's to bring down any incoming aircraft once they are inside Cuban air space and that is my official order that is to be made known to press agencies and published in our 'International Granma'. Fidel's thoughts raced through his mind. "Also I want the city of Santiago and the airport blacked out, even though it's nearly dawn....no need to help Yanquis map read. Sound the air raid sirens. Open the shelters and bunkers. Curfew immediately, no schools, work, get the word out to the C.D.R...........strictly enforced. Mobilise all state security and reservists...call up the conscipts. Also I want all Cadre units deployed. Let's keep the world on our side except maybe the tourists already in Santiago and also at Cayo Coco, no wandering...keep them in the Hotels. Switch off Cubacel and the landline phones network. Cancel all flights internally and all international ones. Grattan would love to blame us for shooting down a European civilian airliner. President Grattan-utang!....I like that name better!"

Fidel then stood up from his desk and was joined on his feet with the rest of the commanders around the conference table. Fidel walked over to the map and stretched his arm high to run his forefinger along the Northern coast from Havana all the way along down to the very tip of Cuba at Punta de Quemado. "Activate all the missile batteries along this coast and lets give them a taste of our missile systems. In the meantime I want the American Interests consular mission in Havana shut down and you can put all the staff under house arrest as enemy collaborators. One more thing Raul, tell those Mig pilots they have my personal good wishes. Use our best. Lets see what damage our heroic aces can do against the U.S. Airforce. We are not going to give the U.S. airforce the pleasure of destroying our Air Force as well as violating Cuban territory in a ground incursion. Just two more Migs and first targets are those fake UN transporters on the ground in Santiago. Otherwise, let the airport battery do what it is supposed to do, protect the airport! What's the latest from there?"

From the rooftop of the terminal Cuban officers continued reporting frantically on the chaotic scenes on the airfield, with several fire fights between units of the Cuban army and U.S. marines. Both Cuban and U.S. forces were also being shot at by the Guantanamo prisoners, either from inside the airport terminal building or at the airport perimeter fence where several prisoners were defending themselves while attempting to break out of the airfield and into the scrubland beyond.

Maceo Airfield, Santiago
Slowly the dawn sun was casting wide shafts of gold

light across the airfield lifting the vale of cover that so far kept the casualties on all sides to a lesser number than it might have been in broad daylight. Simultaneously the two transporters engines throttled up, signalling their take off was imminent. Some marines instantly ran to the armoured personnel carriers dropping prisoners they had been dragging along leaving them in the middle of the airfield. Other marines defiantly stood their ground, determined to fight to the end without any armoured back up; some had arrived in Cuba to avenge the forced exile from Cuba of their parents, fleeing Castro's regime to start life all over again, penniless. With marines leaping on board the armoured personnel carriers and jeeps they raced for the cargo ramps which remained down as the planes began to move along the runway.

Immediately Khalil ran up to the Camello cab and pushed a prisoner who had been firing under the cover of the camello cab out of the way. Khalil started up the camello, now riddled with bullet holes and shattered windows. He got the huge vehicle into third gear going down a taxiway heading for the planes that were beginning to move along the runway. Speed was slow to increase but as he wrestled with the floor mounted gearstick with great difficulty he finally reached fifth gear then sixth, seventh, and eighth gear finally allowing him put his foot to the floor. He reckoned he could build up enough speed to get to one of the planes in time before the pilots advanced throttle levers for take off.

The pilots however saw the camello swing around the bend of the taxi way on to the runway and head for them. The pilot of the second plane screamed down the radio to the first transporter ordering the pilot to take off immediately. There was every chance they were going to be rammed and never get out of Cuba.

The first plane's engines had throttled up to full power becoming a deafening scream and began to move faster down the runway. The Pilot winced as prisoners some still clutching souvenirs were lifted off their feet and hurtled pass his cockpit into the sucking jet turbines on full power. The spinning fanblades also vacuumed up marines as they made a run for the plane. Chasing Cuban soldiers all dived to the ground as the plane approached only to be also lifted out of the grass like leaves rolling in the breeze and spun into the vortex of the fans. As the first plane gathered speed it was raked with gunfire by both the Cuban military on the terminal roof and from the prisoners on the ground. The pilot ducked down as some bullets hit the front windscreen of the transporter but with the ramp drawing up he managed to take off, a wounded monster screeching as it struggled upwards. Behind on the runway were neat lines of minced fleshpulp seared black by the engine heat. Bones had been scraped clean in the turbines, sounding like smashing crockery before being shot out of the exhaust cowls in a shower of marble like chippings. The planes engine blades rattled with the damage caused by the larger bones on take off. Lift was uncertain and with throttle levers fully advanced the pilot had used every last metre of the runway before leaving the ground, the fuselage peppered with continuing gunfire. Any altitude would be a luxury. The transporter just cleared some palms when the fire alarm sounded for port engine 1 and then starboard engine 2. The pilot continued heading for Guantanamo Base with both engines shut down and running on the two that still functioned.

Once the first plane had left the ground, the second plane turned onto the runway and began to pick up speed down the runway. Sucking in the debris left behind by the first plane, it too struggled to achieve maximum thrust demanded from each engine. Racing behind it were another two armoured personnel carriers desperate to catch up before take off. Behind them now was Khalil in the camello who had earlier swerved off the runway to avoid a head on collision with the first plane. The enraged Khalil had other ideas. The pilot roared that he had to bring up the ramp as they were going for lift off now and that unless he brought up the ramp all the armoured personnel carriers with the prisoners on board would fall out of the cargo hold as it took off. The marines on board realised that the plane was building up speed for take off and hugged the body straps tightly along the side of the plane's hold. The marines on the ramp frantically waved away the APCs and as they duly veered off the runway, Khalil right behind grabbed the gearstick again and jammed back with both hands to find ninth and the last gear notch giving him a final surge of power. He crashed up the ramp straight into the cargo hold of the transporter and despite jamming on the brakes inside, the camello smashed head on into a line of 6 APCs shunting one into the other, the last APC bursting through a foreward bulkhead into the flight crew rest area. The prisoners inside the camello were hurled to the front with the impact. Stunned for a moment, they were brought to their senses by the marines opening fire on the camello.

Khalil was in the cab slumped over the steering wheel. As the camello began to roll backwards a marine jumped into the cab to pull up the handbrake as the plane climbed steeply. Although he pulled up the handbrake, the steep ascent of the plane still avoiding a hail of ground fire caused the camello's 18 wheels to slide further down the cargo hold. Before the prisoners had time to jump out, it had slid backwards and hit hard the rising ramp buckling the ramp's centre plates. A quick thinking marine grabbed the release handle of the cargo ramp and as it opened back down again, the huge articulated vehicle with it's terrified prisoner load fell out of the plane; the trailer fell into a near vertical backwards descent, the prisoners inside crashing in a pile towards the rear and then on out through the back windows breaking instantly under their weight. Bodies somersaulted downwards, cries of terror and pitiful shrieks trailing off in the wind.

On board the C130 one of the marines holding a grab rail on the lowered ramp roared uselessly in the raging turbulence of the jet exhausts blasting past the open hold "JUST LIKE JUMPING FROM THE TWIN TOWERS…….ENJOY THE VIEW!"

Following the prisoners out of the rear of the camello were their trash bags, emptying into the sky their cherished belongings. New clothes and shoes from the liner's boutiques, shiny coffee pots, tins of sweets, soaps, perfumes, boardgames, Fantasea bathrobes, boxes of cigars and cigarette packs by the hundred, cameras, and other luxuries scattered, like heaven sent gifts, around Cuban fields. The heavier weight of the cab pulled the articulated trailer out of it's backward near vertical descent, causing the entire vehicle to start to nose dive before the cab disengaged from the trailer. Falling almost 800 feet, the cab plunged into a ploughed field like a giant's hammer, shooting a craterful of clay high into the air with the impact. The trailer landed horizontally seconds later but half a kilometre away on a road in front of a long line of early morning workers waiting to hitch lifts, unaware of the curfew. The weight of the heavy trailer crashing onto the tarmac, all tyres exploding together as it hit, lifted the workers bodily off the ground, the shockwave blasting them flat onto their backs.

The marines on the transporter still battled to manually winch up the ramp which had been damaged further when the camello slipped out of the plane. Inside the cargo hold the remaining marines in the Humvees and APCs had leapt out and strapped themselves along with the remaining captured prisoners to the side frames of the fuselage. The plane was climbing erratically, too steeply until levelled off by the pilot, then yawing and pitching before climbing steeply again. The bent telescopic plates of the lowered ramp meant it would not retract, either automatically or manually even with the brute force of several marines forcing the winding gear. The extended ramp was causing the huge aircraft to become aerodynamically unstable, it's effect like a huge bird's tail stuck in an airbrake configuration. The pilots struggled at the controls to maintain a climb headed South East in the direction of Guantanamo just barely reaching 1300 feet. Suddenly, the plane lurched violently throwing the marines working on the winding gear to the fuselage floor. Scrambling to grab wheel chains to avoid falling out, they waited for the plane to stabilize but instead it went into another steep climb. The marines heard chains snapping and looked up aghast at the rows of APCs and Hummers breaking free. As soon as one of the forward vehicles broke its holding chains, it would set off a domino effect. Again the pilot levelled the craft but called out a Mayday over the radio, giving his position and advising Guantanamo base of his endless use of aileron, flaps and power to maintain altitude, with the ramp still extended.

Suddenly out of the sun just rising over the lip of the horizon came the unmistakable silhouette of a Mig-29 closing fast. Within seconds the Mig had soared clear out of the path of the transporter having first released two heat seeking missiles homing straight in on the transporter's engines. Both starboard engines exploded, the force shearing off the entire wing, falling away in large pieces. The transporter flipped over, belly side up, then exploded into a one winged fireball. Spiralling downwards, trailing a glowing meteor tail, the doomed aircraft thundered into the ground quaking Santiago city and it's hinterland . Above a 100 metre flaming crater a black mushroom cloud blossomed into the clear sky, like a death fungus, climbing hundreds of feet, the echoing rumble and atomic bomb plume alarming the Cuban soldiers in convoy en route overland to Guantanamo.

On board the Fantasea of the World, the martyrs had heard the clear dawn sky rumble and took the sound of war as an ominous portent of combat to come.

Zador hurriedly marshalled all the remaining hostages to carry what they could towards the front of the ship which was being heaped up with sun loungers, mattresses, drums of cooking oil, suitcases, loose clothes and rolls of carpeting that Zador had pulled up in the casino and The Kings Galleon restaurant. As the tables and chairs were fixed to the ship's decking Zador and his comrades had no time to unscrew them and use them as firewood. To the Jews some had begun whispering about being burned alive on the bow which was filling up with such a large amount of combustible materials.

Branagan was making his way towards the Bridge when he heard the sound of water dribbling on the deck. Glancing around the corner of the deck housing he saw Alif having a piss and instantly Branagan lunged at him. Bowie knife in hand he pushed the blade shaft up under Alif's chin, fully through the axis, on up skewering through his tongue until it hit the roof of Alif's mouth. Alif gargled his own blood as Branagan held his hand over his mouth, head pressed against the deck housing. He then pulled the knife out and shoved it in under Alif's left ribcage, into the peritoneal cavity through the diaphragm to penetrate the lower chambers of his heart. He held the knife in position, the blade fully jammed up until Alif's eyes rolled up and Branagan felt the weight of Alif's body collapsing. Branagan intended to show the martyrs that there were U.S. forces on board who could match the martyrs' brutality. He lay Alif's body out flat and lifting up the long blood soaked beard rested the blade on the plateau of Alif's Adams apple. Branagan softly sliced into the thyroid cartilage, then the spinous process avoiding the vertebrae much like a butcher segmenting an oxtail. As Branagan cut the windpipe, Alif's trunk convulsed to reject and spurt out blood welling in his lungs. Finally Branagan prolapsed the discs to sever the head cleanly from the neck. Tucking it under his arm, Branagan opened out a deckchair and picking up a discarded life jacket, placed it upright in the deckchair. He then put Alif's head into the neck of the lifejacket, a pale hairy lump resting on a luminous thin torso. This armless and legless broken puppet waited to greet the next person coming down the steps from the forebridge door.

Branagan leaving the scene saw the activity of Zador below him hurriedly dragging stacks of sunloungers and foam cushions to the pyre which Zador had just ignited with his flame thrower. Branagan knew there was little time left. As he sneaked quickly past a lifeboat trunk he heard a noise and suddenly he was grabbed from behind. Although surprised, he hit his attacker with brute force with an elbow in the ribs which knocked the attacker back allowing Branagan space to highkick the figure in the chest. 'Son of a bitch' the figure gasped collapsing to the floor. Looking down Branagan saw a huge black passenger, his vest covered in blood. The attacker's wounds oozed in little pulsations in rhythm with his heartbeat.

Branagan, stood over him "You're not one of these marshals are you?"

The black passenger replied that he had been shot and had to repay a debt to a squinty eyed terrorist. Branagan lifted up the man with great difficulty and helped him up the stairwells up into the forward deck crew quarters. He entered the 'Sick Bay' to find a Cuban nurse busy collecting bandages.

'Out' she demanded but Branagan went straight over to a bed and laid 'The Titan' down.

"I am a United States Army commando, this man is a passenger and needs immediate attention; the nurse looked at Branagan and nodded. Branagan then left immediately. He was determined to frustrate efforts to set the whole ship ablaze.

On the Bridge Hakeem scanned the horizon with his binoculars looking through the clouds of grey smoke billowing past the Bridge. He ordered the Engine Hall crew to speed Full Ahead. As the ship's speed came up to 28 knots in the calm conditions he looked for signs of activity along the Cuban coast two miles away. Hakeem considered his options. It would be an hour before the liner reached the deep water of Guantanamo Bay where they would use the Hexogen explosive to hole the ship and when they could also expect an attack from U.S. forces trying to rescue the Jews. Or he could sail directly into Guantanamo Bay, run the ship aground at the US Naval Base at full speed, ripping open the liner's double skin hull plating until coming to a halt. The ship could be driven toward the sea huts of the old Camp America in the base. The martyrs would die on the burning ship or with luck they could wade ashore on Windmill or Kitley beach as warriors of Islam to fight the Great Satan on his own territory, and lay siege to 'Freedom Heights' and the homes of the Infidels. He then realised that the liner if beached could be recoverable if the sprinklers inside the main areas put out Zador's spreading inferno. That would not be acceptable.

In the dawn light he could see the peasant farmers coming out to work in the fields and trailers being saddled up to horses. It was 06:00. On the Bridge with Hakeem, were Samia, Hamilton, Hidalgo and one other Bridge deck officer when one of the medical team rushed in, cell phone in hand. On the line was General Raul Castro looking for Capitan Hidalgo. Hidalgo asked again if it actually was General Raul Castro, the brother of El Comandante Fidel. Hidalgo took the call and listened in silence intently, nodding his head occasionally. As the call continued, the only words uttered frequently were 'si General'. Hakeem was watching Hidalgo closely and Hidalgo knew it.

Finally Hidalgo turned off the phone and returned it to the doctor. Hidalgo walked over to Hakeem and putting his arm around him announced that the U.S. had attacked Cuba and they were now brothers in combat against the U.S. Hakeem looked unconvinced and asked him what role the 'General' expected of Hidalgo. He explained that the Chief of Cuba's armed forces told him to offer the hijackers asylum in Cuba if they surrendered the ship to Cuban forces in Santiago. Neither the Jews nor the remaining crew were a concern for the Cubans authorities any longer he said.

Hakeem nodded but said they were martyrs for whom the only true asylum was by Allah's side in paradise; He said the ship was a symbol of Infidel power and and was a Satanic idol, a creation of evil which had to be destroyed as God willed.

Hidalgo replied that he never heard of a God giving such an order. "Is it an order from thin air?....a whisper in your ear or just your own order to yourself? If God issued the order and you do not carry it out, then I can execute you for insubordination and cowardice?" Hidalgo continued, "but then all I am doing you is a favour, no?.....sending you like a missile off to paradise?....then what happens?....how does your God punish you?...does he send you back again? .....as a

Palestinian? or maybe a Jew?" Hidalgo finished with an arrogant smile.

"Shut up atheist! Hakeem retorted angrily.

"Okay, okay, don't get angry, I don't understand your war Hakeem...but as far as orders go I give the orders to the Cuban team on this ship, you and your God are in command of your destiny only, not ours. For now I am calling off the medical team's assistance to the Jews as evidence of our comradeship. Hidalgo about turned and left the Bridge. Within seconds he had returned.

"One of your martyr's has become separated from his body! If this is the work of U.S. forces hiding on this ship then we would be delighted to see them rot in a Cuban jail. Let us sail the ship back to Santiago?"

Hakeem replied with a firm no as he went down with Samia to the corpse. Hidalgo left again to find the medical team, to the sounds of Samia croaking followed by vomit splashing onto the deck. The sky boomed a second time, less loudly than the first and all heads turned in the direction of Guantanamo. A small column of smoke puffed up from the air base as the first transporter crashlanded across Guantanamo's airfield.

Hidalgo continued on his way for the medics. Returning to the Bridge with a doctor, both men stopped to look closely at the head of Alif, lying on the deck. Hidalgo then placed the toe of his black boot under the head. Lifting it onto the flat of his boot he chipped it over the deckrail into the sea like a footballer.

"That's the Cuban burial ceremony over" he remarked

indifferently, "the arabs can bury the rest of him, probably collecting his blood in some sort of ritual" he added sarcastically.

The doctor shrugged, he had seen similar pieces of human on the battlefields of Angola.

The two men entered the Bridge and the doctor explained they would attend to the martyrs now. Hakeem was in deep thought considering his options and waved away Hidalgo and the doctor.

About 20 km ahead of him was a headland with contours similar to the chart map of the headland at the entrance to Guantanamo bay. He still had to decide whether to continue into the Naval Base or just scuttle it in the deepwater channel, going down ablaze taking everyone with it.

Hidalgo did not move, insisting the doctors examine Hakeem as a matter of routine and as a courtesy to the team who had risked their lives for their country and in the name of their honourable profession. Two more doctors arrived on the Bridge. Hakeem said they could examine him where he was. Samia said she would go with the two doctors as she was in pain with her back ribs from an 'earlier fall'.

As soon as Samia had left, the remaining doctor began checking Hakeem's thick head of hair. Grabbing some loose skin at the back of the neck, he stuck a syringe into Hakeem's neck, pushing the contents in instantly. Hakeem swung around hitting the doctor, then aimed his pistol at him. A second later, his eyes rolled up and Hakeem fell to the deck, out cold.

As Hidalgo took his pistol, Hamilton struggled to his feet.

"Brilliant, well done", chirped Hamilton. "You'll be a hero in America after this! I'll take command now."

Hidalgo replied quietly "you're not safe yet, get your Sea Marshals or whatever forces are on this ship up here to the Bridge."

Hamilton grabbed the microphone for a ship wide announcement,

"To everyone on board, this is Captain Hamilton, I am in command again, the terrorists have been captured by the Cuban forces, would any U.S. forces or sea marshals come to the Bridge immediately, we need an armed guard over the terrorists, come to the Bridge immediately; the terrorists are sedated"

Minutes later Branagan arrived, gun drawn pointing it at Hidalgo.

"So these are the U.S. forces on board," asked Hidalgo, …"one man?..then put your weapon away, I'm not in God's army"…. Hidalgo declared.

Hamilton wasn't sure if there were any more special forces; he presumed all sea marshals were dead. Hamilton moved over to the console to plot a new course. He then ordered Branagan again to holster his pistol and attend to the Jews.

As soon as Branagan had put his pistol away reluctantly, Hidalgo roared at both Hamilton and Branagan "THIS SHIP IS NOW UNDER THE PROTECTION OF THE CUBAN WAR MARINE!" as he raised his pistol at them.

"IT HAS BEEN REQUISITIONED AND IS NOW

UNDER MY COMMAND". Branagan knew by the time he raised his pistol again he would be shot by Hidalgo. "Hand over your gun commando, you are my prisoner of war. America has invaded Cuba, a moment we have long expected and prepared for since I joined the War Marine. All weapons on the deck, NOW!

The medical team have given an anaesthetic to the martyrs. They will be conscious soon. The doctor will escort you to the other hostages. Go and find them a safe place to hide on the ship, that will be your last heroic act commando, then I suggest you hide yourself". Hidalgo gave a sinister nod to the doctor to follow the commando. Hidalgo then untied Hamilton's plastic ties and ordered him to the Chart desk.

Hamilton though shaken by Hidalgo's proclamation still mentioned enthusiastically, "we use Electronic Chart Display, Capitan, let me show you" "Absolutely not Captain Hamilton, the only toy that interests me on the Bridge is your echo sounder. It looks like we have a whale for company under the ship! A hungry one swimming at 30 knots! Very fast for the fattest and longest whale I have ever seen! But let's not worry unless it comes up for air Captain Hamilton?"

Hamilton didn't comment. Whatever was intended could only be better in the hands of a disciplined military officer following a government's orders than a gang of zealous butchers searching for a glorious death. Branagan was marched out of the Bridge down to the Jews tied to the rails on the Sky deck. Encouraging them to hide immediately anywhere on the ship, he no sooner had untied the last hostage when he felt a sting in his neck and collapsed to the deck, anaesthetised.

CHAPTER 20

Capitan Hidalgo opened the chart of Cuba's South Eastern coast and studied the coordinates in the margin. He held his forefinger for a moment an inch or so above a particular spot and brought it firmly down on the chart.

"Captain Hamilton, give me manual control of this tin giant, I am heading 20 degrees East, no computers!.......it's very close to the coast but there is plenty of deep water, I know every metre of the seabed where American submarines like to hide. Then go and help your commando friend and hide the hostages."

Hamilton was surprised "Aren't you going to lock up these murdering fanatics while they're unconscious? I'll help you put them in the Brig, we've two holding cells."

"No" replied Hidalgo, "so make yourself scarce now"! Hidalgo ordered the second doctor to escort Hamilton off the Bridge.

Zador meanwhile had been untraced by the medical team as he rummaged in the ship's stores for more diesel for his flame thrower. He had retrieved the rest of the Hexogen explosive and was now looking for his fellow martyrs.

None were to be found and no one answered his radio calls. He began his way back up the ship taking a detour through the Engine Hall looking for a place to detonate the explosives that would disable the engines and also blow a hole in the hull below the waterline. Humming with the sound of turbines, the cathedral of aluminium pipes and machine housings was devoid of life save for the two Indian engineers. They were slumped in their control pods and asleep in the oily heat, where they had been confined for the past twenty four hours.

As Zador walked down steps to another level, he let out a roar of agony as a knife was pushed neatly through his lower leg and clean out the other side. He collapsed forwards landing on his chest. Before he had time to pull the knife out of his leg, Kruger had leapt on top of him, rolled him onto his back and rammed a pistol into his throat. Kruger had been guarding the fuel reservoir and after hearing the announcement was heading for the Bridge. "I'll let you go first to paradise….get ready to say Hello Allah………… NOW"! 'Click'. The gun didn't go off. Zador pushed the gun away but couldn't get out from under Kruger. Zador then opened his mouth of rotting broken teeth and clamped it fiercely on Kruger's nose, biting deep and then deeper and deeper still. Kruger winced with the pain but Zador wouldn't let go. Zador had used this defence before and practised clamping the leg of a live chicken between his teeth counting how long he could hold a vice like grip before tiring. As with the chicken leg, Zador now began a side action movement of his lower jaw to saw through Kruger's nasal cartilage, as far back as the concha, squeezing the nose ever tighter the deeper he chewed. Gradually the whole nose vestibule lifted off his face, a slippery bulbous knob of gristle and slimy septum jammed fast between Zador's chipped teeth.

Kruger rolled over, in torment, one hand groping about the floor for his pistol the other covering his face, trying to breath, mouth wide open flooding with blood. In an instant Zador was on top of him and about to thrust Suleyman's Jambiyya dagger into his heart. Kruger upheld Zador's hand, which he could just make out, his vision blurred with blood flowing over his face from the stump of his nose. With his other hand, Kruger then thumped Zador massively with a clenched fist to the side of his head, knocking him off him. Zador got up on all fours, coughing and gasping, with Kruger's nose jammed in his throat, and dropped the dagger. Without realising it, Kruger's decision to then powerfully kick him in the chest relieved Zador's breathing distress. Zador responded by lunging at Kruger and headbutting him to the floor. With Kruger dazed, Zador knelt on his shoulders and shoved his filthy thumb into Kruger's left eye, pressing deep into the socket, bursting the lacrimal gland. He forced his thumb around and under the ball, then levered it upwards, until it abruptly uncorked out of it's orbital vacuum.

"Now American, you also have just one good eye too?"

Kruger was disorientated, one eye with blurred vision and the other dangling at the side of his head by the optic nerve looking into his own left ear. Yet he still could make out the broad shiny dagger blade hanging above him again. Suddenly the dagger vanished and he saw Zador lifted up bodily. He saw the large black figure of the Titan. Kruger immediately got up and as if putting in a contact lens pushed his eye back into it's left cranial hollow.

Bruised, his face stinging and refitted eye swelling up fast, Kruger staggered behind the Titan who was about to throw Zador to the ground.

"WAIT! Lets help propel this animal to paradise!" Kruger gasped while Zador was still wildly flailing hopelessly as The Titan held him by the neck in one hand and by his testicles in the other. Kruger threw open the glass inspection casing around one of the four propeller shafts, a thick silver trunk glistening with oil, spinning close to 20 revolutions a second in it's tunnel tube.

"No, No, NO!," Zador screamed, MY FATHER AMERICAN....FROM VIRGINIA... PLEASE.... The Titan glanced back at Kruger's mutilated face and then hurled Zador onto the spinning shaft and slammed the casing down. The shaft whined loudly meeting the resistance of Zador's bones, while the glass case splashed red in a rinse of blood; within a minute the shaft returned to it's quieter hum. The Titan opened the case again to find the shaft threading Zador's soft tissue up and down into a crimson spool of wispy filaments not unlike red candy floss.

Kruger recovered his breath and thanked the Titan, who had now sat back on the gantry still weak from

Zador's earlier shots.

"Don't thank me, thank those Indian guys up there, they phoned the Bridge and some Cuban Navy guy told me a sea marshal was needing some help." Kruger looked up trying to locate them. A plump balding man waved down then shouted "MY NAME IS NOHOM" and then burst into an apparently operatic song, in a peculiar high pitch, reaching soprano notes, the sound echoing around the Hall.

At that point, a man appeared in a white coat on a link walkway above them.

"That is right, the Cubans have saved you Señor Marshal and now your fighting is finished on this ship. This ship is now under the control of the Cuban Revolutionary War Marine and is war treasure following the invasion by American forces in Southern Cuba. Come with me peacefully and we will attend to your wounds but you will be confined to the Sick Bay."

Kruger was in no condition to resist nor was the Titan, both unsteady on their feet.

On the Bridge Hidalgo was now agitated, walking quickly from the radar screen to the Bridge wing, to the speed gauge , back out to look through binoculars, then back to the radar screen. He had seen a huge echo come up on the repeater. The liner was doing a gauge speed of 28 knots.

At the helm console Hidalgo continued to look at the speed dial and slowly saw the speed increase from 28 to 29 to 30 knots beyond which the digital counter refused to move further. Then, his breath was taken away momentarily as back again on the Bridge wing he looked through his binoculars and a broad smile broke across his face. The First Officer looked at Hidalgo anxiously as to what he had seen. Hidalgo put down the binoculars and turned to the First Officer. "Today will be another day in the glorious history of Cuba. I have found it. We are about to attack the aircraft carrier John F Kennedy!

The aircraft carrier, Hidalgo estimated, was under power at a speed of 10 knots and increasing. There was less than 2 miles between both ships. As he focused his binoculars on the flight deck, Hidalgo could see some frantic activity on the aircraft carrier's deck of nearly three hectares. It looked like the carriers air squadron was getting ready for take off. He immediately grabbed the ship's microphone and warned the Cuban medical team of a risk that the ship would be straffed as he could also see the blades of a helicopter gunship beginning to rotate. Hidalgo then told them to take up positions on the highest deck but to avoid being a target for fighter aircraft and conceal themselves under piles of lifejackets or amongst the chaos of the sunloungers thrown about. Hidalgo reminded them they could volunteer for combat now that Cubans had a chance to exact retribution against the John F Kennedy, a symbol of American power and an unforgettable name in every Cuban household.

Hidalgo wheeled furiously to direct the ship at the carrier to ram it broadside at full speed. "You're totally mad!" blurted the First Officer as the liner heeled, turning 90 degrees hard to Starboard.

Hidalgo replied with a grin "We are at war! Take the wheel! Steer straight for the super structure." he ordered the First Officer. The Officer replied "What chance do you think you have against the aircraft carrier. This is a cruise ship not a war ship, that carrier is Armageddon on water! This great liner will capsize in a matter of minutes. You may want to die Capitan Hidalgo but you have no right to force innocent passengers or crew to their death in what will be a conflagration."

Hakeem staggered into the Bridge, startling both men. In a drunken slur he addressed the First Officer "You need do nothing crewman except continue to wear that blood stained white uniform to remind you that you are a prisoner of Islam and that this ship is no longer a white ship for the decadent rich Zionists or a playground of Infidels. As for you Hidalgo death must mean nothing as you have no God?

Hidalgo turned calmly to Hakeem, "I have brought you to a greater prize, look ahead, the giant Yanqui war machine, a symbol of oppression of the Cuban people and a symbol of Christian domination over Islam! I have my orders from my General and you have your orders from your God......strangely we have the same objective..........go and arm your muslim gang, if they want to die gloriously in battle, then what greater glory can there be than this!

CHAPTER 21

As the liner veered to make for the aircraft carrier the commander of the aircraft carrier immediately radioed the commander of the City of Corpus Christi submarine advising that it looked like a collision was intended but he wanted the submarine to back up an air assault by the carrier's air wing. "If necessary, fire a torpedo at the underside to knock out the rudder and propellers", he suggested. The commander of the submarine replied that any offensive action would need an executive order from the President as it was a deliberate and unprovoked attack on a United States registered cruise ship. His brief from the Pentagon was to shadow the ship and therefore he could not comply. The commander roared down the radio "PENTAGON CLEARANCE WILL BE RETROSPECTIVE AND I DON'T HAVE TIME TO EXPLAIN NOT ONLY WHAT I SUSPECT ARE THE INTENTIONS OF THE HIJACKERS BUT WHAT THE EFFECT WILL BE ON MY AIRCRAFT CARRIER, THAT LINER AND, NOT LEAST FOR THE HOSTAGES ON BOARD!" The commander of the carrier then demanded that the submarine surface and heave the liner off course using the submarine's reinforced upper hull shoulder. The submarine commander replied that these were matters that again needed orders from the highest in the Pentagon and that he would not jeopardise the safety of the submarine and its crew. He added that the carrier's airwing should be deployed in full immediately. The commander of the carrier replied he didn't have a full complement of crew nor pilots for that matter to fly the entire airwing; he had already called MacDill Airforce Base for air support but that wouldn't be arriving in Guantanamo Bay for another 20 minutes. The Fantasea of the Sea with her bow ablaze and billowing black smoke was now heading directly for the carrier's superstructure. The commander now wheeled hard to port in a collision avoidance manoeuvre and ordered full battle stations. Hidalgo estimated the carrier was making a speed of 15 knots now and increasing.

Straight ahead Hakeem standing out on the Bridge wing saw a helicopter gunship and two Tomcats take off one after the other. The two jets banked steeply and headed straight for the liner. Hakeem guessed this was no flypast but they would immediately attack the Bridge and Wheel console. Hakeem roared at Hidalgo and both men raced out of the Bridge down the corridor to the Communications Center but were bodily lifted off their feet by a massive explosion which threw them further down the corridor. Hakeem's forehead was cut while Hidalgo was out cold seemingly landing head first into the door frame of the communications room.

Hakeem roared to Samia to load all ammunition for

an attack on the carrier which was now only 200 metres dead ahead.

As 'Big John' began to complete a half circle Hakeem ran to the Bridge and found parts of the console on fire, every window shattered and a gaping hole where the portside Bridge wing had been. Hidalgo struggled up behind him, dizzy but still grabbed the helm and steered hard to port. He would cut inside the carrier and ram her broadside to port on the flight deck runway. The ship closed quickly on the aircraft carrier while the carrier again turned both her 36 ton rudders 90 degrees, this time to starboard. The commander hoped to only expose the carrier's stern which was reinforced with heavy plating to withstand collisions from jets misaligned for landing due to pilot error or combat damage. The valiant efforts of the carrier's commander to avoid the liner were however too late without more speed. He looked on helplessly in horror as the liner, a blackened shattered battering ram bore down on his portside. The commander ordered all combat units to fire at will at the liner. The carrier's 20mm guns opened up raining thousands of rounds on the Bridge. The relentless hail of metal continued as the liner's bow heaved straight in under the carrier's flight deck to deliver it bow cargo of flaming debris into the interior hangars. The impact silenced all guns momentarily as the carrier's crew were knocked violently out of their combat positions. The unstoppable weight of the liner pushed up the carrier's entire port side, tilted higher by the driving brute force of her turbines still churning out maximum revolutions. The liner's bow buckled and warped to the sounds of grating squeals and pained moans as metal engaged metal, unyielding to the unyielding, then bending, creaking then snapping into sections crashing noisily onto more metal.

The heavy girders of both ships stressed as they were forced against each other, eventually flexing and twisting like pliable beams of lead. Hidalgo had fulfilled his orders from General Raul. This was a clash of giants, of two Goliaths; Big John's 110,000 tonnes and 23 storeys high to the top of her super structure from her waterline. Against her the liner's 114,000 tons had cut fast through the calm sea at almost 30 knots and though only 17 storeys high most of her superstructure looked down upon the carrier's flight deck.

The carrier commander was bewildered. This was not what any aircraft carrier could anticipate. For Hakeem this was ancient history rediscovered. He had read about the ancient Meditteranean sea battles when the Phoenicians fought the Greeks at close quarters. These were the tactics of the Greek and Roman galleys where a burning prow or firebarge was intended to destroy the other's flagship before hand to hand combat took place. Hakeem grabbed the tannoy microphone and chanted extracts from the Holy Qu'ran in the manner of a muezzin from his minaret exhorting the other martyrs to fight to the end, that no one must be taken prisoner. The bow continued to drive into the carrier before it started to crumple and crush downwards dumping the blazing plastics and wood into the carrier's midship hangar. The carrier's fire sirens wailed and on the orders of the commander all sailors opened fire with whatever and wherever on the liner; a dozen sharp shooters lay flat on the flight deck ready to pick off any visible hijackers.

The carrier was being pushed sideways under the momentum of the liner's unstoppable weight. Slowly, the fixing lines holding the 11 aircraft and the three helicopters on the flight deck began to snap as the carrier heeled over at an angled tilt of 35 degrees. One by one the aircraft and helicopters slid off the deck tumbling over the starboard side into the depths of Guantanamo bay. The commander ordered the gunship already airborne and the two Tomcats to "bomb the hell out of the front of the ship" and then rescinded his order immediately until the ships were disengaged. He then ordered the carriers fire teams to do their best to put out the fire on board the carrier first and then the fire on board the liner.

Slowly the rebounding weight of the carrier began to force down the bow of the liner bringing the carrier back to an even keel though an acre of her flight deck was now an unuseable warped grey dome. The carrier weight pressing down on the bow of the liner now lifted the liners stern and its 4 propellers out of the water, still spinning at full speed causing the entire ship to vibrate and come to a halt. The commander now gave orders that the liner was to be boarded and captured at all costs. He instructed the airborne helicopter gun ship and the fighter jets to protect the assault units as they scrambled aboard the liner skirting the flames at the bow as best they could. Creeping metre by metre along the bow foredeck the carrier crew used the cover of the plumes of smoke to make their way forward.

On board the carrier the commander had ordered an assessment of hangar damage from a repair crew of metal workers sent to cut the carrier free. The liner jammed into the side of the carrier at right angles had reduced the carrier's speed from almost 15 knots to 3 knots despite of the carrier's four 25 tonne propeller blades thrashing on full power. As soon as the repair crew entered the hangar they had to dive to the floor as rivets the size of drinking cans were exploding inward from twisting hanger plating. The commander next ordered the two Tomcats to destroy firstly the liner's propellers and then to demolish the liner's upper decks one by one starting at the Sky deck. The fighters acknowledged the order and both flew low less than 20 feet above water level for a practice run before they banked around and came in low a second time to fire off a rocket each aimed for the two outer 18 tonne blades which would likely cause major collateral damage to the inner spinning blades.

Two direct hits were followed by two more hits on the Sky deck. Suleyman on the deck below climbed into an empty hot tub on the balcony of a Grand Suite and aimed his shoulder fired RPG launcher at the tower of the carrier. He fired four grenades, two of which hit the carrier's bridge and one hit the communications tower bristling with aerial masts. Then from several balconies of state rooms, clusters of martyrs opened fire with machine guns at the aircraft carrier's Bridge deck. Each martyr took turns to ensure a continuous stream of fire scattering gunner crews attempting to reload the carriers Vulcan light defence guns.

Hidalgo grabbed hold of the heavy tripod mounted machine gun and rolled the body of Amir out of the way. He sat into a white patio chair, and aimed the gunsights at the carrier's tower.

In clear commandful Spanish the Capitan roared.

"PRESIDENT JOHN F KENNEDY, THIS IS FOR THE BAY OF PIGS" as he opened fire on the carrier's tower. Lost in the thunderous noise of the gun, he sang La Bayamesa angrily as the rest of the bullet belt fed into the heavy gun, the empty casings pinging off the metal panels of the stateroom verandah.

With no ammunition left he fired off his pistol. He then walked boldly along the Promenade deck, sword drawn, wholly indifferent to the rifle shots coming from the carrier, narrowly missing him. He made his way onto the bow, through a shell hole in the liners front plating and leapt onto the carrier deck.

The Capitan's parade ground roar of 'Hasta la victoria siempraaaaaaay' was heard followed by the sound of several machines guns firing in a simultaneous concert, cutting him down.

Suddenly the submarine surfaced, its vast grey bulk parting the waters like a bloated upturned ship. From it's armoured tower, at right angles to the ship small arms fire was directed at the hjackers on the liner's stateroom balconies.

Suleyman took advantage of the surfaced submarine as a target for another RPG attack. He slowly took aim at the conning tower of the submarine and scored a direct hit blowing the sailors shooting at the liner clean over the side of the tower into the water. As he reloaded, the newly conscious Branagan attacked from behind and slit his throat.

On board the aircraft carrier, aircraft were brought up from the rear hangars undamaged during the initial collision. They taxied along the flight deck and turned to face the port side balconies where much of the hijackers had been based directing their machine gunfire at the Bridge of the carrier. On the orders of the commander the jets were lined up on the flight deck and fired off salvoes of rockets into the side of the liner. Each rocket smashed through the accommodation deck state rooms leaving panels melting into gaping holes. The force of the rocket blast on the outer state rooms continued to the inner cabins throwing wall panels, mattresses, loose chairs and tables about as if a tornado had drilled a huge screw into the heart of the ship.

The pilot of a grounded Hornet on the carrier deck opened up with his wing mounted machine gun and straffed the entire portside of the ship. Under the hale of bullets the hijackers retreated to the starboard side. Samia then radioed Hakeem that she was going to fire on the Hornet with another rocket propelled grenade. Hakeem immediately ordered her to bring the rocket launcher into the Wedding Chapel.

There, she aimed the launcher with Hakeem's assistance fixing the underbelly of the Hornet in the launcher's crosshairs. She pulled the trigger and in an instant the grenade had struck the Hornet, laden with kerosene exploding the pilot clean out of the cockpit and onto the deck. Hakeem realised his mission was now effectively accomplished. He had confronted the might of the American Navy and had converted a symbol of Satan into a holy Islamic warship. He had fought at close quarters with the great Satan and shown that with planning, courage and intelligent second guessing he could outwit all the technology and fire power of the enemy. Death would come in holy jihad but this was only a battle in a long war and with an estimated war chest of $10 million dollars in cash he decided to abandon the disabled burning liner. Hakeem ordered Samia to make her way down to the inflateable rib tied to the pilotage door.

En route they grabbed white coats with red crosses on their backs. Jumping in to the rib, they sped away, outmanoeuvring the bullets fired from the chasing helicopter gunship. Both eventually made landfall on a beach near Santiago Port.

Epilogue

The Cuban Government brought a motion of censure against the United States at a specially convened meeting of the UN security council for violating another members sovereign territory. The motion was vetoed by the United States, the United Kingdom and Russia claiming the assault was a preventative measure to protect the United States from two threats; firstly a possible hijack of the UN aircraft and a suicidal dive into Miami or other cities along the US Eastern seaboard; secondly to prevent against future attacks by avenging prisoners.

Four Israeli Sayamet commandos died in the failed mission to board the liner from the pontoons, with two abandoning the mission and surviving. Twenty six martyrs died during the hijack, most in the attack on the aircraft carrier, while Khalil was killed on board the C130 shot down and Badshah shot on Maceo airfield.

Of the ship's passengers and crew, thirteen were murdered on board, twenty six were unaccounted for and presumed lost overboard, while five died of heart attacks when abandoning ship by lifeboat or during the transfer to the pontoon in exchange for the prisoners.

Of the 595 prisoners, seventeen were killed by Kruger and Branagan on board the liner including six killed in the grenade attack on the Security Center.

More were killed on the airfield at Antonio Maceo airport, Santiago and when the C130 was shot down over Santiago province; fifty four died falling out of the plane with the camello; three pilots and forty five marines also went down in the C130. The prisoners surviving the crashlanding of the C130 at Guantanamo were reincarcerated briefly before being flown out to Saskanuit Army Base in Anchorage. Eight Cuban soldiers found on board the crashed plane claimed asylum in Guantanamo but were exchanged for six US marines captured at Maceo airport. All other prisoners surrendering to the Cuban army were deported to Venezuela immediately to prevent a further attack against Cuba. Assisted by the Red Cross, they were returned from Venezuela to their homelands.

During the battle at Maceo airport, an unknown number of cuban troops and twenty three U.S. marines were killed. On board the Aircraft carrier, fifteen crew and three pilots were killed.

The United States filed a claim against Cuba in the International Court of Justice. Compensation was claimed of $3.6 billion dollars for damage to the aircraft carrier and the loss of half it's airwing, damage to the submarine and the Fantasea of the World. No mention was made of the crashed C130 air transports in the claim.

In a victory parade led by the Cuban medical team who were all walking wounded and only repatriated to Cuba from the US after pressure from Israel, El Comandante Castro declared Capitan Fernando Fernandez Hidalgo a national hero and a Martyr of the Revolution. The pilot of the Mig 29 downing the C130 was decorated with a Medallon de Bravura Revolucionaria. The United States Interests building eventually reopened in Havana with the street being renamed Calle Hidalgo by the city municipal authority.

Hakeem and Samia's whereabouts remain unknown.

Gwendolen Hamilton freed herself after four days in a Southampton warehouse and sold her story to an English national newspaper for a six figure sum.

Captain Hamilton never returned to England after retirement and continued his search for Olga in Cuba staying for the maximum time allowed under a tourist visa.

All US registered Cruise ships were required by the Secretary for Homeland Security to fit an anti aircraft gun and to embark a platoon of marines for every voyage.

American registered cruise ships were forbidden to enter Cuban territorial waters. Foreign cruise ships allowing shore visits to Cuba were punished by exclusion from entering US territorial waters or using the Panama canal for a period of 3 years by executive order of President Grattan.

Kruger was pardoned by President Grattan for the second degree murder of his wife and returned to the

Delta Force at Fort Bragg as an instructor with Jack Branagan.

All non American crew of the Fantasea of the World were, after two months of questioning, dismissed by the company. Under pressure from President Grattan, the Fantasea of the World had to be scrapped. Two months later, as her propeller shafts were being removed, a large spent bullet shell was found. Taken home as a souvenir by the one of the wrecking crew, he opened the cap and found a tiny faded note inside wrapped in plastic. It read 'Mosha Sultmann 2113 Dawson Blvd, Langley VA'; American peace corps.'

Forthcoming in 2006 by Niall de Souza

VATICAN JIHAD!

When an Islamic martyrs brigade seize the Vatican City during the conclave of cardinals to elect a pope, all Christendom is plunged into cataclysm. The outrageous demand of the martyrs tears NATO and E.U./U.S. alliances asunder. Opportunist scheming by Russia, the Orthodox Churches and a self appointed African Pope compound the catastrophe. Salvation however, may only be possible in the deployment a unique and unholy alliance of ancient and modern forces.